This

OUT OF SHADOWS

OUT OF SHADOWS

Gloria Cook

This first world edition published in Great Britain 2007 by
SEVERN HOUSE PUBLISHERS LTD of
9–15 High Street, Sutton, Surrey SM1 1DF.
This first world edition published in the USA 2007 by
SEVERN HOUSE PUBLISHERS INC of
595 Madison Avenue, New York, N.Y. 10022.

British Library Cataloguing in Publication Data

Cook, Gloria
   Out of shadows. - (Meryen series)
   1. Women - England - Cornwall (County) - Social conditions
   - 19th century - Fiction 2. Cornwall (England : County) -
   Social life and customs - 19th century - Fiction
   3. Domestic fiction
   I. Title
   823.9'14[F]

ISBN-13: 978-0-7278-6531-1   (cased)

All Severn House titles are printed on acid-free paper.

Typeset by Palimpsest Book Production Ltd.,
Grangemouth, Stirlingshire, Scotland.
Printed and bound in Great Britain by
MPG Books Ltd., Bodmin, Cornwall.

One

Two figures were hunched over the stone fireplace in the little rough dwelling on the downs. An odd pairing, as always they were quiet, keeping to their own thoughts. Sarah Kivell, just twenty-one, had been a widow for the last four years, and for most of that time she had lodged with an elderly spinster, Tabbie Sawle, the herbwife of the village. If not for Tabbie, Sarah would be homeless. It was of no concern to her that Sarah had lived with the much older Titus Kivell, the criminal head of a once disorderly clan, before their disastrous marriage. She knew all about Sarah, but she never offered information about her past and Sarah asked her no questions.

It suited Sarah to live in relative isolation. They could only be reached from Meryen by a series of narrow tracks hacked through straggly banks of gorse, bramble and scrubby willow, off a slightly wider thoroughfare that the villagers called Tabbie's Lane. A lane it wasn't, its length being no more than a thousand yards and wouldn't accommodate even a small dog cart. The abode – it could hardly be termed a house – was built against a formation of high granite, which made up the back wall and incorporated the fireplace, set in a low shelf of rock. Against the wall, hunks and thereafter fist-sized stones made up the tapering chimney piece. The carefully chosen slabs and boulders of the other three walls made the place like a fortress. The roof, of timber and sheets of corrugated iron, slanted gently down from the back wall and was waterproofed by pitch. The door was formed from spliced young tree trunks, and barred inside with metal of an arm's breadth threaded through huge iron staples. The floor was stamped earth but covered from end to end by layers of rush mats and a once

fine piece of carpet. The two square apertures that served
as windows had metal gratings and were covered against
the cold by wooden shutters. In all, it was a dark and
airless place; to many it would seem claustrophobic, but
it was furnished with the gathered curiosities of Tabbie's
lifetime and was not without embellishment and comfort,
and here, among the dark-blue and claret drapes and cush-
ions, the velvets and damasks that sparkled with gold
thread, all booty from shipwrecks, Sarah was pleased to
be shut off from the world she wanted no part of.

It was rare to be disturbed in Tabbie's Shack, and usually
only then by some desperate soul seeking, as a last resort,
advantage of the old woman's remedies or fortune-telling
abilities. Tabbie was considered by the uncharitable to be a
witch. The superstitious feared she could read minds, look
into souls and successfully ill-wish anyone she took against.
Another reason for the solitude was that Tabbie was an
alarming sight. It was known she had been strong in her
youth – it was she who had single-handedly built her home
and brought its trappings home on a hand barrow – but her
height was now bent with age and her joints contorted by
arthritis. Her wrinkled flesh, sallow from decades of peat
and furze smoke, appeared desiccated, and flakes of skin
were always scattered about her shoulders. Her shoulders
had fashioned themselves into a hump and her head flopped
down to her hollow chest. Her darting eyes, however,
remained sharp and clear and her hearing had not waned; it
was rumoured fearfully that she could hear a whisper from
any distance. No one could recall exactly when she had set
up her home, supposedly having done so with the help of
demons, and her age was speculated as being between eighty
and over a century. Always in black, with her bonnet ribbons
flapping loose, Tabbie was not unlike some monstrous rook
chewing on two fat dangling worms. A gruesome-looking
companion, but she was a woman whose heart was big enough
to take in a 'fallen woman'. Sarah was shunned by most,
and the few who had taken pity on her at her husband's death
were disappointed over her refusal to denounce Titus Kivell
despite his evil deeds.

Sarah accepted the contempt, it did not hurt her. Titus's

brutality and the terrible things he had done to her, and the fact he had tried to murder his grown-up son, had robbed her of all need to fit in. She had been left without hope. She existed, that was all, and cared not if that existence came to an end at any moment. She felt tainted and beyond redemption, for the dreadful thing was she had loved Titus deeply and part of her still did and grieved for him. She wasn't fit to be near good and ordinary folk. Isolation she prized and that was what she got, even at work as a bal-maiden at the Carn Croft copper mine. Few people spoke to her and she never made an opening comment, and with her bowed and shut-off manner she was as she intended to be, easy to overlook. There was one thing for which she drew admiration, and jealousy, the remarkable, raven-haired beauty that had led to her downfall, made all the more appealing to men by her unreachable aloofness and the echoes of her sorrow.

When the thick walls of the stuffy shack were heated by the fire the atmosphere could become overbearing. Her throat parchment dry, Sarah rose from the high tapestry stool and went to the pearlware harvest jug on the bench table. She sipped the water, which she collected every day from a former wine cask, fed by a chute underneath a little trickling waterfall off nearby rocks. She moved the chute away from the cask each night so there would be no overflow.

'Would you like a drink of water, Tabbie? Or I could make you some cocoa. Then I think I'll slip outside for a breath of air. It's stopped raining and the wind has dropped at last.' The stormy weather of the last two days had meant no surface work on the ore-dressing floors at the mine. It meant added hardship, especially for families, for if there was no work there were no wages. 'I know it's bitter cold but I'll be sure to wrap up well.' It was nice that Tabbie tended to mother her, and tried to convince her she was as worthy as anyone else; the latter fell on deaf ears. Sarah had nursed her own brain-damaged mother until her death; the rest of her family, an aunt and a younger brother and sister, had deserted her after Titus's death, moving three miles away to Redruth with the help of money offered by her rich mother-in-law, Tempest Kivell. Sarah had refused the same proposal to make a fresh start. She'd rather starve than take charity off a Kivell, even though Tempest maintained the Kivells held a lifelong responsibility to her.

Tabbie did not reply. Sarah had not looked at her for some time and did so now. Chills trailed up her spine. Tabbie was not apt to answer quickly but she had not heard Sarah at all. Her head was thrown back as far as it would go, and her gaze, usually shrewd and watchful, was on nothing. She was in a trance and seemed to be in the grip of some awful vision. From the contortion of her hawkish features it was likely a calamitous premonition for someone. Sarah had witnessed this before. Tabbie would never recount what she saw, offering only a vague or enigmatic statement. One time it had been, 'Pestilence is abroad. A just punishment, some would say.' Sarah had assumed there would be an outbreak of typhoid or cholera, or animal death – perhaps a dishonest farmer and his family the victims. However, forty-eight hours later talk had spread that Squire Nankervis, who had a passion for exotic plants, spending hundreds of pounds on new discoveries from overseas, had mysteriously lost all the contents of his hothouses and many a fine specimen in his gardens. Joshua Nankervis did little for the villagers, leaving charitable works to his young wife, Tara, with whom Sarah had once been loosely acquainted, but he was not a wicked man. The punishment Tabbie had predicted must have referred to the estate's head gardener, the strange and daunting Laketon Kivell.

Tabbie's amber eyes glittered as if in anguish. She was surely seeing something dreadful. *Please don't let it be a disaster at the mine.* Sarah never doubted Tabbie's powers. Could it be that she was seeing her own death? She had remarked she didn't fear it, but if she was now being faced by a terrible end . . .

Minutes dragged by like hours. Sarah returned to the stool and watched anxiously. At last Tabbie emitted a tremendous sigh and her head fell forward and flopped down. She seemed to have trouble wresting herself to full consciousness.

Sarah was about to fetch some water when the old woman turned her beady eyes on her. Her expression was often fathomless but Sarah had never seen her intense and harrowed like this.

Tabbie shuddered, as if she couldn't shake off the horrors of what she'd just seen.

'You must heed me well, Sarah, for I need to prepare you for something,' she delivered in her reverberating husky tones, pointing a tremulous gnarled finger. 'I can tell you were mindful of me being here only in body this past hour. I was out on the downs, with all my limbs working as in my prime. The winds were howling all around me. It was as dark as pitch and the boulders were throwing long, long shadows all around. I knew there was all manner of terrifying things in those shadows and that if I stepped into them I'd never come out alive but be doomed to stay there a prisoner in torment forever.'

Tabbie's eyes grew wide and potent. Sarah, mesmerized, drew in a sharp breath. Tabbie never went in for melodrama, what she had to say she said. She reached for Sarah's hand. With apprehension, Sarah placed her fingers in the bony paw. She was about to be prepared for whatever the fearsome vision represented, perhaps Tabbie's imminent death. Pray God, not that, she didn't want to be all alone in the world.

Tabbie swallowed with difficulty. 'Then he appeared. The devil, or as good as. You knew him, Sarah.'

Fear took its debilitating hold on Sarah. The vision concerned her, and this time Tabbie was going to reveal the exact details. Without a shadow of doubt, she knew her beleaguered life was about to be plunged again into adversity. 'W-who was it?'

'I'm afraid it was your husband, my dear. Titus Kivell. He's coming back and he's coming after you, Sarah. He means you grievous harm again.'

Sarah's stomach turned to water and for a moment the room spun crazily. She snatched at her breath to keep a grip. Her mixed feelings for Titus whirled in an agonizing circle of love, hurt, repulsion and fear. She'd give anything to see him again, even for a second, but also she wanted to throw off the smallest memory of him forever.

'Tabbie, that can't be,' she got out through numb lips. 'Titus is dead. I watched him die of heart failure with my own eyes, me and many others, both Kivells and people from the village.'

'He's dead to this world, I grant you, Sarah. But you forget he was buried at Burnt Oak and that means in unhallowed ground. Now he's back from hell and set on revenge. Worse still, he's not the Titus we knew at his end. The devil's taken him back to his prime. He's young and strong again. He stared at me with burning hatred and I felt as if he had scorched my very soul. He stared right into me and I was able to read his thoughts, and then he tossed that fearsome dark head of his away from me as if I was some loathsome worm. There's great peril ahead of you, my dear, you and others in Meryen, including Titus's mother. Everybody hated Titus, but he hated everyone with more than hate itself. He's back for revenge on those who watched him die. I know the squire wasn't there but I sense danger for him too.'

Sarah was taken back to the worse day of her life, that fateful day at Burnt Oak, the community of the Kivells, where Titus had died. Estranged from Titus then, following his violence over his fury that she was not pregnant, as she'd believed on their marriage, she had returned to ask him to take her back, to give her the chance to love and serve him. She had evoked his further rage; she was barren, the result suffered by a few ill-fated women when exposed for years to certain minerals in mine ore, but Titus, already father of a large brood, had wanted more children. A celebration had been underway in Tempest Kivell's house, of the betrothal of Titus's only legitimate son, Sol, and Sarah's childhood friend, Amy Lewarne. Jealous of his son's joy, bitter that Tempest had always favoured Sol over him, and that she had never loved him because he was the result of rape, Titus had been brooding and getting drunk. After beating Sarah he had sworn he'd kill her and then violate her younger sister, Tamsyn, just a child. Tempest's timely intervention had saved Sarah's life, but Titus had grabbed her gun and pushed through the party and attempted to shoot Sol. Believing his mother, who also had 'the sight', had cursed him, he had dropped the gun and fallen down, stricken. He'd begged for help but no one had gone to him, not even Sarah after his threats against Tamsyn. If Titus really could somehow hurt anyone from beyond the grave there was no doubt great tribulation was ahead. At least he couldn't touch Sol and Amy. They had left Meryen with their young children, and Amy's family, to explore the world.

Although it was ridiculous to be thinking this way, Sarah clutched at one hope. 'If Titus's spirit really does roam and is intent on evil, can't Tempest keep him in line? He greatly feared her powers. The last place I want to go is to Burnt Oak, but I should go there, Tabbie, and tell Tempest what you've seen.'

'No!' As if the energy of her past years had returned, Tabbie leaned forward and bracketed Sarah's face with her knuckly hands. 'Tempest will not be able to prevail against him. No one can. I think it's very likely she's had the same vision anyway. Sarah, you are in mortal danger, you must believe me. You must never drop your guard. You have an enemy who abounds with cunning and burns to make you pay the cruellest cost. I will give you a talisman and you must never go forth without it about your neck, but you will need every ounce of your strength, every scrap of common sense and exhortations to the Almighty to withstand the terrible force that is about to come upon you.'

On her straw mattress that night, in a partitioned corner of the shack's single room, Sarah touched the topaz and silver pendant resting on her chest. It was one of the fascinating treasures Tabbie had procured, most probably from a shipwreck. Could this splendid piece ward off the evil Tabbie swore was relentlessly heading her way? If Titus was about to haunt her, and others, why wait until four years had slipped by? If she had ventured outside today would she have encountered his spirit? Could his spirit not appear to her within these walls? A stab of fear was eased away by the reassurance that nothing bad could happen in here. Tabbie had no doubt placed a blessing or a spell on the threshold.

Sleep evaded her, her mind drifted and laboured. One moment she thought the premonition too fanciful – after all, Titus couldn't really come back from the dead. The next she was beset by anguish and dread, and fear for the others under threat. People might despise her and look down on her, but she wished no one any harm, certainly not her former mother-in-law, Tempest Kivell, who had always been good to her. And still she wrestled with her confused feelings for Titus and how she would actually feel if she ever really did see him again.

Two

U pstairs in the drawing room of Poltraze, Tara Nankervis glanced at the two men in her life and stifled a weary sigh. Both were distracted, neither wanting to be here with her. Joshua, her husband, the squire of Meryen, who rarely joined her at all, was no doubt fretting about either his withered plants or his lover, the thoroughly obnoxious and somewhat frightening Laketon Kivell. Five years ago, he had installed the former master carpenter, also a connoisseur of botany, as his head gardener, but their feelings had died for each other, and Tara was aware of the constant friction that now existed between them. Joshua's crippling blow had seen the end of his normally placid temperament. He met everything with extreme irritation and bawled at the servants unfairly. He was barely civil to Tara. He was only taking tea with her and his brother Michael to retain the illusion to the servants that he had a traditional marriage.

The widowed Michael was Tara's lover and the father of her four-year-old daughter, Rosa Grace, but most likely his thoughts were centred on his burning interest: after painstakingly sifting through old papers and documents to outline the Nankervis history he was recording it in volumes, monastery style. He spent hours buried in the library here rather than at home in Wellspring House, the former dower house, in the grounds, and nowadays less time with Tara. She knew he wasn't bored with her but he had outgrown their affair. She had a suspicion he was turning elsewhere for lovemaking, for he sought her bed less and less. She had long grown bored with the arrangement but had kept it on, for Michael's arms were the only ones to hold her. She hated it when the three of them were together; until Joshua's calamity, with the unspoken agreement that none mentioned the others' infidelity, they had existed amiably enough.

Tara had served afternoon tea and the servants had cleared the room, warily skirting around their master, who had complained the marble cake was stale and the servants clumsy. Now what? Embroidery or lacework or a book? There was nothing else to do. The men were not intent on conversation and the harsh weather and gathering darkness meant a stroll outside was inadvisable. Joshua did not like her viewing his withered trophies, anyway. And the dark heaps of destroyed foliage outside were like mocking tombs. She longed to go far away and to be in some distracting company.

Restless throughout the tea drinking, Joshua rose sharply with a brusque sigh. Verging on forty years – sixteen more than Tara – he looked older than he should; the consequence of his woes and the overuse of brandy and wine. In his youth he had been called a carousing stag; now he could be termed a spent old dog. Grey was stippled through his dark hair and heavy lines pleated his eyes and mouth. He had often been clad in serviceable attire and gardening boots but since the blight he invariably presented himself as a none-too-well-turned-out gentleman.

'If you'll excuse me.' He addressed Tara only. His educated voice, once kindly and slightly drawling, was frosted with the dissatisfactions of his life.

Michael merely nodded. The brothers had never been close and didn't bother to communicate now. He got up in his careless manner, a polite smile on his long, studious face. 'I too will take my leave, Tara. Thank you for the tea.' In crisp steps he reached the door before Joshua did.

'Can you not stay?' Tara aimed the question at Michael. 'Rosa Grace will be brought down shortly.'

'Huh!' Joshua strode past Michael and left the room. He tolerated the little girl's presence in his home but the only input he'd had in her life was to insist she be given a floral name, as society might expect of him as her supposed father. Her tinkling voice, pattering feet and fair looks, so like her mother's, seemed to increasingly irritate him.

Tara was offended by what she saw as an insult to her daughter but she was glad Joshua had gone.

'I can hardly stay now,' Michael said, and she could see his relief. 'It wouldn't look right if the uncle stayed and not the father.'

Tara was dismayed at his protest. Michael cared for Rosa Grace, as he did his two older daughters, but he merely saw them as pretty young beings to be allotted only momentary indulgence.

'You are Rosa Grace's father. It seems I have to keep reminding you of that.' Tara's dark-blue eyes glinted with accusation.

'I'll never forget it is so,' he replied, not without impatience. Tara was of a pleasing gentle disposition, intelligent and still quite fascinating, and with a flawless, pale-skinned, fair beauty that made her wholly desirable, but she was in danger of turning into a nag. He kept up with Rosa Grace's progress and enjoyed a few moments with her now and then, making an effort when his three girls joined together for special occasions like birthday parties, but children, and people in general, held little appeal for him. It would be different if Rosa Grace had been a boy, his son set to inherit the squire-ship, it would amuse and motivate him about Poltraze's future rather than its past.

Anyway, he liked to come and go as he pleased, preferring long hours in his own company. Today, he was eager to reach a new interest. A few weeks ago while out riding through the woods he had emerged by the gatehouse. The gatekeeper's wife had been outside and he had halted to pass a word with her for she was a comely, curvaceous woman with a certain gleam in her eye. She had offered him a drink of porter and he had quickly found she was well versed in the art of lovemaking. The follow-up encounters had been equally as exciting. Her passion was of a distinctly improper sort, she did and said things Tara had no knowledge of and wouldn't dream of doing if she did, and he couldn't stay away from her for long. The fact that the gatekeeper didn't mind because he was conducting an affair of his own with a parlourmaid meant Michael didn't have to skulk about and it made it all fantastically wicked.

Watching Tara's finely shaped face fall, he gave way to guilt. He had a fond devotion for her. She treated him with care and respect, unlike his bitch of a late wife, who had berated him for not being ambitious and for choosing to shun a high social life. Tara did not deserve her empty marriage and her stifled life. 'A few minutes, then,' he offered. He closed the door, unaware that a footman was obscured behind a giant-sized fern on a side table in the corridor

When Michael had gone and Rosa Grace had been taken back up to the nursery, loneliness fell on Tara like a shroud. The bleakness of her life seemed to grow with every passing day. Michael would not return and join her tonight. They had grown apart in much the same way as many married couples seemed to do, but she would never regret their affair. If not for him she wouldn't have her wonderful child – Joshua had never consummated their marriage. Rosa Grace was all she had. She had lost her close friend Amy Kivell to adventure. She missed Amy so much and envied her, travelling the colonies, sharing the long-held dream of her husband, Sol, while she didn't really have a husband at all. She would never know the love of a soulmate as Amy did.

How was she to abide this lonely evening, when she would have to dine alone yet again? It wasn't worth the effort to change her dress but she would have to go through with the social nicety. She didn't want to upset the servants' routine and cause more unease in the house. Michael grumbled about the miserable atmosphere. He swore the house exuded feelings of its own, and that in the last few days it had taken to brooding again. Poltraze was not a glorious piece of architecture. Pre-Tudor in origin, graceless extensions had been tacked on during each change of style. Before Tara became its mistress it had been gloomy, and like many old structures it was said to be greatly haunted. Tara didn't doubt there were ghosts. She had seen and heard many inexplicable things herself. Now gloom lurked again from its many rooms to the picture gallery and the Long Corridor; everywhere. The five years of Tara's marriage, the young Queen Victoria's reign, had seen modernizations, tiled floors and walls of bathrooms, and trompe-l'œil effects that simulated more expensive materials to give false grandiosity to glass, walls and fireplaces. The new comfort and brightness had been fleeting. Tara found her home a cold, lacklustre prison.

She went to her bedroom to idle the time away until her maid came to her. The lanterns and the fire kindled under the plaster mantelpiece cast a rosy glow and appealing shadows but did nothing to dispel her melancholy. She stared at the bed that Joshua had forsaken and felt cheated and angry. She had been a mere pawn in their marriage, arranged by his controlling, amoral father, Darius, and his second wife, her Aunt Estelle, for the fortune settled on her. Darius Nankervis had not known the truth of Joshua's sexuality. He would have destroyed him if he had. Soon after Tara's wedding, Darius and Estelle had suffered a horrific death in the west wing, burning in their bed; Joshua now occupied the rebuilt suite, his lover using it arrogantly, at will. Now Michael, to whom she had turned after she witnessed an encounter between Joshua and Laketon Kivell and learned the truth of Joshua's reluctance to be intimate with her, had forsaken her. Tara made few snap decisions but she made one now. Her affair with Michael was over. He could go his own way. If only she could do the same.

What was stopping her from getting away from Poltraze and starting a new life with Rosa Grace? She paced back and forth on the Persian carpet. There was no one here she would miss. She felt hollowed out and it was time she did something about it. She had always been loyal to duty but she was beyond that now. Joshua was unlikely to insist she stay, in fact he'd probably welcome her permanent absence and not really care what people thought. He didn't seem to care about anything any more. He had once been proud to show off his gardens to the gentry, but since exalting Laketon Kivell as his aide he had jealously kept them to himself, or had that been the controlling Kivell's decision? The gardens were a wasteland and the house was increasingly suffocating and morbid. It was not a place to bring up her daughter. Joshua had always been generous to her. If she could persuade him to settle an allowance on her, enough to live in a suitable house in a pleasant spot, with a maid, cook-general, gardener and nursemaid, she and Rosa Grace would do very well. It wasn't easy to gain an audience with Joshua. She would write him a letter and get her maid to pass it to his valet. A new life for her and Rosa Grace raised her hopes and put a lift in her step. If Michael objected, too bad, he had taken too little interest in Rosa Grace for his opinion to be considered.

She went to the window and pulled aside the drapes and lace, aiming to capture a hint of freedom. Lights from the downstairs rooms and the lanterns outside the front door lit up a section of the lawn below. Halfway down the sweeping green began an avenue of towering conifers, casting shadows, which unlike those in the room threw foreboding murkiness. A small movement among them made her gasp. Somehow she knew it wasn't one of the dogs or a groundsman, or anyone else who had the right to be there. She pressed her face to the cold glass to make sure she wasn't imagining a presence.

She gripped the curtains. There was a figure, definitely someone there, a man. She let the curtains fall so she was only looking out through a wedge. Well set and tall, the trespasser was still. Apparently, he was just watching the house. Sense told her to ring and order the intruder dealt with, yet she peered and tried to make out more about him. He stepped away from the bushes and her heart leapt in worry he might see her, but she held her course now she could see him better. He wore a gentleman's clothes. Perhaps he was an acquaintance of Joshua's. Joshua had not long left the house and she'd assumed he'd gone straight to Laketon Kivell, but this man could be waiting for him. He might be a new lover. No, that couldn't be so. Joshua quarrelled with Laketon Kivell but he was nervous, even afraid of him. She had overheard him grovelling for understanding and forgiveness on more than one occasion. He wouldn't foolishly take another lover.

Tara tightened her brow. The stranger seemed familiar somehow. Then she knew why. He was a Kivell! Easy to tell for they all shared the same strapping dark looks. This man was not one she thought she had seen before. Even Laketon Kivell, who dressed rather like a fop and behaved above his station, did not own such fine attire or show such a definite touch of authority. The man came forward again, as if flaunting his trespass. He lifted his chin and Tara knew he was staring straight up at her. She shot back, a hand to her mouth. She had seen his face quite clearly and he was very

much like the rogue Titus Kivell. Memory of that evil individual brought her to abhorrence. The stranger must be a
Kivell relative from somewhere but why was he lurking about
Poltraze? If he had wanted to see Laketon he would have
gone to his cottage in the grounds.

She rang the bell and a short time later heard the dogs
barking and the shouts of the footmen and grounds staff.
Returning to the drawing room she waited for the report. Her
thoughts wandered to Titus Kivell's widow. She had known
Sarah Kivell briefly. As a girl, Tara had met Amy in a quiet
place on the downs and sometimes Sarah had accompanied
her. Sarah too had lost her only friend when Amy left. Sarah
was a tragic figure but a proud one too, refusing the help
Tara had offered through Amy. Tara compared her life with
the bal-maiden's; she had a privileged life with all the neces-
sities and comforts but she was nearly as miserable as Sarah.

The report was a long time coming. The ageing butler
entered on an important glide. Upright, thin and disagreeable
of countenance, he intoned, as if he had dipped his tongue
in vinegar, 'The dogs picked up a scent but I'm afraid the
intruder managed to slip away, ma'am. The men are stationed
in the grounds for the night as a precaution.'

'Thank you, Fawcett.' Tara dismissed him with a swish of
her hand. She loathed the sanctimonious shrew-like flunkey.
All the servants were aware of the true nature of their squire's
interests but all except this horrid smirking little man were
wholly respectful towards her, obviously sympathizing with
their mistress, who treated them well.

'Shall I order word be sent to the master, ma'am?'

Tara withheld eye contact with him for a moment, but she
could well imagine his hard eyes twitching and the raising
of his superior nose. Fawcett would know where the squire
was and why. The servants had been ordered never to disturb
him while he was not in the house. Fawcett would enjoy his
master being embarrassed. In a glacial voice she replied, 'As
everything is under control the squire need not be informed
until the morning when he is in the steward's office.'

'Very well, ma'am.' Fawcett withdrew and closed the door
after him without the slightest sound, but Tara felt there was
a triumphant simper in his action.

'You're certainly one individual I won't miss,' she seethed. She returned to her room and the window.

The intruder had successfully stolen away, an easy task for a cunning Kivell. Their line led back to nobility, long intermingled with the lawless. Living under their own rules, the land they dwelt on belonged to them. During the last few years they had branched out from their close-knit community, Burnt Oak, to seek respectability in the ever-expanding world. Many businesses in Meryen were now owned by a Kivell. The locals had begun to marry into the family, but others complained they were covetous and planned to take over the entire village.

The village . . . Tara turned away from the window and sank down on the couch. In her hopes to get away she had forgotten her duty to the inhabitants of Meryen. Little would have been done for the poor labouring classes in recent years if she hadn't persuaded Joshua to provide a doctor and a school, and some land to build other public buildings. She had set up a number of charities which drew scant support from among the neighbouring ladies now that Poltraze had lost its past glory and boasted no up-and-coming men of importance. Without her, the poor would almost certainly be abandoned altogether. The sick, the young and old would suffer if she went away. She had a duty to them, but her first duty was to Rosa Grace.

Her heart was sore and burdened as she wrote the letter to her husband.

Three

'Hello, Sarah, I've come back for you.'

Titus was there in front of her. Just as Tabbie had predicted, he had come. He was strong and forceful, in clothes of leather and fine linen, but he was not young again. He was as she'd last seen him, his long black hair touched by silver, his striking swarthy face scarred like a warrior's from fighting, fights he had mostly instigated himself. The breath clamped inside Sarah's lungs and her insides iced through with fear. Her work apron and croust bag fell from her hand. She was on her way to the mine and had been looking all around, as she'd done for the last week since Tabbie's vision, in case Titus appeared somehow. Now he had and he was inches in front of her. A moment ago there had been no one ahead. He had materialized out of nowhere.

A bitter wind had been plastering her skirt against her legs and tugging on her bonnet, but now it dropped away and the cold dawn sky was suddenly friendly with warmth, the dull grey changing to tints of roses. She had no idea why this should happen and she was still afraid, yet she wanted to stay and gaze at the man she had loved so much. She had felt more than infatuation for Titus. He had been the love of her life.

Titus was smiling as with affection but his smiles could not be trusted.

'A-are you going to hurt me?' To be actually speaking to him brought her to panic. She tried to back away but her feet were like blocks of lead.

'Hurt you, Sarah? Why would I want to do that?' His deep gravelly voice was gentle, beguiling.

'I was told you would come back for revenge.'

'Revenge, my darling? On you, you mean? Why would I

want to hurt you? You're my darling girl. I've come back to love you, Sarah, like I should have before. Come to me.' He beckoned with his hands and big coaxing smiles. 'Let me hold you, Sarah. I've missed you so much. Have you missed me?'

'Yes, Titus,' she admitted. It was hopeless to say otherwise. 'More than I'd ever thought possible.' It was foolish to respond to him. She feared him and she didn't trust him yet she longed to go to him. Panic shot into her like darts of burning liquid. Her legs were moving, but she wasn't walking of her own conscious will, she was being propelled by some strange outside force straight towards Titus.

His muscular arms were outstretched towards her and the tips of his rough fingers were beckoning to her. He was smiling at her so tenderly. His dark eyes were like the softest velvet. She felt blissfully happy because this was what she had wanted more than anything. Going to him was the right thing to do. He would never hurt her again. 'I'm coming to you, Titus.'

'Good girl. Let me hold you, Sarah.' His voice floated to her as if on waves of silken love. 'Let me love you. I so want to love you.'

'Yes, yes.' Her heart overflowed with dizzying joys of rapture. All along he had loved her and now she would be his in the way she had always wanted. This was what heaven was like. She had been wrong to believe she would never be worthy to go there. Real love was wonderful and untainted and she was worthy to receive all heaven had to offer. She peeled off her bonnet and shawl. As if she had reached some magic zone her drab dress metamorphosed into a shimmering gown of silver tissue and her long black hair sparkled with gems, rippling down her back and lifted by the breeze like a bridal train. On bare feet she was walking on soft luscious green grass scattered with rose petals. Titus was now in white and bathed in a golden peace. He had come back to her purged of sin and evil and at last she was to receive his devoted eternal love. 'Titus . . .'

'Sarah, my only love . . .'

A sound deafened Sarah's ears and shattered the heavens. The light vanished and darkness swooped down from the sky. Winds lashed from all directions and howled about her head and pounded on her body, pushing on her as if to press her to the ground. Shadows formed in a dark inky avalanche behind Titus, great chasms of black shadows, but of a living substance, with writhing, hissing serpents and creeping, twisting vines. Vile winged gargoyle-like shrieking creatures flew out of the shadows and with talons as sharp as daggers snatched at her hair and ripped off her gorgeous dress, leaving her in the tatters of her own shift. She screamed to Titus to help her, imploring him with splayed hands. The ground beneath her feet was oozing a freezing, lumpy tar-like substance and her flesh was being slashed by razor-sharp stones. She was leaving a stream of blood behind her. 'Titus, help me! Help me!'

He was staring at her with a peculiar smile about his mouth, twisting his wide lips as if into a tangle.

'Titus, you've got to help me!'

'Help you, Sarah? I've got to help you?'

He put his hands on his hips. His clothes turned black and all his hair was black and tangled. He threw back his magnificent head then thrust it forward, and his eyes were wild and crazed. His hair became painted through to white straggles and his skin was riddled with rotting flesh and burning coals were in his mouth. His eyes were monstrous crimson orbs inside a staring skull. It was all a sham! An evil deception, and just like before with Titus, she had fallen for it. On the day he'd died, after raging at her he'd seem to soften and had coaxed her into his arms, but then he'd held her down and boasted maliciously about how he was going to violate and then murder her. How could she ever have believed she had loved a man like that? How could she have remained a slave to his memory? She must flee.

Using all her strength she tried to force her feet to turn around so she could race away. She fought against the colossal power that was taking her ever forward to Titus, but the malevolence was too great for her, it refused to let her go.

She was nearly there, nearly to him. He only had to curve one huge decomposing hand and he could flay her head clean off her shoulders. She saw her next moments, her last. Her head being sent hurtling through the air to sink down into the squelchy hell's mud and her body plunging down to this hell's ground. But the force that was taking her to Titus refused to let her go. She opened her mouth to scream but no sound came out. Terror consumed her, she was no longer a being of flesh and blood but one of fear and panic and torment.

Then she released a scream, a scream sharper and more terrible than a banshee's. She was screaming and screaming.

'I'll help you, Sarah. Let me hold you, hold you.' Titus's voice was disjointed and saturated with hate and his contemptuous mocking echoed like iron clashing on iron all around her, and even inside the being she was being reduced to. 'Then let me kill you, Sarah. There will be no peace for you even then. I'll pursue you in hell for ever and ever.'

'No! No!'

'What? You don't want me now, Sarah? I thought you loved me. You mean you don't love me any more?' His dreadful uproarious laughter echoed through her.

She had reached him. She screamed and pleaded to God to save her. Titus's devilish hands pounced on her throat. He had a new plan to kill her. He pushed in with his thumbs making two indentations of burning agony in her neck. She couldn't breathe. She was about to die. He had won. This monster, who had stolen her innocence, her reputation, her confidence, her family life; and had turned her into a shadow, was squeezing out her mortal life to torment her for all eternity.

Suddenly she hated him as much as she had loved him, even more. The intensity of the hatred made her scream with rage in the depths of her soul. He would not take her soul. A new strength rose up in her and she fought against him, clawing his hands and trying to wrench them away. If she was to die she wouldn't die passively. She'd fight him with every last drop of this new strength.

'No! I won't let you!'

His grip round her neck weakened a little.

'I hate you! I hate you! Do you hear me?' She could barely breathe but somehow she could shout. Darkness was filling her head. And still she shouted and with each shout the beast's terrible hold grew fainter.

'*Keep fighting, Sarah,*' a voice said from somewhere. '*You can do it. You can win.*'

'Yes, I can do it.' Somehow she found her full voice. 'No, Titus Kivell, I won't let you take my life.' She pushed between his raised hands and grasped the talisman round her neck. 'I hate you and you have no power over me. I hate you! I'll hate you for ever! You have no power over me, no more power, no power . . .'

His hands fell away from her. Exhausted by her terrible fight for life she fell in a heap on the scrubland and darkness took her.

'You've won, Sarah,' Tabbie whispered from where she was bent over beside her mattress. 'The brew's worked at last. The fever it gives finally brought out the right nightmare.' While enduring the dreadful pain in her back and joints, Tabbie had held Sarah's hands around the talisman while she'd tossed and writhed. She laid Sarah's hands down at her sides. 'Sleep well, dear one. You'll need your strength for what's ahead. I won't be here much longer to look out for you.'

Sarah woke to find Tabbie was up first for a change and had the oatmeal made ready for breakfast. 'You should have called me,' she yawned, in her calico nightdress, feeling as if she had been pummelled by a pair of fists all night, Titus's fists. She was raw and angry and was prepared for a fight but kept it hidden, though perhaps not successfully, for Tabbie kept aiming knowing looks at her. It wouldn't surprise her if Tabbie knew the harrowing details of her nightmare and its grim and victorious outcome, and that she was in no mood to be cruelly abused ever again. Every memory of Titus was now corrupted. How dare he treat her without respect for her freedom, her life and the very breath in her body? She was angry with herself for allowing herself to be maltreated for so long and then to cling to the memory of the degenerate beast. She should have realized all this long ago. Nothing that had happened to her was her fault. It was perfectly understandable, that she, living in crushing poverty, depressed and weighed down by responsibility, should have been won over by a wicked man's ploys. Titus Kivell had cunningly used

kindness, providing food, clothes and nice things, anony-
mously at first, for her and her family. After he'd gained her
total trust, he had taken her virginity in a rough manner,
under his mother's roof. A ruthless manner, she saw it know.
He had controlled her from the start. A man proud of his
virility in producing children, he'd only married her when
she'd believed she was pregnant. He had violently turned
her out of Burnt Oak for her mistake. And she had foolishly
allowed herself to go on suffering these last four years, but
no more. Titus Kivell was justly in the torments of hell and
she'd not waste another second revering his disgusting
memory. She flopped down on her stool at the bench table.
What was she doing here? Not in Tabbie's home, but in
Meryen? Why hadn't she got away with Arthur and Tamsyn
and old Aunt Molly when she'd had the chance?

'Eat it all up, Sarah.' Tabbie used her gravelly burr kindly,
while ladling out bowls of oatmeal. 'You had another bad
night, twisted and turned throughout most of it. You need
to be well set up to go back to work today. The rain's
moved off at last but 'tis mortally cold. Will be hardship
in Meryen come Christmas. Loss of wages will mean a
good deal of hungry bellies and the dangers of disease that
go with it.'

Sarah left for the seven o'clock start in the bucking shed
at the Carn Croft Mine, carrying her work apron and gook
– a double-thickness bonnet with long protective flaps – and
wearing metal-tipped shoes, petticoats and a calf-length
dress, the traditional length for a bal-maiden to allow for
the dirty conditions. She had wound canvas bands round her
legs for decency and protection from flying shards. Round
her shoulders hung a long black woollen cloak that Tabbie
had given her, then also the gift of a rabbit-fur wrap. With
woollen gloves and stockings she had knitted herself she
felt fortunate to be quite warm and better kitted out than
many of the workers. Tucked inside a canvas bag was her
croust for the morning break, a pasty for the midday meal
and some pennyroyal herb for a mug of tea.

Tabbie hobbled to the screen and looked down on Sarah's
mattress. Sarah had left it tidy, as were her few belongings.
'Dear maid. It was good to see the lift in your chin and your

new determination. May God give you all the strength you'll need. But I've got more than one way to help you.'

When a young woman, Tabbie had been taught to read and write by an indulgent gentleman she had been mistress to. She made the painful journey to a cupboard built by her own hand and took out a sheet of paper, a quill and ink pot; the stationery items stolen for she had been a successful sneak thief. Taking them to the table she eased her hurting bones down to script a document.

Sarah made the short journey from Tabbie's shack on dry feet – Tabbie, and then she in later times, had wisely covered the ground with stones. It was two and a half miles from Meryen to the mine and Sarah was usually the last to arrive, hanging back so she could walk alone. She was soon on the outskirts of the village. She had timed it well. All was quiet. The main exodus of surface and ancillary workers tramping from their mean cottages, their boots and shoes ringing out a heavy tattoo on the cobbles and rough ground, was over. Sarah never went through the main street but slipped onto a well-trodden path that ran in a roughly straight line, parallel to a wide stream, at the back of the dwellings. Exposed stones offered a fairly dry but bumpy passage needing careful attention.

Her mind was on the calculating brute she had married and Tabbie's vision of him. Titus was dead and rotting in his grave in unhallowed ground and he couldn't resurrect himself, so of course, Tabbie hadn't literally meant Titus was coming back, but if anything *of* him in some shape or form *did* turn up, it would have no power over her. It couldn't hurt her. And she would not give way to improbable fears. If Tabbie's vision did come to pass soon she was ready for it.

'Looking out for someone, Mrs Kivell?' The reference to Sarah's married status was a jibe.

Deep in thought, Sarah had not noticed the latecomer, a girl of sixteen years, and the two women with her. She did not reply. The mocker, Dinah Greep, squat, with a sneering nose and blocked pores, never missed a chance to get at her. Dinah's older brother, Jeb, a tribute miner, had pursued Sarah before her marriage and was one of those who made a point of speaking to her kindly. Dinah had warned Sarah to leave

Jeb alone, as if believing she only had to show him a little interest and he'd forsake his wife and two infant children and run away with her. The whole thing was ludicrous. She had made it plain she would never seek love and marriage again. She stopped, stone-faced. The two women were hanging on out of nosiness but their expressions showed they were not happy with the mollusc-like Dinah's spite. Sarah would let the harpy have her say then bring up the rear. She would not have insults aimed at her back.

Dinah went on in a jeering sing-song voice, ending with a peal of laughter, 'You're done up like a dog's dinner. Hoping to attract someone, are you? Got some new fancy lover? Someone old and corrupt like Titus? I bet old Titus was a beast in bed. You must have enjoyed it. You must miss him all through the nights, eh, Sarah?'

The low opinions of others were unimportant to her and she had not bothered to defend herself before but this mocking was a torment. In the light of her new attitude Sarah felt sullied to have been intimate with Titus, she saw now that he would have raped her the first time had she not submitted to him.

'You should cleanse your mouth out, Dinah Greep.' One of the women, a drab young widow supporting her family, turned on her sharply. 'What would your brother say? You're a disgrace to him. And your poor father and mother would turn in their grave if they could hear the things you say.' Her companion nodded in pious agreement.

Rebellious, quick-tempered, Dinah snarled, 'Mind your own business, Elizabeth Coad. We can't all be good Bible Christians like you, and she there with you, and Jeb.' Then her rubbery sour features narrowed and darkened on Sarah. 'Don't you try giving my brother the eye. Jeb don't want you. He and every man left in the world are too good for you, the village trollop. Why don't you get yourself another Kivell? There's plenty of 'em in the village to choose from. Far too many, in fact. They breed like ruddy rabbits. They're taking us over. Getting rich in their shops on our poor wages, that's what they're doing. Thought you'd like to be a part of that, *Mrs Kivell*. Why don't you fix yourself up with another Titus?'

A click went off inside Sarah's mind, as if a tiny door in

a forgotten corner had been opened, releasing all the emotions she had buried for so long. Her bland expression grew to fiery wrath, her beautiful dark eyes blazed. Striding up to Dinah, she glared and hissed, 'I hate Titus Kivell! Don't you ever dare mention him to me again, you vile little tyrant. The Kivells are loyal to their kinfolk, even those that disgrace them, so you be careful, Dinah Greep, that a Kivell doesn't get you! Their revenge is quick, ruthless and long lasting. You'd deserve every second of it.'

The unexpected onslaught made Dinah quail and gulp down a sob. She backed away, a typical bully, afraid when confronted by someone stronger. She and the others stared at Sarah, shocked by her admission about her late husband.

'Good for you, maid,' Elizabeth Coad said in a hearty manner. 'The village will be glad to hear what you just said. Now you must forgive all that's gone on before and you'll find peace.'

'Why don't you walk on with us?' offered the companion, a gawkish old spinster, and turned on Dinah. 'It was time someone put you in your place, Dinah Greep. Your tongue's full of poison. Mind it doesn't bring you down.'

Sarah met her opponent's hostile gaze. No longer snivelling, Dinah was steeped in malice and adding up a score against her. She didn't forgive anyone, least of all those who humiliated her. Sarah wasn't afraid of the little shrew. 'From this moment forward I renounce the name of Kivell. I'm returning to my maiden name, Hichens. Be sure that it's the only one you use when addressing me in future.'

She went on with the two women, allowing them to chat to her as if she was a lifelong friend, replying with the odd word or two. She didn't need their friendship. She didn't need anything from anyone in these parts. Not long ago she had passed Chy-Henver on the opposite side of the stream, the carpentry business owned by her old friend Amy, willed to her by her father. Her husband, Sol, had bought into it, leaving it to another Kivell to run; an investment for them to come back to. She had looked forward to seeing Amy again when her travels were over, now she might never do that. She was not sure how but she would leave here soon, go far enough away to shed every bad memory for ever.

Four

So this had been his father's home? The once anarchic community he had lived in and governed, under his mother's matriarchal influence, until his death at the age of forty-six. Heart failure had claimed Titus Kivell's life, and according to the information, he, Kit Woodburne, had gleaned, Titus's heart had been corrupted by drink, bitterness and hatred. Kit understood how a heart of such darkness could betray and kill a relatively young man; his half-brother, Charles Howarth, who had only recently come to know of his existence, had warned him that he was in peril of succumbing to the very same thing. He cared not about that.

Burnt Oak was set off Bell Lane in a large plunging valley, with the land behind supporting a farm. Sitting astride a mount from the property he was renting in the nearby prosperous copper-mining parish of Gwennap, Kit was spying on the Kivell holdings. Through the hawthorn bushes on top of the rambling hedgerow, he watched the activity below of the quiet, industrious sort as men, women and children went about their enterprise in the several workshops, the forge and the farmyard: people content in the knowledge they belonged to generations of a strong and formidable family; cosy scenes which even the bleak frosty weather did nothing to dispel. No doubt down there were fathers teaching their sons their given craft or trade. Kit made a pained expression.

The property was flung amid the far-reaching estate of Poltraze, and no doubt was an open wound to the Nankervises. There was an ancient reason why the ten-acre Kivell land was bracketed within the squire's territory. In the time of the Norman Conquest a Nankervis and a Kivell knight had ridden for the prize of the manor. The Kivell had lost, taking a fall from his horse, and had grudgingly had to make do with the smaller lot. He had gone on to form a remote clan that had married into undesirables, becoming troublesome, until a few years ago when it suited them to break out into the expanding world of business. Kit was here to cause trouble for the clan, more than that, pandemonium, if he could, and for one Kivell in particular.

A few nights ago, thinking how different things would have been if the original Kivell had won that race – for one thing Kit would probably never have been born – he had been led to spy out the squire's despoiled grounds rather than coming here as he'd first intended. The wits and cunning he'd developed during his appalling childhood had enabled him to slip among the blackened hulks that had once been prestigious camellia shrubs and the like, but he had not gone unseen. The lovely young woman – who had to be the squire's sadly neglected wife – peering out of a bedroom window made him chance a closer look at her. The lamplight had given her an aura of enchantment. He could have stared up at her for hours. He would engineer the pleasure of gazing at her in close quarters. A woman like Mrs Joshua Nankervis should not be allowed to be neglected by male company. A little earlier he had followed the squire's departure, finding him soon to be met by another man – a Kivell, indeed – who had taken him into an intimate embrace. The squire being of that sexual persuasion was interesting. Finally he had returned to his secluded house. His manservant, the only person he had ever trusted, had seen to it he was provided with diverting and experienced female company, and opium. A prolonged drugged daze had delayed his visit here to Burnt Oak.

Half a dozen large and attractive dwellings, thatched or slate-roofed, were also part of Burnt Oak and all were protectively encased inside a fortress square of granite walls. It was both something of a tribal arrangement and a medieval court, with, Kit's good sight made out, dashes of ostentation in the new Victorian manner. There was the added sheltering of a few proud oaks. All in all, it was a marvel and an outlandish curiosity, with the strangeness of a graveyard at its far end. For generations Kivells had been buried in the grounds and somewhere down in that unsanctified sod were his father's remains.

What would it feel like to stand over Titus Kivell's decaying bones? The man who had been as corrupt as his now putrefied flesh? Kit could not suppress a fierce, angry shudder and next came the hated and all too familiar sick hollowing out in his gut. Would his hatred of that scurrilous individual burn even more intensely than it had for the main of his twenty-seven years? It would be hard not to dance on and foul the grave of the man who by force had sired his existence, imparting to him a life that had been wretched and blighted in its almost every moment.

Down there in the grandest house of the pack, sweetly named Morn O' May, dwelt his grandmother, Tempest Kivell, the she-witch who was the original source of his distress and desolation. Kit hated her with a passion that sometimes sacrificed his reason. He knew all about her. She was a lady by birth, and she was a murderess who had never been brought to the law. Her heart was good and kind to some, dark and heartless towards others, the latter towards his father. From a wealthy Quaker family, she had been ravished by Garth Kivell and forced into marriage, kept practically a prisoner until Garth's death at her own calculating hand. She had turned much from the Bible, yet still followed parts of it.

'Well, here's a verse from the Good Book for you, Grandmother,' he hissed between clenched teeth, making his darkest of dark eyes fragment and burn, 'Jeremiah, chapter twenty, verse fourteen. "Cursed be the day wherein I was born." That sums up my life and my heartfelt feelings, Tempest Kivell. Now your turn has come to say the same thing.'

On resolute feet, Sarah was heading for Burnt Oak, passing through the village on her way rather than skirting around it over the soggy downs. She no longer hid herself away. She had been a victim of her circumstances, not the instigator of them. She would be a victim no more and she had the worth and the right to wander where she might. She took her time, head up ready to meet any curious gaze. Her change of heart about her dead husband had brought much comment, some haughty and unforgiving, '*It's about time!*' '*Doesn't mean she's no better than she ought to be.*' Some, like the two women she had walked with to the mine that day, were genuinely pleased. The truly God-believing had rejoiced, the Bible Christians exhorting her to forgive Titus and fully repent her ways. She would change when and how she chose to.

It was Sunday, and the journey through the straggling slopes and dells of Meryen led her past her old family home, tiny Moor Cottage, next to the Nankervis Arms, one of the four drinking establishments. Further on was the Anglican church in its usual subdued voice. Most notable were the new villas, here, there and everywhere, beautifully crafted but pieces of blaring showiness by their Kivell business owners. They employed servants from the village, a reason for envy and resentment, the workers seen by some as turn-coats. The two Methodist chapels, at suitable distances from the church, one in the main thoroughfare, the other cutting off down a little side street, were singing their hymns more stridently. Louder than the three congregations put together, at the far end of the village the Bible Christians were 'being happy'. Jeb Bray had kindly invited her to join his family in the new sturdy chapel, rendered much by his own hands and funded by him and fellow miners and some interested better-off Quakers from Gwennap. The pleasantries Sarah had been offered had fed her desire to better her lot at last. Why shouldn't she live well and have nice things? There was no need to go on denying herself. She had never deserved Titus Kivell to come into her life. Tempest Kivell had entreated her to come to her for help at any time, but as Titus's widow she had the moral right to have part of what had been his anyway. So she was off to her marital home, without telling Tabbie where she was going, knowing her friend would implore her not to go, but to perhaps write to Tempest Kivell instead; she had learned to read and write during the short time she had lived at Burnt Oak. She wanted her due and she wanted it as soon as possible. She had already wasted too much of her life. Then, as someone of means, she could approach old Aunt Molly and Arthur and Tamsyn. She yearned to see her family again. She had left them hurt and bewildered by refusing to accompany them to their new home at Redruth. Her five-year silence must also have caused them pain. How could she have forsaken her only family?

She would plead to them for forgiveness. She wouldn't simply pack up and leave Tabbie, but it would be wonderful, after Tabbie's death, if she could live again with her family. A better future was beckoning.

She was nearly there. A couple of bends, a long, roughly straight stretch of winter-desolate hedgerow, then she'd reach the wide iron gate before the trek down the dipping muddy cart track to the community. She smoothed at her centre-parted hair where it emerged at the front of her best bonnet, a ruche-trimmed, second-hand affair. Her two-piece dress and Tabbie's cloak were both well worn but she hoped she looked good. After years of not caring about her appearance it was important again.

She sighed in impatience to discover a man, a gentleman by his appearance, of tall, broad and a slightly stooped stature, about to lead a horse through the open gate. She came to a sharp halt.

'Mama, why are you peeping out of the window? It's good to see you out of bed again but I can see you're all tense. You should be resting. What are you looking at?'

Tempest Kivell did not turn round to her only daughter. The knuckles of her shapely fingers were white from gripping the sill, but not from fear of her unsteadiness. 'Come and see for yourself, Eula. Be careful he doesn't see you. It's *him*.' The voice that had once flowed like honey was dry and feeble. The once-proud shoulders sagged. 'He's arrived at last.'

'Who has? You don't mean *him*? He's really here?' A doughty mother of seven, and living under her mother's roof, Eula, still a Kivell, having wed a cousin, did not doubt her mother's breathless statement, and she whispered fearfully, 'Oh no.'

Several days ago her mother had been seized by a terrifying vision. 'We're all in great danger,' she had declared in frenzy at the end of it. It had been unknown for Tempest, normally so regal and calm, to be in hysterics, and Eula and the rest of the community had been alarmed. Her account of Titus's imminent return from the netherworld, hell-bent on retribution, had been rapidly followed by a loss of all

Tempest's strength, and until now she had been too weak to lift a foot out of bed.

'It can't be Titus, Mama. That's impossible.' Eula had tried to renounce the vision at the time, but she had found it hard and had crept about in trepidation. Her mother's powers were unshakably accurate.

'I know that,' Tempest had gasped in mortification. 'But someone of Kivell blood is coming for us. Even people beyond our boundaries won't be safe.'

Tempest could also not be moved from the belief that the end of her life was not far off, but she kept that to herself. She feared for her soul, having deliberately shot her violent husband to death, but it was the anxiety for her loved ones and innocents outside Burnt Oak that had filled her with dark horrors and sapped her strength.

Eula joined her at the cross-leaded window, staying concealed behind the jade-green tabby silk curtains. 'See him, up there behind the hedge?' Tempest croaked. 'He's been watching us for some time. I don't need a spyglass to know he's a young man, just as I saw in my dream. And he looks very much like your brother did.'

Having the better eyesight, Eula related that the stranger was clad in fine apparel. 'A Kivell, yet not a Kivell. How very strange.' She could not bring herself to offer more than that.

'Strange?' Tempest's voice was a mere rusty echo. 'We have much more than strangeness ahead of us. We must not drop our guard for a moment. Eula, help me get dressed. I will receive this individual in my sitting room.'

'Mama, you will not even make it down the stairs,' Eula cautioned.

'Then I will be carried down!'

'Let me get the men together,' Eula pleaded. 'They can see him off.'

'No! That sort of strength and unity is not the way. He wants to see inside my soul. It's something I must allow. It is our only hope.'

Kit heard light steps approaching from the direction of the village. Was a relative of his arriving home? The old woman herself? No, she never walked the lanes. She was a sprightly sixty-year-old but saw herself as too grand to go anywhere on foot. He swung round, straightening his back and holding his loftiness at his most intimidating. He beheld a most pleasing sight but retained his belligerence.

Sarah almost dropped to the hard hostile ground from sheer alarm. She couldn't have been more shocked if she was facing Old Nick himself. Tabbie's vision had been absolutely and chillingly correct. Titus was back from the dead and had been returned to his youth. The brute in him was whole and evident. She stared at him, horribly expecting his next move to be an attempt on her.

Kit was bemused by this gorgeous creature of splendid midnight and dull autumn colouring being so troubled by him. She was near panic yet something mysterious was preventing her from taking flight. Her crystal-dark eyes never wavered from his face and were saucer-like and threatening to swell from their sockets. She was in a state of utter disbelief. Despite the barrier of her cloak, he could tell her chest was rising and falling in over-breathing. She must be tingling from head to foot and surely would soon faint. He was pretty sure he knew why she was in a frightened stupor, and in fact, who she must be. Sarah Kivell, née Hichens, his widowed young stepmother, the foolish mine girl who irrationally glorified his father's sordid memory. And she was as superstitious as most of the Celtic breed that inhabited this bleak and lowly county of Cornwall, and right now she was imprisoned by the belief he was actually her dead husband. The stupid little thing . . .

'Don't you know it's rude to stare at one such as I am, girl,' he snapped.

Sarah came to with a cruel start which sent her gasping for breath and fighting to keep her balance. She threw out a hand and received only the harsh comfort of the winter-ravaged hedge. She had been caught in the echoes of her dream but her senses cleared and her mind was sharp. This wasn't Titus. How could she have thought he could raise himself from the dead? Only the Good Lord could do that and He no longer had business with Titus. This stranger had the stamp of Titus about him, more so than any other Kivell, apart from Sol, but she should have seen the dissimilarities. There was the tendency to stoop, while Titus had stood stock straight. A far paler skin tone, a softer jaw, blue eyes and not black, the lack of scars on his more refined face. One thing he did share with Titus was his sense of menace. Could this man be a 'turn of a blanket'? Titus had sired many children by his first wife and two common-law wives and he'd boasted he had many more brats scattered about. The most striking difference was the man's cultured tones, unnerving in their low, supple delivery. Titus had spoken with a deep gravelly burr, as common as he had been.

Suddenly she felt the talisman hanging about her throat, as if the silver and topaz itself was reminding her of its protective presence. It topped up her courage and new higher self-esteem and she formed a sense of outrage. Whoever this man was she wasn't going to meekly bow to his higher station and animosity. 'I don't care to be spoken to like that,' she fired the words at him, the creamy skin around her eyes and mouth drawn tight. 'You might be togged up but I don't take you for a gentleman.' She turned on her heel and went back the way she had come. She would knock on her mother-in-law's door another day.

Amusement and deeper interest were Kit's reactions. The girl had some grit in her after all. 'Sarah Kivell!' he called at her fast diminishing back. Rough and ordinary she might be but she walked with a grace beyond her humble status.

Burning with ire, Sarah stamped back to him. 'I do not acknowledge that name. I am Sarah Hichens. I hope never to chance upon you again, but if I do, and you choose to speak to me, address me as such.' She made to march off again.

While marvelling that she could speak so well, Kit was overtly curious about this. 'I beg your pardon, Miss Hichens. So you no longer wish to use the Kivell name?'

'No, and I wish I'd never had the cruel misfortune to have taken it.' She was baffled by the turn in his stance, and the almost melodic variance in his voice, but she was struck again by the fact that he must be the man in Tabbie's vision. Fear pricked her nerves but she was determined not to be overwhelmed by him. She demanded, 'Are you one? A Kivell?'

'I do not have the Kivell name but I do happen to have

Kivell blood.' Kit was careful, almost confidential in his answer. He saw a possible ally here. For some reason the girl had a worthy amount of bitterness in her concerning Titus Kivell. Such a tremendous change of heart usually led to the sort of bitterness that was apt to seek revenge. She could be useful to him. Good, now a look of perplexity was marking her exquisite features. Nature had kindly bypassed the jadedness it usually endowed on one steeped in much hardship and sorrow.

Rather than give in to natural inquisitiveness, Sarah retained her senses. 'I do not really wish to know who you are, sir.' She was foolish to have come here and it would be foolish to remain with this man. She must hasten back to Tabbie.

Kit tapped his well-barbered chin with his knuckles. What had caused the girl's enormous turn against the devil Titus? At some time he would press to learn all there was to know about the delectable Sarah Hichens-Kivell. But now, to pay his respects to his grandmother.

Five

The instant Kit was through the gate a company of barking lurchers raced up and formed themselves as an escort. No doubt all visitors received this dubious honour. He didn't care for dogs. Apart from lapdogs and well-trained hunting hounds the creatures were invariably territorial, intrusive about one's person, and some were vicious. He knew about vicious dogs. As a boy, he had been guarded by a pair of edgy, cantankerous mutts, guarded in the manner of being kept in on the small country property where he'd been raised, and to keep visitors out. He had never received visitors, it had been strictly disallowed.

The grey, wire-haired, sharp-nosed lurchers were well kept, and no doubt, trained to be suspicious and could easily turn nasty. He trotted on down the steep gradient of the valley, but after a cursory sniff close to the horse's legs the lurchers did no more than keep close. The second steadfast iron gate, incorporated in the lichen-clad granite walls, was open wide and he went into the compound with the horse's hooves crunching noisily on the circular gravelled court. It was an alien sound that burrowed deep inside his ears, as did all new sounds wherever he went, for he had never belonged anywhere, and here, where he had blood kin aplenty, it felt the most alien of all. A silent childhood cry of aching loneliness, the desperate plea of old for comfort and acceptance emerged from his hidden depths. He stamped it down with the ruthlessness he'd acquired to survive another wretched day of isolation. He must lock arms only with one companion, hatred, and the friend it brought along with it, revenge. They were his reason and purpose for being here. He'd come to see that Tempest Kivell paid for her crimes against him, the grandson she didn't know had existed for all his miserable life.

He enjoyed the effect he had on the Kivell clan, open-mouthed stares and small gasps, until he realized he was being regarded not with the avid curiosity for a stranger of their breed suddenly coming among them. These people, who crowded out of their homes and workplaces and gathered on the stone-chipping courtyard, seemed to be expecting him. Despite keeping to the house at Gwennap his notable resemblance could not have gone unnoticed by the staff left there and likely it had been carried here, or perhaps even by the doxy brought to him. If that was the case, Kit could understand their suspicion. They would want to know why he'd taken so long to make himself known to them. But why the disquiet, hostility even, glittering from every frosty eye and every bold frame? Were they so easily offended? They were devil-may-care, supposedly. But family was everything to them and they must be offended that he had been keeping his distance. There were a great many children here, the Kivells being prolific breeders. These well-fed, well-dressed brats imitated their parents' unreceptive stance. This was not a puritanical clan; they had small respect for God or the law. So if they'd heard of his drunken womanizing and resorting to opium it wouldn't be that which was making them so unwelcoming. The dogs were still in watchful formation about him, and while he was still wary of them, these people did not scare him. Some of them might have a hidden firearm on their person; so did he.

Reining in, he swept friendly smiles to one and all, cloaking the supercilious jibes lurking beneath his surface. These people thought themselves individuals but here they were in distinctive muted shades of homespun cloth, fine stuff, but a uniform nonetheless. The women, most were comely, for poverty was not their enemy as with the labouring masses, more or less favoured the same hairstyle, a centre parting with looped braids about the ears, and white aprons edged with intricate lace. It was something like a secretive religious cult here but without the religion, and the women did not seem particularly subservient to the men. The men looked to the last one capable of repelling any invader or of readily desiring to storm another's stronghold. The Kivells were known for their brawn, intelligence, wits and cunning. Tough stuff, Kivell blood, and he had it running through his veins, but he would be very careful how he conducted himself here. 'Good morning,' Kit shot brightly to the entire gathering. 'Please forgive the liberty of my unannounced arrival.'

An ancient Kivell, poised slightly in front of his kinfolk, with a thick white spade beard and a blast of white hair to his hefty shoulders, scratched his leathery hook nose, making the point of delaying a return greeting. 'Good morning to you. What might your business be here?'

His brogue was so heavy and rural that at first Kit failed to understand him and he thought he was getting a rebuff. He reached inside the top pocket of his riding coat and proffered a card to the elder. The details stated: *Mr Charles Howarth, Howarth Shipping Line, Bristol.* His half-brother's identity. 'Charles Howarth, sir. I am hoping to be received by Mrs Tempest Kivell.'

'I'm Genesis Kivell,' the elder said, after reading the card. He gave a brisk nod towards the prime house. 'She's waiting for 'ee – Mr Howarth.'

Kit frowned. So he definitely had been seen in the area and his grandmother was expecting him, and not simply as someone who resembled her son but as someone she saw no reason to trust.

His horse was led off, and Genesis Kivell showed him to the threshold of Morn O' May. He passed the card to a woman waiting on the doorstep. She glanced at it but showed no interest in the details. She looked Kit up and down and with each movement of her pretty hazel eyes her expression grew graver. In her late thirties, of large frame, and a good figure nourished by good cooking, he got the impression she was normally a kindly woman who'd not shy from Good Samaritan acts, but right now she was stiff and pursed-lipped.

Silently, she ushered him inside but did not offer to take his hat and gloves; he was not welcome to stay for long. All she said was, 'This way,' but Kit knew she was bursting to confront him, to warn and threaten him. He had the notion she had been cautioned to say very little.

She was not unattractive, and as he followed her into the

hall he gazed up the stairs, which divided at the top onto an arced landing, and he pondered behind which of the many doors up there was her bed. Then he snapped off the thought, for if she was Eula Kivell, as he believed, then she was his aunt and such a musing was disgusting. More importantly his mind should be only on his reasons for being here.

It had been easy to gain an audience with his grandmother. Her so-called powers of witchery didn't frighten him even though they had his villainous father – that scrap of information had greatly surprised him. Kit didn't believe in all that supernatural tosh. He had seen spectres and visions himself, but only while in his cups or under the influence of opium. It came to him suddenly – disjointed thoughts were apt to rush into his mind – these people might believe he had come for money. He had money, a sizeable fortune left to him by his remote guardian and money of his own making, and he looked as if he was wealthy. He had made many lucrative investments and significant gains at the gaming tables. He wanted nothing from these people except to bring them down, starting with his damnable grandmother. Damn these upstart people, damn them all! They had a little land and through enterprise and deviousness were well placed but it didn't qualify them as gentry, even though they thought themselves above the middle class. The people of Meryen consorted with them but only because they were the weaker element. The Kivells weren't wanted in any society. They were misfits. So was he, and he hated his late father and Tempest Kivell because of it.

As if aware that he had dropped his pretence of cordiality, the woman glanced round at him. He avoided her stare – she would see the bitterness in him. She sighed, an angry sigh. He was as welcome here as the plague, but he was used to that from the other branch of his parentage. Her feet made a light tap along a stone-flagged passage spread with berry-coloured woven runners; his step was heavy and brooding, and she kept glancing behind her as if fearing he might rear up on her.

They passed rooms and each door was shut against him. He noted the paintings, carvings and ornaments as they went along. The Kivells were highly skilled craftsmen but some of their fine acquisitions must be from smuggling and theft.

The massive tapestries caught his eye. One portrayed the Kivell origins, entailing the first owner of Burnt Oak falling off a horse during a race to secure either this land or the manor of Poltraze.

The woman stopped at the end of the passage at carved double doors and put a hand out to bid him wait. She entered the room. Kit put his ear to the solid wood and heard her talking to another female, his grandmother at last. He clenched a fist, felt dizzy and let out a deep breath of excruciating tension. He breathed in deeply, once, twice, three times, sighing out as he exhaled, as a former mistress of his had advised when he succumbed to light-headedness, brought on by his dark thoughts. Why did this have to happen now? He'd have a fainting fit like a woman if he wasn't careful. He must clear his mind. Never had it been more important. Ignoring the racing of his heart he raised his shoulders. He had an awful habit of stooping, a legacy of the relentless put-downs he'd suffered as a boy. He'd hated being tall then, it had made his presence all too obvious.

In her most stylish day dress, a lilac affair with exquisite lace, it took all her strength but Tempest was on her feet to receive the visitor and she would receive him alone. She knew she was in for an ordeal but she had to present a strong front from the beginning because she sensed the stranger's issues were mainly with her. She was about to be faced with a man who bore a close likeness to the son she had despised from his birth, whose only good deed on earth had been his children, the ones who hadn't turned out bad, that was; Sol was her favourite. She missed Sol so much, and now she must be faced with Titus's evil replica. She had been ill since her vision and the strain was killing her. She felt a stab of fear – *killing her literally?* She didn't want to die soon. She wanted to see Sol and his family again before she left this earth.

Eula was urging her to sit down and to allow her to stay in the room. Tempest lifted her pince-nez and glanced again at the visiting card, then clearing the lump of dread in her throat she said, no higher than a whisper, 'Send him in, Eula. Then go, do as I say. This is the right way.'

'If you insist, Mama, but I'll stay just beyond the door in

case you need me.' Eula gripped her mother's hand, anxious at how fragile she was.

Tempest lifted her once-regal chin. What was she about to be faced with?

Eula opened both doors and motioned with her hand for Kit to go in. She wanted to glare at him, make it a warning, but she mustn't interfere with whatever her mother was about to do. Her mother was at her weakest but she did have her powers, and Eula prayed they would not fail her.

Kit held himself as straight as a military man and, thankfully, he felt strangely calm, his mind quick and able to calculate.

At the other end of the thick carpet, Tempest pulled off a stately bearing, remembering to hold her hands together lightly and not too tightly. She must not for a second show how unnerved she was by his coming here. She moved her head to left and right. How much of Titus could she see in this man? He allowed her examination with accommodating passivity. Tempest was taken aback to find the Kivell he most favoured in appearance was Sol. Sol had been wild and arrogant in his youth, but without any of Titus's malice. This stranger was summing her up in return and there appeared to be nothing particularly adverse about him, but he was no doubt being careful.

Kit found himself in a distinctly feminine room, a lavish room of glass display cabinets, tabernacle-framed mirrors, lush greenery on elaborate jardinières and opulent drapery. He found Tempest Kivell prepossessing and noble-featured, with high distinctive cheekbones and jewel-blue eyes. Her black hair was showing the first transition towards grey. She was not hale and strong as his intelligence had reported, but as pale as summer mist and clearly unwell. He had been ungallant towards Sarah Kivell only minutes ago, but it would not amuse him to be uncivil to this woman right now. She was regarding him steadily, an intelligent, shrewd woman, who had survived a brutal marriage, and he was stunned to actually feel some sneaking admiration towards her.

Each was curious about the other on a far deeper level than they had first imagined. Neither felt the need to draw battle lines for the time being.

'You have my sincere thanks for receiving me, Mrs Kivell,' Kit said in the polite voice he would have used in any genteel sitting room.

'Your card gives you the name of Charles Howarth,' Tempest replied, her honey tones scratchy. 'But obviously you have connections with the Kivells. Who, sir, are you exactly?'

'Ma'am, let us not make pretence this is an ordinary occasion. You are curious about me and I will gladly answer all your enquiries. I, in turn, am curious to learn why I am so unwelcome here among the people whom I not long ago became aware as being my kin. Mrs Kivell, I have very good reason to believe your late son, Titus, was my father.' He watched her closely, there was no need, this wasn't a revelation to her, but she was trembling. 'May I be so bold as to suggest that you seat yourself? I am happy to remain standing, as I think you would prefer. Please accept my apologies for coming at an inopportune time. I would have understood if you had sent a message that you were indisposed.'

'Yes, I will sit, Mr Howarth.' Tempest made her feet perform their usual graceful task of conveying her to her tapestry cabriole chair at the window. 'Sit, if you would like.'

To loom over her was what he'd prefer but to gain exactly what he wanted it might be worth a try at gaining her trust. He took the edge of a matching sofa where he was close to her. He wanted to see her face every moment.

Tempest was of the same mind. She felt compelled to gaze at him. 'Would you have understood, Mr Howarth, if I had sent word to say I was indisposed? I think you are not here for the good of this family.'

Kit hated that remark and hated her for saying it. Was this all she had to say to someone so clearly connected to her own flesh and blood? 'Have you ever heard of me, ma'am?' he asked in a grim tone. 'Do you know something about me that you do not approve of?'

'I have never heard of you before, Mr Howarth.' Tempest realized how lame that sounded. The only basis she had for being the slightest offhand with him was a dream, and that would sound ludicrous and mad to those of no belief in matters spiritual. She had foreseen and dreaded this moment, it had made her ill, and although this young man actually existed and was here, even to her it seemed outlandish. He looked a lot like Titus but he was *not* Titus. On the other hand, dreams were for interpreting, and it seemed more than coincidence that although he could have found out at any time he was of Kivell blood and got in contact he had come now. Surely she must trust her psychic abilities and heed the terrible dread that had come upon her. Most of the family had wanted to warn off the stranger who had turned up on their boundary. But to Tempest, that was not the way. And surely he should at least be allowed a hearing? What would Sol have advised? He would have been interested to meet this man who was possibly his half-brother.

Kit frowned darkly. How he wanted to rail against this superior woman. She had never heard of him yet she and her wretched people had chosen to treat him like dirt. Then he was worried. During his drunken or drugged state he might have revealed the true purpose behind his presence in Cornwall to the doxy. She could have run to the Kivells with the information for payment. That must be it. Tempest Kivell had lied, she must have known he had not been far away for the last few days. He should have been rigidly circumspect. He would not make that mistake again.

Tempest saw the trouble darken over him. She sensed some inner torment, and because he reminded her more and more of Sol she was moved by the stirring of guilt. If he was Titus's son, that made him her grandson. But she must not give way to sentimentality. On the other hand, need she fear him so? Her powers had always manifested to help her when she really needed them. She should take heart and explore the vision. Shadows hid good things as well as bad. The image of Titus might be a mocking from beyond the grave but to concentrate only on that might cause her to miss something it had wickedly endeavoured to disguise. This man might simply have come to look her up, his grandmother. People invariably longed to trace their roots to discover who they really were. There was a great sadness in him, more than that, and if he was genuine, her attitude and the fears she had cast upon the family were unjustifiably adding to it. She cleared her throat and found her voice had regained its strength. 'It seems you may very well have a connection to my son, and therefore to the rest of us. How did you come by and how long have you had this knowledge, Mr Howarth?'

Kit raised his straight black brows at her honeyed tones. What was her ploy now? She was no longer trembling in the attempt to sit upright but rather was sagging like a sack of straw. She had relaxed. He fancied that in another minute she would be smiling and offering him tea. Hell's teeth, she was a witch of sorts. He had the horrid sensation he had walked into a trap. He knew then that he did not have all the advantages, as he'd so arrogantly believed. He had set himself up against a witch and her coven. He'd been foolish to believe he could breeze into their lives and upset, even destroy, a centuries-old stronghold.

'Altogether, for about three months. I happened upon a captain of a Falmouth packet in Bristol port, in a certain drinking establishment. He was shocked by the strong resemblance I bore to a man he had known from Cornwall, a man going by the name of Titus Kivell. I have known from a very young age that the man who gave me his name was not my real father.' A lie, he'd thought he'd had no family at all. His real surname Woodburne had, apparently, been plucked out of the air. 'Naturally, my curiosity was whetted. I paid an enquiry agent of good repute to investigate for me. It took a while for the story to be pieced together.' This was how he had come by the truth of his maternal parentage. 'I looked up old records and I tracked down some former servants to obtain details. My parents had never mentioned they had been to Falmouth, but it turned out that they had stayed there on shipping business in 1818, nine months prior to my birth. There was a brief affair.' A lie, he had been sired by Titus in the same brutal manner as Titus had himself. 'My mother, it seemed, was dazzled by Titus Kivell's good looks and wild ways, and apparently by how he could turn on the charm.'

Tempest nodded, reminded of how her son had beguiled Sarah. 'Did her husband discover the affair or did she confess it to him?'

'My mother confessed the moment she knew she was with

child. There had been no physical closeness between her and her husband, a much older man, for some time and she knew she must tell the truth. He had always adored her and he forgave her. He accepted me as his own. It pleased him to have an heir.' Complete and utter lies, it cut into his soul to be saying them.

A similar set-up to the one at Poltraze, Tempest mused. 'How did you discover the truth?'

'There were always whispers among the servants or so it seemed to me. A footman was dismissed for stealing and I came across him quarrelling with the butler while he was being shown the back door. The vengeful footman blurted out that he'd broadcast the fact that I was, forgive me saying this, a little bastard, and he'd drag the Howarth name through the dirt. He was eventually paid off, and my parents answered my earnest questions with the whole sorry truth. They had always been rather remote from me, now I knew why. My mother felt guilty, and Mr Howarth, as I came to think of him after that, chose to keep me in the background. My mother refused to divulge who my real father was and I did not press it. How could I? I was just a child. My nurse kept reminding me how fortunate I was that Mr Howarth had not had me cast off. Well, I could not really grumble, I was well clothed, fed and educated, with an inheritance to look forward to, but it was hard and I was always very lonely.' More lies, except the remoteness and the loneliness. No one in the Howarth shipping line, except the real Charles Howarth, knew of his existence, and he was not desirous of publicly acknowledging Kit, full name Christopher.

'I'm sorry,' Tempest said. The sadness was on him again, it was a crushing melancholy, and part of her wanted to offer him more sympathy. 'Well, Mr Howarth, you were fortunate, as your nurse said. I find no problem in accepting you to be my son's son. What do you hope to achieve by your visit here?'

The worm of loathing that had gnawed in him for so many years caused his gut to constrict and his temper to rise. He had to bring it under control or he would have snarled, 'To make you suffer! To see you go through a similar sort of hell to mine.' He shrugged his shoulders. 'I had to come. I thought I would like to see Titus's grave but now I'm here I'm not sure. I'm not sure what I feel. I'll return to the house where I am temporarily residing. I suppose what happens next is up to you, Mrs Kivell.' His shoulders slumped. It wasn't a ruse. The deep, dark depression was pressing down on him again. He didn't belong here or anywhere else on earth and his time here had reinforced it. He needed to get away, to be on his own, and to seek a way to forget for a while. As for Titus Kivell's grave, if he saw it now he'd rip off its memorial stone and kick the ground apart.

Tempest thought about what she should say. He was giving her the chance to send him away for good. How could she do that? He was her flesh and blood. It was obvious he had led a life without the least affection, making him sorrowful and with the need to present a confident facade when he was in fact unsure of himself. He had known loss and rejection.

Kit got up and caught a glimpse of the well-kept garden beyond the window. Most of the plants were in winter slumber but all seemed healthy. Something struck him as strange, and then he had it; the blight that had hit Poltraze's grounds had not done the same deadly job here. He couldn't care less about it, but the destruction at the grander property had obviously been wilful.

'You like gardens, Mr Howarth?' Tempest wanted to know a little about him, actually, a lot about him.

Kit was confused by the question. 'What? Oh, yours shows a splendid aspect, Mrs Kivell. I shall take my leave.'

To Tempest it seemed a shameful thing for a grandson of hers to come and go without the smallest offer of hospitality, but she mustn't be soft, and Eula and the rest of the family would disapprove. She could at least give him a kind word. 'Thank you for coming to see me. You must think me a very poor hostess . . .'

'Not at all. I can see you are unwell.'

'I'll see you to the door. May I ask where you are staying?'

'Trengrove, in Gwennap, fairly near to the church.' He bowed, and allowed her to reach the door before him. It was a peculiar feeling to be this close to her, to look directly down on the lace cap on her upswept hair, to smell her light floral perfume. Her marble-toned skin had just a few feathery wrinkles. He had thought she would be hard and cold, as the rejection of Titus suggested, but after an initial frostiness, there seemed kindness and even concern in her. 'Perhaps . . . perhaps I might call again? By proper arrangement, if that is agreeable, when you feel more able to receive visitors. I've thought to remain locally a while longer yet.'

'Yes, I think you should.' He had the right to be interested in his new family. 'Perhaps you could come this time next week. Come for luncheon, Mr Howarth.' She nearly went on to say, 'And meet some of the family.' But that was inappropriate. A week would give time for some enquiries to be made about the Howarth Shipping Line; if it was a real and successful enterprise there would be business connections at Falmouth. A few select members of the family round the dining table could make up their minds about him, and she would have time to consider if he really was a threat.

'Thank you. I shall look forward to it.'

Tempest opened the door. 'Eula, dear, Mr Howarth is ready to leave. Please see him to the door.' She smiled at Eula and then at the man she knew as Charles Howarth, to show her daughter his visit had not worried her.

'I can see you're eager to see him again, Mama,' Eula said minutes later, when she and Genesis and some others were gathered in Tempest's sitting room. 'But are you sure your judgement isn't clouded because he reminds you of Sol?'

'I admit I am confused about my thoughts concerning Charles, but if he's genuine I have done him a terrible disservice by becoming hysterical after a simple dream.'

'It was hardly that, Mama.'

'But we don't know all the mysteries. We should at least get to know him a little better.'

'I don't trust him,' Genesis said gravely. 'There was something about him. He looked at us as if we were a bad smell under his nose. Other times he was edgy, strange. And another strange thing – one of the boys was sure he saw Sarah talking to him by the gate just before he rode down. She hasn't been near us since the day Titus died. What was that all about, then?'

Tempest shook her head. The shivering prickling of dread was creeping over her again. She ignored it. She found herself wanting Charles Howarth to be misunderstood and no threat at all. 'I don't know, but we should find out. I think someone should pay a call on Sarah.'

Tara was returning home from church, alone in the carriage except for Rosa Grace, and after being subjected to an after-service sherry at the vicarage. The former vicar, a doddering old second cousin to Joshua, had died last year, and the new incumbent, the Reverend Oswald Hobden, quite young, dull and monotonous, was devoid of social wit. His childless wife was equally boring, with a tendency to retell the same stale anecdotes. Tara had only accepted the invitation today because there was an empty house waiting on her return, its morale at the lowest. Her request to Joshua to leave Poltraze with her daughter had been met with rage.

He had stormed into her boudoir, unforgivably scruffy, flinging out the hand holding her letter and sending a vase of silk roses crashing to the carpet. 'What the hell is this all about?' Quivering in agitation, his whole face gleaming ferociously, he had balled the paper in his palms and thrown it at her feet. His forehead and chin showed bruises clearly above the discoloration of his temper. 'You dare to ask me for money so you can leave me? Have you no shame, woman?'

'Shame?' Tara's shock had gone in a flash and she had leapt up off the couch to defend herself. 'Leave you? You are the one given over to a life of shame and it was that shame that made me turn to your brother. And as for money, my marriage settlement brings in three thousand a year. I ask not for what is yours but what is morally mine for you have been no husband to me and never will be!'

'I had no choice but to take you to wife any more than you had to marry me. My despicable father and your conniving bitch of an aunt saw to that. And what life did you have before my father recalled your greedy aunt out of exile to continue as his wife? She had left him and plunged you both into near poverty.'

'I'd rather have that life than this except for—'

'For your bastard spawn?' Joshua hurled. 'If you want to leave you can ask her father, my lazy brother, to provide you with the means. You'll find he'll give you nothing more than his seed, and you don't even get that nowadays. He's too busy bedding the gatekeeper's wife, did you know? As it is, you will stay here and you can rot for all I care. If I must stay then so will you!'

Tara's temper rose to a ferocity that threatened to bring the house down and shatter it to its uninspired foundations. In two smart steps she flung back her hand and slapped it across his cheek, adding another mark to the ugly bruises on his chin. 'How dare you speak of my child in that vile manner? I will never forgive you for that. Rosa Grace's existence has served you well, remember, masking your deviance. And you do not have to stay here. You have no desire to rebuild your gardens, so why not take your money and your corrupt and dangerous lover and go somewhere far away? Michael is more than capable of filling your shoes. He is lazy about the estate but he would find a way to rebuild something of it. I don't care who Michael sees, our association is over and I'm glad. All I care about is Rosa Grace, and come what may I shall find a way to get her and myself away from this desolate place.'

Joshua had not listened to the end of her tirade. 'What do you mean by Laketon being dangerous? Why do you say that?' He was embarrassed and seemed afraid.

Tara viewed him dispassionately. He was a man brought down, and until his terrible insult about Rosa Grace, she would have been sympathetic, for he had once been kind and thoughtful, someone who did not readily seek to hurt another. Laketon Kivell's obsessive jealousy and controlling ways, and then the devastation of his plants, had just about destroyed him. 'Is he not dangerous, then?' It was her turn to curl her lip.

'I asked you why you said the word dangerous.' Joshua's attempt at authority was betrayed by the jitters in his once-confident frame, the nervous licking of his dry pale lips.

'Oh, for goodness' sake!' Impatience was on her now. 'Only an imbecile would not notice how frightened you are of him. I'm frightened of him and so are Michael and the servants. It can't always be a coincidence that bad things happen to anyone who crosses him. There was the wood-cutter whose axehead flew off and cut into his body after he'd ignored Kivell. And the well water of the tenant farmer fouled by a dead fox after he'd been rude to Kivell, after Kivell had complained about his sheep delaying him in the lane? I wouldn't be at all surprised if he didn't poison your precious plants. It's inexplicable why some of them died suddenly and why some of the same species have remained untouched. He did not allow you to call in experts to discover the cause. It's obvious he beats you, and now he's not even bothering to keep the evidence of his brutality unseen. Wake up, Joshua, the man is dangerous. Rid yourself of him before he's the end of you.'

It was as if she had watched her husband fragment one tiny piece at a time. None of her words had rung hollow to him. With his head bowed to his chest he turned as disjoint-edly as a puppet. 'How am I to do that?' he whispered to himself.

'We could work together.' Tara did not want to be his ally but she grasped at a way out for her and Rosa Grace to start afresh.

Joshua turned back and raised his head and stared at her as if she was mad. Then he shuffled around again and shuffled out of the room.

Tara had informed the Reverend Hobden that the squire was indisposed to explain his lack of attendance at church for the first week of Advent. Where Michael was only he knew, and his girls and their governess had travelled to the church and back in the trap. It was probably true that Joshua was ill, suffering from a hangover somewhere, or he was lying abed, more or less a prisoner in Kivell's cottage – ironically the beast had renamed it Paradise Cottage.

She had another problem concerning Joshua. His valet had suffered a stroke through the night and was no longer fit for service. Would Joshua want a replacement? It was hardly necessary. He spent so little time at the house and even then had rarely sought the valet's services. If he did require a new valet he would do nothing about engaging one himself. Why should she care? But Joshua growling about the house like an angry bear if one of the footmen wasn't up to the task was not a prospect she wanted to entertain. She'd ask Fawcett to procure a suitable valet. He was good at that sort of thing.

The carriage was jerking over the lesser byway of Bell Lane. A fallen tree had blocked the main route to Poltraze. 'I like this way better, Mama,' Rosa Grace said, her sweetheart face pressed to the window, while clinging to the door strap.

'I certainly don't. There's too much jostling. Sit back properly beside me, darling, before you are thrown over.' Because she'd had a rigidly restrained childhood, Tara indulged her daughter. Her love and affection, her careful protection, meant Rosa Grace was a bright, unharried child.

'We'll be passing that strange place again soon. Do you really think it's true Burnt Oak got its name long ago from witches being burnt at a tree?'

'I suppose so. But it's not a pleasant topic, Rosa. Oh!' There was a shuddering lurch and Tara reached out just in time to prevent her daughter being hurled to the floor. 'Sit beside me, young lady, and stay still.'

Rosa Grace giggled, but she was not wilful and she obliged. The carriage came to a sudden stop, which threw the pair forward and then slapped their backs against the buttoned back rest. 'Goodness,' Tara cried. 'We must have a loose wheel.'

The coachman, thickset, a nasal breather, with watery eyes in a foxy visage, and in need of a shave, pulled open the door. 'Sorry about that, ma'am. There's a village woman lying in the road. The ponies nearly ran her over. The boy's gone to see if she's 'live or dead.'

'Poor creature,' Tara said, vexed he should be so blunt in front of Rosa Grace. 'Report back to me, Sampson.'

'Yes, ma'am.' He closed the door with a clumsy bang. Since Joshua's plunge into depression some of the servants showed less care and respect.

If Joshua or Michael were here, uncaring of the locals, they would have ordered the poor unfortunate, no matter what her condition, to be dragged to the verge and for someone to be fetched to remove her.

'If she's hurt, Mama, we should help her. Like the Good Samaritan in this morning's sermon?' Rosa Grace said seriously, crossing the carriage and peering out of the glass.

'Of course we shall,' Tara replied, glad her daughter had not inherited her 'father's' or her real father's uncaring trait.

Sampson returned. ' 'Tis a young woman, ma'am. She's up already. Said she was running and plunged down but not really hurt. She's standing back. Boy's back up top. We can go on now, ma'am.'

'Bid her come to the door, Sampson.'

An insolent irritation crisscrossed Sampson's sharp hide. He paused before sighing, 'Yes, ma'am.' He made to bang the carriage door before plodding off.

'Leave it open!' The underling was eager to get back to the stables and his pipe. He'd order the stable boy to unhitch the ponies and brush them down and oil the carriage and stow it away. 'And Sampson, do not present yourself for your duties in such an ill-kept manner again.' Afraid in her anger she would display a red face, Tara alighted to the uncivil ground. The coachman might have no heart but she did. She would hold them up all day if it pleased her. 'Rosa Grace, stay inside.' Her strident tone ensured her daughter obeyed. She strode the few yards to the woman in a shabby cloak waiting, with her head bowed, for the carriage to pass by.

Tara recognized the muddied person at once. 'Sarah! It was you. What happened? Are you hurt?'

Sarah wanted only to get home to Tabbie and tell her about the encounter with Titus's younger lookalike. The fall to the ground from running too fast had knocked all the breath out of her. Conveyances along this road were rare, indeed only Kivells and the odd tenant farmer used it, and she had taken a moment to get up. That decision had nearly proved to be her last, so the foul mouth of the fuming coachman had told her. 'Miss Tara . . . .' She dipped a hurting knee in a curtsey. 'I mean Mrs Nankervis. I apologized to the coachman.'

'There was no need for that,' Tara said softly, looking her over, noting the blood on her palms, a graze on her nose and chin and a rip in her skirt. Sarah had retained her haunting

Arthurian beauty, and Tara expected to find her remote and dejected. It was a surprise she should be shot through with some kind of uneasy energy, and a surprise that she should be in the vicinity of Burnt Oak. Seeing the girl who had been as close to Amy as she had been made Tara miss her friend once more. She had no one to turn to and she had reached a time when her life couldn't get much worse. If she had made a friend of Sarah too, perhaps they could have been some sort of comfort to each other. 'Sarah, are you sure nothing is wrong? If you ever need help . . . Would you like to get into the carriage and come to Poltraze with me to have those grazes tended to?'

'You're very kind to offer but I have to get home.' Sarah saw Tara's sad-eyed eagerness. Amy's genteel friend must be very lonely to make a gesture that her husband would hate and her servants think totally wrong.

'Yes, of course. Sarah, if I can ever help you please don't hesitate to come to Poltraze.'

Tabbie woke from a nap. The fire was burning nicely, she was warm and content. Sarah had been a different girl for the past thirty-six hours, full of spirit, a determined bounce in her step. She talked about the mine and why people were speaking to her now, and even sharing their croust with her. She had even taken to singing cheerful folk songs and hymns; she had a sweet singing voice.

Sarah had mentioned she did not expect the vision of doom to materialize. Tabbie wasn't so sure about it now either. The vision might have solely been one of those things where the bad had worked for good, like it said happened in the Good Book. Sarah had been purged of her hero-worship of the evil Titus Kivell, she had resumed her maiden name and she was at last planning a life for herself. Tabbie was sure she would tell her about her plans by and by. She could die a happy woman now.

Suddenly dread slammed into her, consuming her every last particle. She saw Sarah as if she was actually standing in the room, surrounded by blackness, with her clothes torn off, her beautiful hair ripped out of her head and blood on her face. Someone was trying to strike the life out of her, someone not unknown to her. The vision had been right after all.

Tabbie reached out towards this new vision. 'Sarah . . .' Her cry was no more than a gasp. Her heart stopped beating and her body slumped down in the chair.

Six

Joshua watched from the cast-iron tester bed as Laketon Kivell preened in front of wardrobe mirror in the main bedroom of Paradise Cottage. It was a plush room, enlarged by the removal of the wall to the next room. It was well ventilated with the register fireplace allowing a healthy through draught, and with tiles at either side depicting peacocks. Highly patterned carpet covered the floor. The ceiling beams and supports were painted white and festooned with china plates painted with flowers and fruit, bearing their Latin names. A fussy room, with screens and embroidered fabric in the Eastern style, but one fit for the squire to sleep in, and all done to Laketon's precise requirements. Thanks to his unending demands, Laketon had an enviable wardrobe and today he was wearing a pleated shirt, check trousers and a check cravat. His thick hair was curled about his face and the sideburns and small beard circling his chiselled jaw were faultlessly neat. Black was popular for men's coats but he put on one of light blue with dark-blue frogging. The final flourish was a generous splash of rich French cologne.

'Anyone would think you were slipping away to an assignation,' Joshua muttered sourly, wrapped up in the bed linen.

Lifting his chin, Laketon peered into the smug reflection of his own black eyes. He was exactly how he looked, a selfish man of stealthy properties. He was more distinguished in appearance than his male kin but there was an insidious roughness about him also. People got the chills just by receiving an under-eyed glance from him. He strutted about the estate, arrogant in the knowledge that it was he who really was in charge. 'I can make myself presentable without a valet,' he mouthed in a polite voice, but it carried an accusation. Then he snapped, 'I can't abide you looking like a vagrant any longer. Get up to the house and try out your new valet. He starts work today. I won't have him idling his time ravishing the maids.'

'You don't know anything about him. He might not be fast and loose.' Joshua took a shot at his lover – he must try to keep his superior position – but he threw back the covers and started to get dressed. He was sweaty and itchy all over. He would welcome a bath and shave and clean clothes. Hopefully, the new man would be good at his job. He'd allow himself to be pampered and try to relax, try to forget his miseries. Pulling on his shirt he knocked a bruise on his upper arm. He had bruises on his back and thighs too. 'What will he think of these marks?' He would be embarrassed to strip before a total stranger.

'Explain that you're a clumsy bastard,' Laketon puffed impatiently. 'Your skin would be as clear as marble if you were more acquiescent to me. Wouldn't it?'

It rubbed insult into indignity for Joshua to be forced to admit *he* was to blame for the harm done to him. 'Yes, Laketon.'

'Aren't you curious about where I'm going?' Laketon lit a Turkish cigarette, and showed his white teeth in the manner Joshua knew was deriding him.

'It's obviously not somewhere in the immediate locality. To Redruth? To Truro?' Joshua wished he'd go out and never return. He had deeply loved the handsome Kivell, after meeting him years before his marriage, when Laketon had been trespassing in the grounds, there to admire the rare plants. Joshua had thought they would last a lifetime. But Laketon was not his soulmate; rather, his intense jealousy and underlying malice, and perhaps even a touch of madness, were destroying Joshua's soul. There were times Joshua wished him dead, or himself. A death seemed the only way out of this increasingly one-sided relationship.

'To Falmouth,' Laketon declared, boasting.

'Why there?' Joshua realized how hungry he was. He had not eaten a proper meal for days. All he wanted was to go home and order a decent breakfast in his room. He edged towards the bedroom door. Laketon gave him a harsh look of reprimand and he retraced his steps. Oh, how he hated the fiend.

'Have you forgotten the delivery we've been expecting for months? I heard yesterday that the ship has just moored. There will be ferns, vines, orchids, camellias and much more.'

Joshua's heavily shadowed jaw fell. He had forgotten something that had once been vital to him; nowadays his mind was in a dejected fug. 'That should be my prerogative.'

Laketon's eyes glowed. 'You should have made sure that you behaved yourself, shouldn't you?' The look of acute dark anger made him appear demonized – the look Joshua feared so much.

'Y-yes, Laketon. I shall look forward very much to seeing how you will restore everything.'

'Go and get yourself restored to something of the gentleman you used to be,' Laketon ordered coldly. 'I'll restore everything else. Now, I want some money.'

In a quarter of an hour, Joshua was in his dreary, oak-panelled dressing room with his head lowered in his hands. He was exhausted and his head thumped with tension but he was wholly relieved to be away from Paradise Cottage. He couldn't take much more of Laketon's scheming and brutality. Once he'd had gardens the envy of all but the greatest estates in Cornwall, and the freedom to follow his heart's desire thanks to his agreeable young wife, who had produced a child which staved off questions about his virility. Now his grounds were in ruins and only to be restored on Laketon's decision, and Laketon would ensure he received all the glory when all was flourishing again. That would take years, years of living under his demands, of him deciding what to plant and where. Tara was probably right about Laketon destroying his plants. Laketon was malicious. He was a devil. He was dangerous and terrifying. Tara, the calming influence in his house, was desperate to leave it. As for Tara's child, if only the girl was any other man's but his brother's. He felt Michael smirked over the fact and considered himself more as the squire. Michael saw to all the business of the estate now. He had no family to turn to and no friends. His life wasn't worth living and there was no hope of it ever improving. 'I hate you!' he fumed at the cold-eyed image of Laketon in his mind. He burst into tears of desperation.

Moments later he wiped the tears away with the heels of his hands. There was a way out, one that would not benefit his rotten lover at all. He would kill himself. He'd take his razor and slash his throat wide open. Michael would be the squire then. He was welcome to the beastly place. He'd order Laketon out of Poltraze. If his suicide brought the estate down, good! Michael deserved it. He could add the tragedy to his records. Tara could do as she damned well pleased.

He strode to the bathroom, picked up the cut-throat razor laid out neatly on the shelf above the marble-topped wash-stand and basin. He looked into the mirror and blanched at the blotchy-skinned, wild-eyed creature staring back at him. Was that really him? He had been reduced to a crazed, unkempt gargoyle. He couldn't bear the sight and whirled round putting the razor to his throat.

'Sir! Let me do that.' Joshua had not heard a discreet shuffle at the adjoining door nor it being opened and someone coming in.

'Who the hell are you?'

'I'm your new valet, sir. Aaron Hobbs. Forgive me. I did not know you were here. Mrs Nankervis engaged me. I was just looking over where I shall be waiting on you.'

Joshua's hand fell. His brain couldn't take in the rapid change. He had been about to kill himself, to splash his blood all over the black and white tiles. Now he was surprised to be facing a slim young man with an ivory face framed by a veil of curly blond hair, and immaculately dressed in starched high collar and a dark suit. There was a softness in his voice and a softness in his demeanour, and rather than the grov-elling look of servitude or stiff discipline of many servants, he seemed to portray genuine concern. After being with the devilish Laketon, Joshua fancied he was in the company of an angel. Instead of being distressed or embarrassed to be caught in a disgraceful state of dishevelment, he was just numb.

'Shall I order hot water to be brought up for you to bathe, sir?'

'What?' Joshua blinked, his mind clicking in a daze before

it returned to working order. 'A bath? Yes, of course.' He could hardly cut his throat now. The thought was so ludicrous it made him want to smile, to laugh, but he was sure he'd go into hysterics. Yes, he'd allow himself to be scrubbed, shaved and smartened up and then commit suicide, go out looking like a gentleman, and by some poison or pills; less messy and more dignified.

He wondered if a smile had creased his face, for the valet smiled at him, a small smile and a pleasant one, and Joshua saw how pretty his new servant was. A smile from anyone else would have been offensive. It was out of place, but for some reason he didn't mind. 'What did you say your name was?'

'Hobbs, sir. Aaron Hobbs. Shall I take the razor, sir?'

'Well, Hobbs,' Joshua said, handing over the instrument that had nearly carved a wide gash in his neck, 'I've been rather out of sorts, as you can see. Are you experienced in your post?'

'I was three years with the recently deceased Lord Hampton of Bath, and before that with Mr Maurice Astley of London.' Hobbs gave him a long particular look.

'Lord Hampton. Maurice Astley?' Joshua knew of these men and the particular clubs – *molly houses* – they had frequented. They had not been accepted in conventional society. Hobbs would be very acceptable as his new valet. Suddenly life seemed worth taking a new chance at. Thoughts of suicide left him for now. His bathroom was one of the pleasanter rooms in the house. It was functional, with no ornamental excesses. He would unwind a little and allow this young man to pamper him. 'I shall require a hearty breakfast after this, Hobbs. I'll eat in my chamber.'

'Yes, sir.'

'Tell me more about yourself, Hobbs.'

'The Kivell woman's got no right to be burying that old witch tomorrow!' Dinah Greep thumped cheap pottery plates down on the table. 'She should've waited till Sunday, like the rest of us do for a funeral. She hasn't worked since the old woman died. Rest of us have had to work extra hard to get the quota done.'

'If you're so worried about the work, maid, then you should stop your complaining and just get on with the job,' Jeb, her brother, sighed, shaking his head and casting his eyes down on the stone-flagged kitchen floor. He had worked early morning core at the Carn Croft Mine, and until ten minutes ago had been seeing to his smallholding, complete with goats and two pigs, at the back of the cottage. A devout Bible Christian, he was to go soon to prepare the chapel for a prayer and worship meeting. He was tired from the physical work but his weariness came from having to endure his sister's constant jealous sarcasm and mischief-making. It seemed no amount of patience and praying could bring about a softer, repenting side in Dinah. He never got to sit for a few minutes in peace at the hearth, where he was now, cradling his sleeping baby daughter. 'And you shouldn't be so uncharitable. Sarah had a terrible shock finding Tabbie dead like that.'

'Trust you to take her side! You're even going to the funeral. Anyone'd think you still had feelings for her,' Dinah spat, seeming more and more like a cross between a newt and a shrew.

'That's enough!' Jeb raised his voice, waking the baby of one month and making her cry, and alarming his year-old son, sitting on his wife's lap and slurping down milky sops. Miriam Greep reached for the baby, but Jeb held on to her. 'It's all right, my love, I can manage.' He shushed the baby back to sleep then put her down in the cradle. Thank God, Miriam took no notice of Dinah's jibes. She was everything his sister was not, patient, hard-working, generous and a good Christian. Like him, Miriam would prefer to have the little whitewashed cottage, rented, like most houses in Meryen, from the Poltraze estate, to themselves, but she never grumbled about it. Unlike Dinah, who resented Miriam's presence in what had been their late father's home. His father used to say that if Dinah could, she would put two sticks to fight. Jealous that her unfortunate looks and spiteful ways discouraged the young men from seeking her as a wife, it could be believed Dinah would be happy to cause a rift in his happy marriage.

The unusual sharpness in Jeb's reprimand brought Dinah

up with a start and she carried on with her job quietly. She had passed a nasty comment only a moment before, hinting that Miriam should have laid the table and not herself. Miriam had not long walked back in the freezing weather from the mine. She was in for more than a ticking off this time, but she didn't care. Jeb was too mild-mannered to worry her. He was soft, and so pathetically honest that if he found lost property he returned it to the owner – what good was that to the family? And as for charity, he helped out so many people it sometimes made them short here. 'You can't out-give the Lord, who sees all things done in secret,' he'd say, and Miriam, the idiot, would nod and say, 'It's the truth. He sees that we always get by.' They might be happy to scrape through life but she wanted a lot more. She'd turn a deaf ear to what her brother had to say now, which, no doubt, would be full of Bible quotations. It made her sick the way prayers were said for everything and over everything, and the way she had to be dragged to chapel every Sunday without fail. It was a wonder her brother put his shirt on without asking God's permission first.

'If one more nasty word comes out of your mouth, Dinah Greep, I swear I'll put you out of this house.' Jeb's tone was as inflexible and deliberate as his expression.

'What? You can't do that. You wouldn't.' Dinah laughed in his face. She had brought her brother to real anger at last. She would enjoy this quarrel. She'd provoke him to shout at her. Make his scrawny daughter and snivelling son bawl their heads off. What fun if she got him so mazed he even swore. She stifled a giggle. From then on she'd be able to accuse him of unchristian behaviour and make him feel guilty.

'Dinah, you go too far.' Freckle-faced Miriam was placid and pliable, something Dinah wilfully exploited, but she wasn't going to have Jeb mocked in this manner. She put her now-sleepy little boy to lie down beside his sister, and then stood at Jeb's side with her arms folded to show she meant business.

'What are you both going to do?' Dinah smirked, swaying her bony hips. 'Call on a thunderbolt from heaven to strike me down?' Now for a full-blown row, she'd bring up every last thing she could think of to make sure her brother's voice would be heard shouting halfway across the village.

'I don't have to do that, Dinah,' Jeb replied in a cold quiet tone. 'You're in great danger of doing that yourself. You're bitter and hateful, yet you foolishly wonder why you have no friends and the young men run a mile rather than return one of your flirting smiles. You're jealous of the slightest joy anyone else has. The only reason you have such a loathing of Sarah is because she's pretty, and even though her marriage turned out so badly for her, at least she'd got herself a husband. I know you've been teased for your plain looks and that's awful, but you're the one who's made yourself ugly and undesirable. Now you've got all bitter and twisted because Sarah has gained some respect. She was once shunned because she had principles, believing she should have loyalty for her husband. The reason you're shunned is because no one *wants* your company and it's entirely your own fault. People only speak to you or do your bidding because you bully them into it. You're your own worst enemy, Dinah, and you always will be unless you wake up and see yourself for what you really are.

'I won't have my children growing up near you while you're like this. You're their aunt but you don't take the least bit of interest in them. In fact Miriam and I are afraid to leave you in the house alone with them, afraid you'll neglect them. My job is to provide for my family and to protect them, and Miriam's job is to nurture our children in a godly atmosphere. Either you change your wicked ways, maid, or out you go. You have my word on it. The choice is yours. Well, what's it to be?'

All the way through the chastisement Dinah had scowled more and more at the couple. Damn their self-righteous hides! 'You're only angry with me because I said something against your precious Sarah. You can't never turn me out. Father made you promise on his deathbed to look after me.'

'Not exactly. What he actually said was that I should do my best for you. Well, I've done that and you've pushed me to the limits. Father said what he did because he sadly knew what you're like. You broke his heart, and Mother's before his, but you're not going to do that to anyone here. There's not a soul who would blame me if I showed you the door. Most wouldn't have put up with you for as long as I and Miriam have. I'm not kicking you out, Dinah. What I'm saying is that if you want to remain under this roof, you must still your spiteful tongue for good and mend your ways. And that goes at the mine as well. Torment the other bal-maidens, issue one more insult to anyone and you won't be welcome here again. You can be a part of this family or you can go your own way. You've been warned. I'll repeat what I said. The choice is yours. What's it to be, Dinah? Shall I pack your bags for you?'

She was beaten. The shock of her brother's firmness, the humiliation of it all and the fear of ending up in the work-house or begging or having to sell herself on the streets reduced her to tears. 'N-no.'

'Am I to take it you'll repent your ways?' Jeb wanted to be absolutely sure he had won the day.

Dinah nodded wretchedly.

'Then you can start by giving me and Miriam an apology.'

She had gone too far, so Miriam had said. Now her brother had. Bastard! He was demanding she grovel to him. She had no choice but to obey and to live a hellish life of watching every last word that came out of her mouth. So he and everyone else thought her ugly and horrible? Well, no one was going to put her down and keep her there. It wasn't her fault that God hadn't given her a lovely face. It wasn't fair at all. Everyone, even God, was cruel to her. Sarah rotten Kivell had all the beauty, but after allowing herself to be used as a whore, she did nothing with it. She could easily get herself another husband. She would never know the humiliation of being undesirable. Dinah quelled her tears and lifted her chin. She'd say sorry to her beastly brother and his sickly sweet wife, and after that, God had better help them and their brats too. And, just for good measure, Sarah Kivell too.

Seven

It was another day at work but it was different from any other, it was the day after Tabbie's funeral and Sarah was feeling all alone in the world. The vicar had been against Tabbie being buried in the churchyard, but thankfully Tabbie had put her papers together and Sarah had produced her baptism certificate to show the self-righteous misery that she had the right to be buried in sanctified ground.

Sarah was up on the high exposed ground of the Carn Croft Mine and had been toiling away for nearly an hour. As she was young and strong she had one of the hardest jobs for the women and girls in the ore-breaking sheds. Bucking involved standing in line at a long table and using a long-handled flat hammer to crush the ore, already broken into birds'-eye sizes, into small granules. The continuous blows sent shock waves up through her hand and arm, and at the end of each shift she went home with an aching back and shoulders, and inevitably a headache. She could tolerate the hard labour, with its dangers of flying shards, and the harsh dirty conditions, under a roof but with no sides to the shed, but she hated all the noise. But today she didn't take in the hammering of each stage of the ore dressing, the rhythmic thumps as the steam pump in the engine house raised gallons of dirty water each minute, the clanking of heavy chains on the whims, or the trundling of huge barrows laden with lumps of ore brought up from the depths. Her mind was centred on the grief of suddenly losing her dear friend, and how she intended to be gone from here for good after Christmas. During croust time today she would give in a month's notice.

She cried in pain as a splinter of ore flying off the bucking iron of the girl next to her burrowed through a flap of her gook and pierced her neck. Putting her fingers up to pull out the splinter she realized Dinah Greep was next to her. Absorbed in her musings she hadn't been aware of Dinah changing places with the other girl. She must have caused her this pain on purpose. She never made cutting remarks to her directly now but had been taunting her by saying things loudly to others. Sarah glared at her.

Dinah exclaimed, 'Oh, sorry, Sarah!' putting a hand of regret to her flat chest.

The sarcastic bitch, never mind though. Sarah wouldn't give her the satisfaction of biting back at the derision. Tabbie had left a will and she had bequeathed to her all her possessions, many of high value, and the amazing sum of twenty pounds. Dinah really would have something to be jealous about if she knew. Sarah dabbed at the blood with a clean scrap of cloth then turned away to resume her work.

Dinah tapped on her arm, pulled her round a little and shouted above the clamour, 'No, I really am sorry. I'll tell you why at croust.'

Sarah sighed. What was the little witch up to now? She'd avoid her like the pestilence during the mid-morning break.

Dinah left Sarah be. To convince everyone she was a changed girl, and that she had been truly 'saved', as she'd pretended to be at last evening's chapel meeting, she needed to show a repentant attitude towards this damned woman. She grinned to herself. While Sarah had cleaned up her neck she'd noticed the silver and topaz pendant hanging there. It looked an expensive piece. Everyone knew she had taken nothing from her marriage. Old Tabbie Sawle had been rumoured to have treasures hidden in her shack, she must have given the jewellery to Sarah. What else might be in the shack? Other stuff of value? Money? Dinah was in urgent need of money. She'd already drawn subsist on this month's fifteen-shillings wages.

When the count-house bell rang for croust time, Sarah gave her notice to her tribute leader, who expressed his disappointment at losing a good worker. She told no one else but the news would soon be spread anyway. She ensured Dinah Greep couldn't offer some mocking explanation for her apology by sitting in the middle of a group of bal-maidens and young children. Outside, in the shelter of a storage shed, she hugged her mug to warm her hands and sipped her penny-royal tea, nibbling on a rock bun she'd bought as a treat at the village bakery.

Dinah sat as close as she could get to Sarah. After stuffing her face with half of her lunchtime pasty and gulping down her hot drink, she started up a hymn, singing with vigour. There was always a lot of singing at the mine. Others joined in, and some were smiling at Dinah in delight. Sarah stayed silent but was amazed.

'Isn't it wonderful,' Elizabeth Coad whispered in a reverent pitch to Sarah. 'The maid has seen the light. She went to chapel last night and during the altar call she fell to her knees and gave her life to the Lord.'

'Yes, wonderful,' Sarah said drily.

'You must come along on Sunday, Sarah,' Elizabeth said, her leathery hands clasped in enthralment. 'There could be rejoicing in heaven for one more.'

'Mmm.' Sarah wondered if heaven really was rejoicing over Dinah Greep. Dinah was attempting to catch her eye, and the ragged lines of her thin lips were pulled back in the widest smile. Sarah doubted it was a sincere smile. She knew better than most not to lightly give away her trust.

The next day was pay day, market day in Meryen, some-thing that had grown up in recent times out of the expan-sion of the village as the copper trade had grown. Stallholders, wagon traders, pedlars and quacks turned up each month and set up their wares in a clearing on the edge of the downs, in shouting distance of Chy-Henver, Sol and Amy's Kivell carpentry business. The tribute leaders doled out the money individually to the male surface workers, women and chil-dren. Those who didn't work on tribute were paid by the purser of the mine as a whole and had to buy something at the mine shop first to receive it, at up to twenty-five per cent mark-up.

Sarah's wages were docked for the three days she'd had off following Tabbie's death. It meant no hardship to her. She had plenty of food in store and all that Tabbie had left her. The question was how she could sell the valuables, and there were a lot of them, without being accused of stealing

some of them, as Tabbie certainly had done. Close examination revealed that a few of the items, including glassware
and tea caddies, bore the Poltraze crest. She would have to
work out what she could comfortably sell and the rest she
would bury deep out on the moor. But where could she find
a buyer she could trust and who would give her a fair price?

Looking about at the market traders there were none that
dealt in the valuable stuff Tabbie had concealed in battered
old chests and the nooks and crannies of her makeshift walls
– she had left Sarah a detailed description of where all could
be found. Sarah had been astonished at all the wealth: pocket
watches, candlesticks, miniature pictures. Why hadn't Tabbie
sold up – her resourcefulness would have found suitable
buyers – and lived comfortably in more traditional surroundings? She could even have afforded a maid. Tabbie had obviously been content in her unorthodox life. Knowing her as
she did, it must have pleased her simply to relieve the rich
of some of their trappings. Sarah wanted to get away from
Meryen and start afresh, to leave all the tormenting memories behind her. It was a great relief not to have made it
inside Burnt Oak, to have gone cap in hand to Tempest Kivell.
The sight of Titus's lookalike had purged her of ever wanting
what might be her moral right. She would never have left
Titus and his cruelty behind if she had taken anything of his.
She was cross with herself for putting aside her pride that
day. Now that a stranger who bore his looks was about locally,
the man from Tabbie's vision, she wanted to move away as
quickly as possible and go to her family. Unfortunately, it
couldn't be done in a tearing hurry. She had no wish to
continue at the mine but was working out her notice so as
not to arouse suspicion about her intentions or what might
be in Tabbie's home. In the past she had heard people remark
that they were waiting for 'the old witch' to die so they could
look over her shack, ransack it they'd meant, hoping to find
stuff of value.

On paydays she usually bought herself something small, a
handkerchief, a scrap of lace or ribbon or a cheap household
item needed in the shack and some food, perhaps a pie or a
saffron cake to share with Tabbie. She didn't want anything
for herself today but stopped at an aged olive-skinned gipsy

laden with a huge basket hanging from her neck, packed with haberdashery, clothes pegs, combs and other items. There were twists of cloth which contained spells and concoctions to cure various ills or to lure a sweetheart. 'What will 'ee have, little bud?' the gipsy grinned, making rugged furrows in her inscrutable, weather-beaten skin.

'I'll take a look, Peg.' Sarah took her time choosing presents for her family. A lace-edged handkerchief for Aunt Molly, a painted comb for Tamsyn, now aged twelve, and a jointed dog puppet for Arthur, one year the senior. While she looked, Peg, who had astonishing white teeth glowing through crinkled lips, rattled off Sarah's fortune.

'I see mixed fortune ahead of 'ee.' Everyone has that, Sarah thought. 'Them as should won't. Them as will, you won't want.' Why did those of Peg's ilk talk in riddles? Even Tabbie's sayings had needed to be interpreted. If only Tabbie hadn't been near accurate about Titus's return. Who was the stranger who looked so much like him? Her mind had been in a fever while hurrying home after their startling encounter. Discovering Tabbie dead, slipped away into the next world whilst alone, and looking none too peaceful, had meant she'd given little thought to the stranger. She must forget about him. Let the Kivells deal with him. It was none of her business now. She would move away under her maiden name and leave her wretched past behind without looking back. Just one thing she would do, write a letter of thanks to Tara for her kindness in Bell Lane. She smiled while imagining Amy's delight at her good fortune. She'd wait until after the reunion with her family and then fill a letter with the wonderful story. She had money of her own and if Aunt Molly, Arthur and Tamsyn allowed her to live with them it would be on the same level and not as a burden. She paid Peg the price of three farthings.

'You shouldn't be smiling, m'dear,' Peg said in an urgent tone. 'You should be on your guard.'

'Not this again,' Sarah wailed. Why couldn't the netherworld let her be?

'Then you know what I'm talking about. There's one who wishes you terrible harm. There's great upset ahead for 'ee.'

Sarah couldn't bear to hear any more. It had taken years

for her to become positive, to believe she had a future worth living. She hastened away from the gipsy. At least she hadn't been told she would fall in love again. She would have screamed if she'd heard that ridiculous notion.

Within a minute she was faced by a Kivell.

As Sarah was walking away from the gipsy pedlar, Dinah was making her presence known to a Johnny-go-Fortnight. A man of about thirty, in a rough suit and faded yellow- and green-striped waistcoat, with sallow skin, crooked yellow teeth, a thick, tobacco-stained moustache and a chin thrust out pugnaciously, he was one of those traders who talked the girls and women of less foresight into taking out fortnightly terms on expensive wares. Dinah had bought a pair of shoes and petticoats from his wagon, and a brooch, supposedly of a real ruby. She hadn't understood that if she got behind on a payment, at a very high credit price, she'd owe twenty-five per cent interest on top. She had avoided him the last two fortnights when he'd arrived expecting instalments from his customers. Today she marched up to him boldly.

'You've been hiding from me!' Abner Jago accused gruffly. 'You'd better have money for me t'day and it'd better be in full.'

Dinah handed over nearly all her wages to catch up on the belated weeks. She only had a few pence left to give Miriam towards her keep. 'Sorry to have kept you waiting, Abner.'

Ignoring her confident grin, Jago snatched away the money and counted it on a sweaty, grimy paw. 'There's still a shortfall. What d'you intend to do about it?'

'I've got an idea about that. Hopefully I'll soon be able to pay you everything I owe.'

'You better had. Pay up prop'ly next fortnight and I'll let you buy something else. If not I'll go to that Bible-punching brother of yours and demand my money.' He half-swung away from her, his piercing eyes searching for new customers among the milling mine workers, the traders to the mine and the villagers.

Dinah didn't lose her confidence but actually crept up to him, ignoring his stink, and spoke into his ear. 'I know a way we can make a lot of money, Abner.'

'What the hell are you talking about?' he bawled, shaking his head as if her whisper had lodged something abominable in his ear.

'Shush!' She was anxious Jeb didn't see her hanging about him. So convincing was her act as a devoted member of his chapel he actually believed she was a repentant sinner. If he spied her with Abner Jago, known for his shady dealings, he'd change his mind and never trust her again, and she might lose her home. He had urged her in the past to join a dress club with the more careful girls, who to avoid debt bought clothes and took turns wearing them. The Anglican clergy didn't approve of this practice, and Dinah wasn't one to share anything with anyone. She whispered, 'I know where we can get good stuff just for the taking.'

'Go on,' Jago muttered. The girl was a nuisance, but she also had no morals, and she might be on to something.

'See that woman over there by Peg the gipsy?'

'The pretty one? Widder of Titus Kivell? Lived with old Tabbie Sawle, who's just dropped off the edge.' Abner had always admired the beauty of the young woman who had never come near him to do business.

'Yes,' Dinah replied sourly, going on harshly, 'she wears a silver pendant round her neck, a very expensive piece, if you ask me. It's been said for years that Tabbie Sawle was stashing away things she got from shipwrecks. Where else could Sarah Kivell get such a good piece of jewellery? Come from a ship's rich passenger, I shouldn't wonder. Or the old hag stole it. Tabbie hadn't worked in years but she always had money. Bought well at the shops. Seen it myself. Abner, the Kivell woman is working out her notice. I reckon she'll be off then, probably on the proceeds left by the old woman. She got Tabbie Sawle her own coffin, you know, made from good oak. There must have been money lying around for that. When Sarah Kivell's working at the mine, someone could break in and take away what she's got. Would be as easy as falling off a log.' *And it'll serve the bitch right*, Dinah thought, the malice shining out of her beady eyes.

'Someone? You mean me?' Jago muttered in poor temper.

'If you're not interested I'll find someone who is,' Dinah said, disappointed, but hoping to talk him round. There was no one else she knew as dishonest as Abner Jago, there was no one else she could approach like this, to relieve herself of debt and to make enough money to get away from the hard, dirty life of a bal-maiden. She burned to wreak a glorious revenge on the high and mighty Sarah Kivell. 'But think of it, Abner. It could be easy pickings for a great reward.'

'I'll consider it,' he said, not quite so antagonistic now. 'I need to know exactly where Tabbie's Shack is. Tell me where to go. You can meet me there later today. You sure we can creep up on the place without the lovely Sarah knowing we're about?'

'It'll be as easy as breathing.' Dinah was so happy she didn't consider that Abner Jago would surely know where Tabbie's Lane was and that it would be easy to find the shack from there.

In Sarah's path, Jowan Kivell stood tall and resolute, but not in a confrontational manner. 'Can I talk to you please, Sarah? It's very important.'

Sarah was annoyed to be waylaid by one of Titus's illegitimate sons, but she knew Jowan as an agreeable Kivell. At nearly twenty, he was in charge of Sol and Amy's business and lived at Chy-Henver, with two carpenter kinsmen and a sister. 'Is it about Amy? Have you heard bad news?' Sarah was always in fear of dangers for her friend from shipwreck, foreign diseases or natives.

'Grandmama Tempest asked me to talk to you. Can we go somewhere quiet? There's no one at Chy-Henver. The others are looking round the market.'

'If I must,' Sarah mumbled, frowning. She marched off towards the cottage where she had spent many good times with Amy. She could have lived there. Amy had begged to take her in. But it was Sol's home too, and Jowan's. Other Kivells had always been dropping in. Sarah couldn't have borne that. Jowan followed her, a respectful thing for a Kivell male to do. They didn't usually walk behind a woman, or anyone else for that matter. She reached the back door of Chy-Henver then turned round and faced him.

He smiled. It was a smile one could easily return for he was light-hearted in the main and had smiling eyes. He had the Kivell dark good looks, and firm, strong expressions, which made him a prize worth catching to many a local girl. It would be years before any girl was likely to succeed with him for he was flirtatious and free-willed. 'Would you like to go inside?'

This was probably about the stranger she had met outside Burnt Oak. It was a serious business and she accepted this. Jowan swept out a big dark hand to intimate she should lead the way. It had been ages since she'd been in Chy-Henver's large, comfortable, well-furnished kitchen, where she and Amy had sat at the hearth and drunk tea and chatted. She was hit by envy of her friend's happy marriage and two healthy sons. Amy had all her family, including her mother and little sister, with her. Sarah missed Amy more than ever, and now, bereft of Tabbie, she was hit hard by loneliness. Then she remembered that she would soon be reunited with her own family. Nothing else mattered. She had no reason to be off-hand with Jowan. He had been horrified at how his father had treated her and he had always been respectful towards her.

'Would you like to sit, Sarah? Can I get you something to drink?' Jowan eyed the kettle warily. His sister Rachel hated him touching things in here. She complained he always left a mess, which was true.

To show she was not hostile, Sarah sat at the table. 'A drink of water will do, thank you.'

On the table was a blue and white china jug of water, covered with lace that was weighted round the edge with glass beads. He fetched two cups off the dresser hooks, poured the water and sat opposite her. He couldn't help taking a lingering look. He admired not only Sarah's loveliness but her strength of will and he felt sorry for all her suffering. As his father had taken little notice of him Jowan had not had any strong feelings about Titus until he'd tried to murder Sol. Now he hated his father's memory. If he had his way he'd have Titus's body dug up from Burnt Oak's grounds and buried in the loneliest spot out on the downs. 'I'm sorry about Tabbie. You must miss her.'

'I do, a great deal. Jowan, what's this all about?' She told him about her guess.

'Yes, it's partly about him. His name's Charles Howarth. It seems he's my half-brother. He's due to dine with us at Morn O' May in a few days. He told Grandmama he was the result of a brief love affair between my father and some married lady. Her husband owns a shipping line at Bristol. He accepted the child as his own. There are no other children. Grandmama has had his background checked. Apparently, he's of excellent repute; a philanthropist. He runs the Howarth Shipping Line now his adopted father is old and doddery. The mother sadly became deranged and ended her days in a sanatorium. I got a strong feeling Grandmama was hoping Howarth would turn out to be trustworthy. I'll be interested to meet him. The other thing is, Grandmama was wondering why you were near Burnt Oak on the same day as Howarth. Can I ask, did Howarth happen to make himself known to you beforehand and you went there to speak to him? Or had you gone there for some other reason and the meeting was just a coincidence?'

'I just happened to be walking that way,' Sarah lied. She would never reveal the truth. It would probably lead to Tempest offering her some help and she would have the bother of turning it down. 'I was shocked to see someone who looked so much like . . . your father.' She couldn't bring herself to mention Titus's name now. Disgust and loathing for him had replaced all her love. 'I can tell you, Jowan, that I didn't take this Charles Howarth as a worthy man. He shouldn't be trusted. He was offensive to me and looked at me as if I was dirt. I know this isn't unusual due to our stations but there was something really horrid about him. He knew who I was; I found that chilling. You should tell your grandmother all this.'

'I will, Sarah. She won't be happy to hear it. She was quite ill before Howarth's appearance but since then she's returned to her former self. Thank you for disclosing this to me.' He sipped his water, his head bowed.

Sarah saw he was troubled. 'Did Tempest by any chance see this man before he arrived? You know what I mean?'

Jowan met Sarah's concerned eyes, stretching his long legs out under the table. How beautiful her eyes were, the sort of eyes that stayed in a man's mind long after he'd gazed into them. 'Yes, she had a vision. It's what made her ill. She warned us about all sorts of bad things happening. It was like she was expecting the end of the world for the Kivells. Now she seems to be allowing a hasty judgement to cloud all that. I hope I can convince her she should be suspicious of Howarth. Are you hinting that Tabbie saw something too?'

'I think she saw the very same thing. Tabbie gave me dire warnings too. Well, I shan't be round here much longer to worry about it. I've given in my notice at the mine.'

'I know.' He smiled at her. 'Word gets round. Good for you, Sarah. Listen, please don't think me forward, but if you need help with anything before you go, I'm here. Sol and Amy would like me to help you if I can.'

'I'll be fine. Thank you anyway, Jowan.' She was about to go, then hesitated. Could she trust him? He ran the business here very well indeed. Sol had said he'd trust Jowan with his life. Jowan might be the one who could help her. 'I, well . . .' Taking a deep breath she told him about her need to secretly sell some valuables. 'Would you know of anyone? Someone discreet?'

'A job with no questions asked and a fair price given, you mean? Leave it to me, Sarah.' Jowan smiled at her again. He knew his reputation for being a charmer, but he wasn't out to charm Sarah. He really liked her. 'Give me three or four days then let me know when you're ready to offload the goods. I'll oversee everything for you.'

'Thank you, Jowan.' Sarah couldn't resist a smile coming on. 'I've packed up most of the things. This person you know can look over the goods and take them away as soon as he pleases. It's better he looks over everything away from Tabbie's place.'

'We'll call on you soon.' Jowan was thoughtful. 'You'll have to take a day off work. Sarah, take my advice and leave as soon as you can. Go somewhere and start again. I'll be happy to take you anywhere you choose. You and Amy are sure to keep in touch. I'd like to stay your friend too. I promise no one in my family will ever know where you go, if that's what you want.'

Sarah sipped from her cup to give herself time to think. She had just put her trust in Jowan. Would it hurt to keep on trusting him? Amy wasn't here and she had no idea when she'd be back. She had lost Tabbie for good. Tara had made a kind offer but their different stations meant a friendship was impossible. She would be with her family soon but it would be good to keep one local reliable friend. 'Thank you again, Jowan.' She returned another of his stunning smiles.

Darkness was drawing in when Dinah met Abner Jago at the entrance to Tabbie's Lane. He'd left his wagon elsewhere and was on foot. 'You found it all right, then,' she whispered, her insides bubbling with the excitement of planning a crime that could change her life forever. 'It's down there. Ground's good but you'll have to watch out for gorse and brambles hitting your face.'

Jago glanced all around, his neck protruding forward as if he was in the habit of skulking about and looking to see if anyone was in the vicinity. 'Is she at home?'

'Got back more'n two hours ago. Well, you know where it is for sure now. How much will I be getting out of it? My debt will be cleared, won't it?' Dinah was shifting on her feet, eager to get home. Jeb would be wondering where she was. He'd chide her for not being there to help Miriam with the supper. Dinah hated having to be sickly sweet in apology, to have to spout 'the Good Lord this' and 'the Good Lord that' after she'd lied about going off alone to meditate about Him.

'Depends what I find there. You'll get what you deserve, maid, never fear. Go on, lead the way.'

'What? I have to get home. It'll soon be dark. You'll easily find your way to the shack in the daylight when you come back.'

'I s'pose so.' Jago used his gruff voice. 'Just take me along a little way, so I can get the feel of the ground.'

'Just quickly, then.' Dinah set off down the short lane. At its end she entered the neck of overgrown track. 'See what I mean? You have to watch your head. 'Tis only a few twists and turns then there's a small clearing with the shack. I've spied it out. Can we go back now?'

'In a minute.'

'What else do you need to know?' she sighed.

'Nothing. Nothing at all.'

'Then why can't we go?'

''Tis nice and private here. Thought we'd have a little kiss or two first.'

'What?' She'd never been asked for a kiss before. She wondered if Abner Jago was married. She wasn't likely to ever bag herself a husband but she could overlook this man's unsavoury attributes for he'd make a good provider. 'Do you have a wife?'

'What's that got do with anything? I got a woman and five children. Come on, I'm eager to get on with it.' The next instant she was in Jago's clutches and his face was coming down on hers.

'Get off me!' she struggled, swearing as foul as a drunkard, knocking off his billycock hat. 'I'm not kissing an ugly swine like you if you're married.'

Jago grabbed her by the roots of her hair and yanked her head backwards, twisting her neck to the side, making her scream in pain. 'We'll leave out the kissing, then. You're as ugly as a frog anyway and no one'd want to kiss you unless it was pitch dark.'

He pushed her down to the ground and flung himself on top of her, putting a hand over her mouth. He yanked up her skirt and petticoats. 'I always keep my promises, maid. You're about to get exactly what you deserve.'

Eight

Next Sunday, Tara had a welcome excuse to miss church when Rosa Grace developed a cold, with a high temperature. She was in no mood to be a cold place listening to an uninspiring sermon. She thought the shouts and hand-clapping and foot-stamping of the Bible Christians inappropriate at any time and utterly disrespectful on the Sabbath, but she rather envied their joyful zeal. At least they had something to lift themselves spiritually and mentally out of the miseries of their hard and meagre living. While travelling slowly through the village in an open carriage back in the summer she had heard one of their street preachers in full stride: 'What does it matter that I live in a little cottage with not much in the way of furniture and decoration, and sometimes find it hard to put food on the table? One day I shall live in my Father's mansion and feast at his banqueting table!' Well, she lived in a mansion packed with fine things and comforts, things she had taken for granted all her married life, but she had never known personal happiness. But she had Rosa Grace, and her charitable works as a distraction.

She was arranging a Christmas bazaar, of scented gifts and lacework, to raise funds for the parish needy to have meat on their Christmas tables, a few provisions in their larders, perhaps a new blanket or some woollen cloth to make clothes. She already had a collection of mufflers and gloves and hose to distribute, made by a team of ladies, and some middle-class wives and daughters of tradesmen, who had little to do each day. She held meetings at different times, of course, for the women from each station in life. Rosa Grace and this work gave her some satisfaction, a lot actually, she decided. There was no point in self-pity. If love wasn't meant to enter her life, if she couldn't get away from

Poltraze, if Sarah never came to her to form a friendship, then she had to accept it, just as the poor of Meryen had to accept their lot. At least Amy would come back one day. Please let it be soon.

Joshua had attended matins and had returned home in a very good mood, as he'd been for the last few days. He sat down, all smiles, at the head of the dining table and tucked into the four-course luncheon, clearing his plate of game soup, chomping on the ham and the beef, taking a second helping of suet pudding, while liberally quaffing down various wines. 'Tell cook everything was delicious and perfectly presented, Fawcett.' Once someone who had taken to only toying with his food, he did not leave a morsel.

'I congratulate you on the choice of menu and the sauces, Tara,' he drawled with charm, when they were finishing off with coffee alone in the winter parlour.

'Thank you, Joshua.' Tara was pleased to receive a compliment. Joshua was a different man to the one who had attacked her over her desire to leave and end their sham of a marriage. Very much his old self again, he had led a jolly conversation with her over the meal table. He was immaculately groomed, and there was no garden dirt under his nails even though the clearing of the grounds and the restoration of the hothouses had begun; instead they were painstakingly manicured. He seemed to care more about his appearance than anything else nowadays, perhaps, she supposed, to compensate for his earlier disregard of it. He changed his clothes several times a day, wholeheartedly approving of the new valet. The atmosphere in the house had taken a turn for the better, and she secretly agreed with what she assumed would be Michael's sentiment, that the old timbers had eased into sighs of relief. It was good that now her affair with Michael had ended he no longer availed himself of meals with them, requesting trays to be brought to the library. Joshua was obviously finding the new arrangement more acceptable. Because Michael crept in and out to his old books, one could almost forget he existed. 'Are things going to plan in the grounds?'

'Yes, I think so. I'm leaving it all to Laketon,' he replied enthusiastically, although his keenness did not lie with the cartloads of young plants and shrubs, saplings and delicate specimens that Laketon had brought back from Falmouth, with insufferable pride. Laketon was spending long hours supervising the team of gardeners, and stressing to Joshua that he would watch over the hothouses himself to protect the precious cargo, which at all costs must be kept at the same temperature. Laketon could crow all he liked. Joshua had found a new interest. Hobbs had given fresh breath in his body. He felt sure that Hobbs felt the same way. From the first, Hobbs had kept a tentative but steady eye contact with him, normally insolence in a servant, and when Joshua had not reprimanded him, he had gone on to give him many meaningful looks, taking his time when dressing him and helping him to disrobe. It was dangerous to be even thinking of embarking on an affair but the risk of Laketon finding out was small. He didn't make so free wandering into the house now and he had never disturbed him when he'd been with his valet, so he could spend lots of time with Hobbs. Laketon was pleased he was looking his old self again, espe- cially as Joshua had told him it was all for him. Right now Laketon was totally absorbed with the gardens; it pleased him that Joshua took no more than a gentleman's usual interest in them. It hurt to have to virtually ignore his great love of botany, but it pleased him that this way made Laketon more like a servant. Some day, somehow, he'd get rid of the evil swine responsible for sadistically wrecking his beautiful gardens.

'Why leave it all to him?' Tara had wondered about this. She'd wondered about Joshua's change of mood. Was it because he was spending less time with Kivell?

'It's better this way.'

'Yes, I understand.'

'Thank you.' He passed his cup to her for more coffee. 'Tara, I'm sorry I was so short with you before. I hope you have been finding things a little more agreeable lately, and that you won't find it so hard to stay here. I've been thinking. There is no reason for us not to live separately for part of each year, many couples do. Now you have ended your asso- ciation with my brother it will leave you free to take another lover. Look for someone who'll adore you, Tara. Someone you can dance with and have fun with, not some dreary bookworm. After Christmas you could stay at the house in Truro. The widowed Lady Worth will make a respectable companion to attend the Assembly Rooms with and see you about society, and as she hasn't her full wits about her she wouldn't hold you back. You can take your little girl and her nanny with you. You'll be able to shop in the best shops. It's not good for either of you to be shut away here all the time. Forgive me for being so thoughtless and selfish. In fact I'll escort you there myself and stay a night or two.' Laketon could not object to him making a show of keeping up the pretence of his marriage. Hobbs would come with him, of course. He'd have him more to himself. And if there did turn out to be something between them, as he hoped, he would buy some secret gifts for his new young love in Truro.

'The last thing I want to do is to take a lover,' Tara said. How could that possibly lead her to happiness? She would still be tied to Joshua. 'But it would be nice for Rosa Grace and me to have a change of surroundings. Goodness knows the grounds are in a bleak state with all the removal of dead trees and foliage.' The rest of the winter spent away from here and some socializing was wonderfully appealing.

'That's settled, then. I do hope Rosa Grace will be well again soon. If you'll excuse me, I'll go up and change.'

Joshua did not have to ring for his valet. Aaron Hobbs was waiting for him in his dressing room. He gave a little bow. Joshua loved the way he did it, a smooth flowing movement, as graceful as a swan. 'I have your outdoor attire ready for you, sir.'

'Thank you, Hobbs. I need something to wear for the afternoon. I shan't be going out.'

'Very good, sir.' Hobbs quietly set about pulling a pair of soft trousers and a smoking jacket out of the vast wardrobes.

Joshua watched him avidly. 'Your first week in my service has proved to be a success.'

'Thank you very much indeed, sir.' Hobbs's mild eyes were fixed to his. He was quite beautiful; his skin pale and soft as if he need never put an offending razor to it. 'I shall always be ready to please you, sir, in any way that I can. Any way at all.'

It was a blatant invitation to turn their master-servant

relationship into something deeper, Joshua was sure of that. It brought heat to his loins. In Hobbs he could have a lover he would truly be superior to. It was too marvellous. He couldn't help himself. He lifted a hand and laid the palm gently against Hobbs's face. 'Aaron . . .'

'My dear Mr Nankervis.' Aaron turned his head and kissed the palm, placing his hand over Joshua's, closing his eyes to revel in the touch, the moment.

With a sigh of desire, Joshua stepped up and took the youth into his arms. 'We won't be disturbed, we have all afternoon. Aaron, my darling . . .'

Sarah had stowed away the silver items, among them candle-sticks and a coffee pot with the Nankervis crest, into a captain's chest; the latter was shipwreck booty. Now she was filling a decorated tea crate with ornaments, china, glass and pewter. She would keep all the lovely fabrics and take them to her family's home. The more she thought about it the more confident she was that they would take her in. It would be such a happy reunion. It was arranged that as soon as she was paid for Tabbie's treasures Jowan would take her on the carpenter's cart to Redruth to call on her aunt, brother and sister.

There was a light knock on the door. She wasn't expecting anyone to call. Perhaps it was Jowan, come with informa-tion about the sale of the stuff before going on to the dinner to meet his half-brother at Burnt Oak. She looked out of the window and leapt back in shock to see the very man who had insulted her looking back in.

'Miss Hichens,' he called out. 'Please may I have a word with you?'

'I don't want to speak to you. Go away!' The nerve of the man! Finding out where she lived and actually coming here. She didn't like this at all, what interest did he have in her? She slammed the shutters and dashed to the door and drew the bar across it.

'I mean you no harm,' Kit called again. 'I've come to apol-ogize for my lack of chivalry towards you the other day. It was unforgivable of me.'

'You're right there. I'm not interested in your apology or

any explanation and I never want to see you again. Go away now or I'll take a gun to you.' Sarah glanced at the pistol Tabbie had kept in a small box.

'I'll respect your wishes, Miss Hichens. I really am sorry to have offended you so sorely. I wish you a very good day.'

Sarah heard his steps retreating over the stony ground. She peeped out of the window to make sure he really was going. His deportment was slightly stooped. She kept watch for some time.

Kit slunk back into the little lane and mounted his pony. He had made a mistake in upsetting Sarah Kivell. Information revealed that the Kivells regarded her highly and felt they had a lifetime responsibility to her. He had let his temper get the better of him. He mustn't allow that to happen again. He should have come back the following day and offered his apologies. His hope now was that she wouldn't speak to a Kivell and reveal what had happened. He rallied and pulled himself upright in the saddle. Apparently, the lovely creature was a dedicated recluse. She would never have a reason to go to Burnt Oak. He should be able to do what he intended quite comfortably.

It had been a long week keeping his head down before returning to Burnt Oak today. He wasn't a patient man, and stewing every minute over his childhood he had resorted to drink and laudanum to help him sleep, keeping at bay the nightmares he'd had all his life, the terrible dreams of crying out for a mother, for someone, anyone to love him but there was never anyone there.

As a boy he had been shaken awake and slapped across the face. 'Shut up, whelp,' his lazy young nursemaid had shrieked, 'or I'll beat the hide off you. Your real mother don't want you. She hates you. You haven't got a father, you was born a bastard. You haven't got a family. You've got no one. That's why wealthy old Miss Minion is bringing you up as a charity case, and she's been sworn to keep you here in total seclusion. It's no use crying, the old lady's deaf and batty. You're nothing, boy. You'll be nothing. No one will ever want you.'

He had never known what it was like to have a playmate. Observing children in later years he realized he didn't know how to play, to join in with fun. After receiving his lessons from a severe tutor until the age of twelve, he'd been thankful to get away from Miss Minion's stuffy dark house, which had smelled of mothballs, to go to a boarding school in the Bristol countryside. There he'd felt some freedom at last and had been surprised to realize he was strong-willed, and unlike many boys from an uncaring background he did not prove to be an easy target for the bullies. He had been able to stand his ground, fiercely if need be. Intelligent in the classroom and a good performer on the sports field, he had been popular, up to a point. Something had held him back from making friends and he had spent many hours in aching loneliness. Going home on his first holiday the need for revenge had been bred and he had devised a plan to get rid of the tormenting nursemaid. Putting fishing line across the servants' stairs he had enjoyed watching her take a plunge that had maimed her, rendering her unfit for any future employment. He had hoped she'd end up in the gutter.

The rest of his childhood had been no easier, the nightmares of belonging nowhere had continued to plague him. It had seemed to him at the time that every other boy at the school had a wonderful home life. He had hated listening to them enthusing about how they could twist Mama round their little finger, how Papa was so proud of them and about the games they played with their siblings and friends. He had wished and wished he could make friends but always some dark wall inside him had prevented it. He gained a reputation for being strange and the boys had avoided him.

He had seen little of Miss Minion, whom he remembered as someone akin to a waxen likeness of Queen Elizabeth, with a squawking voice and a tendency to hiccup. She had been forced to take to her bed when he'd reached his teen years and he had come under the guardianship of her lawyers. There had been days when he had spoken to no one but the servants, but wanting only to be alone he had brooded over his origins. On Miss Minion's death he had been left her house and a considerable fortune, in respect that he had fulfilled the proviso that he had turned out to be a successful, respectable young gentleman. He'd had no need to seek work.

Investment in the local railway and in ironwork factories had seen that he lived exactly as he willed.

For a while he had been distracted by a life of women, drink and playing the gaming tables but his underlying misery had driven him to decide to seek his real mother. He had hoped the nursemaid had lied, that he was actually the son of some poor girl seduced and deserted. He began to daydream that she had desperately wanted to keep him but had reluctantly given him up, perhaps even taking him to Miss Minion, or abandoning him on her doorstep, so he would have a better life.

He had enquired at every orphanage and workhouse and charity within a wide radius. He had even tried the brothels. He'd asked discreet questions in the houses Miss Minion had been associated with, thinking he might be the child of an acquaintance's servant. Everywhere he had drawn a blank, and he had been left with the worm, of being an unwanted nobody, chewing away at him all the more. Sometimes he thought he'd go mad and eventually he had resorted to drugs to ease his torment. If not for the chance meeting with the sea captain he might never have known who his parents were. The most hurtful thing was hearing from the former Howarth servant that his mother had gone insane after giving birth to him, hating the fact she had carried the result of the rape in her body. Could not Prudence Howarth have felt something for him? She had been the other half of his parentage. Was he so vile? Like something rotten, like carrion? She'd made him feel he was. She had prayed she would miscarry – she had wished him dead. And he had wished that too.

Remembering all this made him feel sick. His head went muzzy and he put a hand to his brow to rub at the tension. He realized he was nearly at Burnt Oak, having led the horse there by instinct. There was a commotion in the hedge. A large feral cat ran across the road ahead of him with a sparrow in its mouth. Impervious to Kit or arrogantly ignoring him, the cat let the bird down on the road but as it tried to flutter away it reached out and played with it with a tormenting paw. Kit dismounted. He grabbed the cat by its scruff as it picked the bird up in its mouth again. 'Drop it!' He shook the cat until it was forced to let the bird go. Kit dropped the

cat down and hissed at it to get away, which it did, and he
picked up the trembling shocked sparrow and closed gentle
fingers round its tiny body. He could feel its heart pounding
but it didn't seem to be too badly hurt.

The cat slunk back, meowed in complaint and circled about
his legs. 'Get away! Cruel bully.' He marched back to the
horse and holding the trembling bird carefully, he rode on.
When well away from the cat he stopped and opened his
palm. The bird flew away at once. 'Ah, thank God.' He knew
the cat had only followed its instincts but he hated seeing
the suffering of something smaller and less powerful.

Jowan was in his grandmother's sitting room, drinking Kivell-
produced mead before the meal. His grandmother was in her
chair, regal and calm, like a duchess. His Great-Uncle
Genesis, and Aunt Eula with her husband, Jack, his eldest
sister Delen and a half-brother, Hugh, were also there to
make up their minds about the expected guest. As ordered
by his grandmother all were dressed formally.

It felt very odd when he was facing his new half-brother
with his clear Kivell looks. No wonder Sarah had received
such a shock. It was an odd and uncomfortable situation
despite the pussyfooting pleasantries, the small talk and
polite smiles. Staying on his feet, hot and stuffy in high
starched collars and a tie, although determined not to let
Sarah's distrust of Charles Howarth prejudice his opinion,
Jowan took a dislike to the man. Howarth was trying hard
to please, which was understandable, issuing witty anecdotes about nothing in particular, but he was vague about
his life and was warding off direct questions. His grandmother seemed keen for everyone to form a good opinion
of him. The others were nodding and smiling a lot. Was he
the only one to have noticed Howarth's reticence? But
perhaps he was being unfair. Howarth was outnumbered.
He had got a cold reception the first time here and must be
feeling ill at ease.

By halfway through the meal Kit had grown more or less
at ease. He had spoken to everyone and had received politeness and hospitality in return. Only with Jowan was he finding
it difficult to strike up a conversation. The younger man's

suspicion of him was plain, deliberately so. 'You run a carpentry business, I understand, Jowan?'

'I do,' Jowan watched him closely from the other side of the table. How genuine was Howarth's interest? 'It's the property of my brother Sol and his wife.'

'I'm sorry not to be able to meet Sol. I'd like to look over the business, if I may. To see where you live.' He had been invited by the others to view their workshops and enter their homes.

'Come when you like. You have left a great responsibility behind you in Bristol.' Jowan wanted to talk about Howarth's affairs.

'Indeed,' Kit included all with a sweeping glance. 'But the Howarths have always retained very good managers.'

'I'd have thought you'd spend time in Falmouth looking up contacts and forging new ones.'

'That wasn't the purpose of Charles's journey down to Cornwall, Jowan,' Tempest interjected. She was aware Jowan was set on an interrogation. It was important that the family should learn all about Charles, she was eager to know all about his life, but she didn't want him feel on edge.

'I know what Jowan means, Mrs Kivell. A good businessman never stops seeking opportunities.' Kit turned back to Jowan. 'I've ridden to Falmouth and done just that, but I wanted to stay fairly close to Meryen and get the feel of the locality you all live in, the mining community included. Gwennap was the closest I could get without infringing on you. Mostly I have kept quietly to myself.'

'Has anyone spotted your likeness to us?' Jowan leaned towards him, his eyes piercing the other man's face.

'Yes,' Kit answered at once. 'Sarah Kivell has. She informed me that she wished to be known henceforth by her maiden name. She stared at me. It's a particular dislike of mine, being stared at, and I'm afraid I was rather sharp with her. At first, you see, I'd assumed she was some insolent village girl. Later, I was ashamed of myself. I called on her prior to coming here and offered my apologies. She refused to accept them and ordered me away and I promptly withdrew.'

'You took the trouble of finding out where she lived and

went to Tabbie's Shack?' Jowan didn't like this. He could imagine how Sarah would have hated being disturbed by this man.

'Of course Charles would do so,' Tempest chided Jowan. 'He's a gentleman. Charles, Sarah actually told you she has disowned the Kivell name?'

'She told me she hated Titus.' Kit looked down for a moment. 'Sorry to have brought it up, but you might as well know.'

Tempest, like the rest, wondered what had caused the monumental change in Sarah's attitude, but this wasn't the time to speculate about it.

'Do you have a wife, Mr Howarth?' Eula put in, and Tempest blessed her for changing the subject.

Jowan had told Tempest about Sarah's intention to leave the village; the sooner the better. It appeared she had finally put Titus and all he had meant to her behind her. Tempest was pleased about that. Jowan had always liked Sarah and it touched Tempest that he was protective of her. Tempest did not have the same strong emotional link with Jowan as she did with Sol, but she loved him a lot. He was the one grandchild who wasn't jealous about Sol being her favourite.

'I'm not married,' Kit told Eula, putting on a sweet sort of smile. 'But I think when I get back to Bristol I'll start looking for a bride. It's time I settled down. I'd like to have a large family.' He couldn't think of anything he wanted less. He didn't ever intend to encumber himself with a wife – one who would surely disapprove of his lifestyle – and he had no care at all for children, he had no idea how to relate to them. He didn't believe he could ever fall in love, anyway. Family life was alien to him, in fact he was rather frightened by it, of the commitment and possible rejection it might mean.

The lunch was eaten with the talk, as if by some silent agreement, centring on the running of Burnt Oak and its many crafts and trades, the Kivells all feeling there would be other times to get to know more about Charles Howarth. Kit was only really interested in Tempest, in finding the best way to bring her down for her crime of rejecting Titus. If she had shown him a mother's love, as all mothers should do without exception for their children, then Titus might have grown up to be a good man, and Prudence Howarth might not have been raped to ultimately bear him and cast him into a life of hell. He felt the food, although delicious, was choking him, and he was careful not to make too free with the wine. He'd drink himself into a stupor when he returned to his house to purge himself of this boring, cringe-making experience. He didn't want to admit he actually admired and was excruciatingly jealous of the family's easy closeness.

The rest of the visit was kept formal, with Kit leaving after making arrangements to call again in a day or two.

'What did you think of him?' Tempest asked the gathering, when back in her sitting room after waving off her guest.

'He seems agreeable enough but I still don't know what to make of him,' Genesis answered first, as was his due as the elder. 'He won't be around for long and may choose to never come down to Meryen again. He's a kinsman, and while we should stay careful of him I suppose we do have a duty to offer him hospitality.'

'It's obvious you would like to form a closer relationship with him, Mama,' Eula said in a reserved tone. 'But I can't forget how much your vision distressed you. All that couldn't have been for nothing.'

'But his character was found to be exemplary. I have thought much about the vision and every possible way it could be interpreted. Charles turning up would have thrown my world upside down anyway. It could be that.'

'It could be anything, Grandmama,' Delen said. 'I shall reserve my judgement for now.'

'Me too, until I get to know him better,' Hugh said. 'I don't think you were impressed by him at all, were you, Jowan?'

'I can't say I was.' Jowan was tight-lipped. 'I don't trust him. When he knew he was related to us, why couldn't he simply have written to introduce himself? To have spent days at Gwennap before coming here means he must have been spying on us. Why all the drama? I shall go to Sarah, keep her informed of events.'

'I thought he seemed rather shy,' was Jack's deliberation.

'That could explain his actions. He might have been deciding whether to actually approach us or not.'

'Yes,' Tempest said quickly. 'We should give him the benefit of the doubt for now. He's not used to mixing in with family life. In a way it was brave of him to come to us. Thank you all for being here. Tell the rest of the family about Charles. We shall hold another council about him again soon.'

Kit's mind was on riding fast to his house and drowning himself in a luxury of fine wines, but at the outer gate he recalled that the opposite direction led to Poltraze. The lady there was lovely and it tugged at the side of him that liked a mystery and a challenge to get to know her. How did she fare with a husband who preferred a man in his bed? The big house was bleak and it shunned entertaining, in parts its grounds were as ruined as a battlefield. Tara Nankervis adored her child and apparently found a little purpose in her charities, but her life must be wearisome in the extreme. How much longer could a young and vital woman go on like that without turning into a sorry drab? He would welcome some distraction right now, and the lady might too.

He presented his false identity at Poltraze's massive carved front doors, was invited into the echoing tiled hall by the stiff and ceremonious butler, who raised astonished brows, no doubt over his likeness to the Kivells, before taking his card up the dismal grey stone stairs to the drawing room. What a discouraging place this was, built by and then added to by philistines.

The butler returned. 'The squire is unavailable, sir. Mrs Nankervis will receive you.'

After the butler had announced him and retired, Kit stretched out a hand, smiling lightly. 'Thank you for—'

'You're the intruder!' Tara exclaimed, distinguishing his broad build and Kivell looks. She hurried to the bell pull at the mantelpiece.

'Please, I mean you no harm.' He put up his hands. He didn't want to be ejected from the house. Tara Nankervis was not only favoured with exquisite snow-white skin, she also had a fascinating spirit, usually restrained, he was sure, but which had come to the fore in her belief her home was under threat. 'I'm sorry about my trespass. I can't explain it. It was something I did on impulse.'

Tara restrained her hand but kept it raised to the bell pull. 'Do you often act on impulse, Mr Howarth? Or should I say Mr Kivell?'

'If you would kindly let me explain the obvious, Mrs Nankervis . . .'

'Oh, you have an explanation.' Tara was shocked to have him here but she was also curious to know something about him. 'I'll allow you five minutes.'

Kit gave a brief account of why he in was in the area. 'Of course, one of my first thoughts was to call on the local squire and I had heard about the splendid gardens here. The light was dimming on my first arrival and I was astonished to see the state of them. I wandered about, in something of a daze, I suppose. Then I left. I felt it wasn't the best time to call.'

Tara knew he wasn't telling the full truth, and that he was an individual always careful in his approach and ready to seize the advantage. He'd had a cheek wandering about the grounds. It would be wise to send him away, but present-able visitors to Poltraze were rare nowadays. 'It must have been strange for you to meet your real family.'

'It was a somewhat emotional event. My grandmother, Tempest Kivell, was very pleased to receive me. I shall be making myself more acquainted with all the members of the family in the next few weeks. I'm looking forward to it.'

Tara nodded. 'May I ask what your family in Bristol thinks about you coming down here?'

'My mother is dead. I confess that the others do not know. It would distress them and I had no wish to do that. I had to come. One has a burning desire to know about one's exact origins.'

'I can understand that.' Tara didn't know how to entirely sum up this man but there seemed no real need to urgently be rid of him. His company was better than none. 'I'm sorry my husband is not here. Would you care for some sherry?'

'I would, thank you, Mrs Nankervis.'

She was pleased he did not gush out an acceptance but had replied quietly and humbly. 'Do sit down.'

Sherry glass in hand, Kit waited for her to take a seat on the end of a striped silk Georgian sofa, near the serpentine fireplace, one of the few splendid masterpieces about the place, and then he sat opposite her, at an angle where he could best see her face. She was like a marble goddess yet soft and tender, as if waiting to be brought fully alive. He saw the sadness edged behind her fair eyes and sensed a need in her to see right and justice done. As with every beautiful woman he met he desired her, but he had respect for Tara Nankervis. There was nothing shallow and conniving about her.

'I see the gardens are being restored,' he said.

'Yes. It was a terrible blow to Mr Nankervis to have lost so much.'

'Was it a blight that caused the destruction?'

'I believe so.'

Kit could tell she had very little interest in the gardens. She had no reason to be proud of anything about Poltraze. She was wasting her life here. He would keep the conversation to the usual topics discussed in a grand drawing room with a lady. He would enjoy this afternoon and hope to be invited here again.

Jowan made straight for Tabbie's Shack. Sarah was outside drawing water. 'Hello. I came because Charles Howarth told me he'd been here. I hope he didn't upset you.' He looked for signs of this in Sarah's expression but she was always difficult to read. It would be good if she was glad to see him.

'He did a bit. How was the meal?'

'I didn't like him particularly, but in fairness I haven't really had the chance to get to know him. Grandmama seems to be quite besotted with him. He's a lot like Sol in looks. I think she sees him as a sort of replacement. He admitted that he'd met you and offended you and was sorry for it. I'll be keeping a close watch on Mr Charles Howarth. He's coming to Chy-Henver soon. I'll be able to find out more about him then without Grandmama jumping to his defence.'

He was gazing at Sarah, enjoying the way her black hair was falling long and free and was ruffled by the wind. 'How are you, Sarah? Could I take a quick look at what you're hoping to sell? I'll be better able to see how the dealer and I will carry it out from here and down Tabbie's Lane.'

'Come inside.' Sarah didn't mind Jowan's company. She was grateful to have his help.

'I've always wanted to see inside Tabbie's home.' Jowan smiled to himself. He would stay here as long as he could. After Sarah had been in her new house for a few days he'd call on her there. He knew it was unlikely she could be enticed back to Meryen, but he was more than taken with her and was prepared to live in hope.

Nine

'So, Hankins, have you anything interesting to report to me today?' From the mahogany twin pedestal desk in the ostentatious little office in Paradise Cottage, Laketon Kivell held the Poltraze footman in a direct stony stare.

Every part of the skinny, fresh-faced youth quivered in trepidation. He'd heard about a practice in ancient times of killing a messenger who brought bad news. He was praying the frightening head gardener wouldn't do something dreadful to him. It wasn't his fault, what he was about to say. He had to tell, to keep secrets from this man would cost him dear. 'Yes, sir, I'm afraid I have. It's, um, about the squire.'

'Go on.' Laketon leaned back in the leather-backed chair, toying with a crested silver paperknife, pressing it into each well-padded fingertip, enjoying the delicious sensation of each sharp prod. He imagined trailing the paperknife down the youth's back and watching him squirm. The last significant information that Hankins had passed on was Tara Nankervis's reminder to Michael Nankervis that he was her brat's father. That was unimportant. From the lowliest servant to the highest in society that was suspected to be true. It caused tittering and innuendo but suspicion alone did not cause a public scandal. It couldn't bring down the house of Nankervis, and thereafter turn him out of his very comfortable living.

'Th-the squire's having an, an affair, Mr Kivell. W-with his valet,' the now sweating Hankins blurted out, leaping back in case the other man went into a rage, a not uncommon occurrence, and grabbed him from across the desk. He'd hate it if the man touched him. Everyone knew about the open secret concerning him and the squire.

The only change in Laketon was a heightening of his dark complexion. 'You are sure about this? Absolutely sure?'

'Yes sir. I heard them. I-I saw them. I peeped into the squire's bedroom. They . . . they were on the bed.' The memory of what he'd seen haunted Hankins's dreams. What if he was at risk of the same treatment? If he refused he would be turned out without a character.

Laketon was using his imagination and the result flayed him to the bone. He looked sharply at the footman. 'Does anyone else know?'

'I don't think so, sir.'

Laketon's eyes seemed to twist in their deep sockets. He wanted the runt of a servant out of the place. He reached into his waistcoat pocket and produced a sixpence and tossed it on the desk. 'You've done well, Hankins.' His voice was as cold as an Arctic blast. 'Keep up your watch with every diligence. Keep a record of any more such occurrences. Now get out.'

Hankins snatched up the silver coin, terrified the paperknife might be plunged through his hand. He bowed and scampered out, latching the low door after him with careful deliberation so as not to antagonize the man in the room.

Laketon heard his footsteps running away as if the hounds of hell were after him. He stabbed the paperknife into the middle of the desk where it pierced the polished wood and shuddered in its upright position. The hounds of hell would soon be on Joshua's traitorous heels. So he had fallen for the charms of the creamy-skinned Aaron Hobbs? Hobbs was a tempting prospect; softly spoken, a well-moulded body; something out of Greek mythology; young and clean and fresh. Laketon had summed him up as one who enjoyed being controlled. Joshua must love that – controlling someone for a change. 'Well, Joshua, I'll let you enjoy your dream for a little while longer. As for you, Aaron Hobbs –' he flicked the paperknife and watched it quiver – 'I'm going to get to know you.'

Dinah Greep crept down the stairs with her belongings wrapped into a bundle. She had made a show last night of being violently ill so she could get out of going to work today. She would never go to the Carn Croft Mine again or set another foot inside this wretched cottage.

She had spied Miriam carrying out fodder to the pigs. With Jeb at work on the night core and not due back for a couple of hours she could slip out through the front door. Her nephew and niece were taking a nap in the cradle at a safe distance from the kitchen hearth. She loomed over them. 'I won't miss you brats! Nor your rotten father and your oh-so-saintly mother.' Jeb had once declared that Miriam was everything she was not, and had held up how wonderful a mother Miriam was. She was a goody-goody bitch! But she was insensitive to others' ears when enjoying rocking in the bed with Jeb, crying out in pleasure. How could she enjoy *that*?

Tears burned Dinah's eyes. She was still sore and bruised after Abner Jago's assault on her. It had gone on and on. He had done depraved things to her and made her do depraved things to him. It had been long after dark when she'd managed to trudge back home, scratched and bleeding, and in terrible pain. She'd given Jeb the line about meditating on God and forgetting the time and then tripping over a stone and hurting herself in the darkness. Jeb and Miriam had been kind to her but they had left it too late for that. Her virginity had been brutally stolen. If they knew how and why they would say it was her own fault and go on and on about repenting her wicked ways. Damn them! Damn their beliefs! Damn their bloody brats! She wanted to scream and smash the place up, make Jeb and Miriam suffer. They deserved to suffer, their brats deserved to suffer too. In a moment of madness she picked up the bread knife from the table and put it in the cradle and pinched the little boy to make sure he woke up.

She met Abner Jago as arranged outside Tabbie's Shack. She didn't speak to him. She scowled from behind the hand barrow he had brought to carry away the goods, keeping back while he grunted and groaned with the effort of hack-sawing through the padlock.

Throwing the padlock on the ground he kicked the door open. 'Come on,' he bawled. 'Let's be quick about it. I don't want my wagon seen out in the lane. People will wonder what I'm up to.' Once inside the shack he let out a triumphant laugh. 'Looks like she's about to leave. Everything's packed up. Makes our job a lot easier.'

'How much are you going to give me?' Dinah demanded. She was to heft stuff out to the wagon while he wheeled the loaded barrow, and she wanted to get the business side agreed before she started.

'There's a tidy lot here. I'll give you a tidy sum,' he barked.

'When?' She hated being in close proximity to him, her vile abuser.

'When I drop you off on the road later on,' he snarled impatiently, cursing wholesale. 'Come on! Let's get weaving.'

Together they lugged one of the chests onto the barrow and he wheeled it, while she carried stuff to the wagon. It was hard going for Jago as the wooden wheel jarred and got stuck between the stones. He blasphemed when she had to abandon her load to guide the barrow wheel over all the obstacles. It was more than an hour later before they finally loaded up the barrow with the last of the individual items and the draperies. There was nothing left but the bench table, screen and some ragged old clothes.

'That's everything,' Dinah said, sighing heavily in relief. 'Let's be on our way.' She was on her way to a new life, soon to be free of this beast's disgusting company. She took a moment to gloat over the shock Sarah Kivell would get when she got back from work and found her home ransacked.

Jago took a final look round to make sure nothing of value had been missed. Then with an aggressive grunt he pushed Dinah further into the room until her back hit the bench. 'No!' she screamed. 'Not that again!'

'Don't be a fool,' he growled. 'There's no time for messing about.'

'Then why aren't we going now?' she wailed.

'Because I'm the only one who's going. I'm not giving you a farthing and I'm not taking you anywhere.' His rough hands shot out and he was squeezing her throat. Dinah screamed and choked. She was terrified. He was going to kill her. He shook her fiercely and kneed her in the groin. 'Don't tell anyone it was me or I'll do for you, understand?'

She nodded, tears searing her eyes.

He let her go and pushed her away so hard she hit the ground. 'Be sure you get far away from this place and never come back. And don't never come near me again. Your debt's cleared. Be grateful for that.' Off he went.

Dinah curled her hurting body into a ball. Tears came thick, convulsing her, and she gagged on them and the bile that had risen from her stomach. She was going to vomit. She scrabbled to her hands and knees and spilled out a mess on the floor. She crawled away. She sat with her knees up, sobbing until she had no strength left. How was she going to get away if she couldn't stand up, let alone walk? She recalled what she had done. Miriam must have discovered the knife in the cradle. The boy might have cut himself or the baby. He might be dead, she might be dead. She couldn't go home. She had no home. She had nothing. She would be hunted down and brought before the courts and hanged for her terrible crime.

'I hate you, Abner Jago! Hate you! Hate you!' she raged and raged.

She had to get away. But she wouldn't get very far. Jeb wouldn't stop searching until he'd found her. She had hurt his children in a most horrendous way and for that he'd forget about God and kill her with his bare hands. She was dead whatever she did.

She screamed and screamed at the top of her voice, smacking her hands against her forehead, screaming until her throat was hoarse and painful and her voice would no longer come. She backed up against the wall, tearing at her hair, her eyes growing wilder and wilder. Where was she? It took moments to remember. She was in Tabbie's Shack, Sarah Kivell's home. The beautiful Sarah Kivell, who everyone cared about and now respected. Jeb had always liked her and preferred her to herself, his own sister. The handsome Jowan Kivell had stopped her at the market and she had gone off with him. No Kivell had ever given her a second look. Sarah Kivell lived here. But she didn't have to. She could live in the wonderful surroundings of Burnt Oak and wear nice clothes and eat the best food. She didn't have to hammer ore all day long, but she did, like a martyr, the stupid, stuck-up bitch. No one called her ugly. Not the wonderful Sarah Kivell.

Beating her fists against the wall behind her, she chanted, 'I hate you, Sarah Kivell. I hate you.'

Some time later she let out a mighty howl like a wolf at full moon. Then she let forth a maniacal laugh and scrabbled about the floor for the discarded clothes.

Sarah saw at once the shack had been broken into. The door was shut, but the hazy glow of her lantern in the misty atmosphere showed the padlock had been sawn off. Stunned beyond measure, her heart falling to pieces, she knew her hopes for the future had been dealt a massive blow. She had been robbed. She didn't need to go inside to know that.

How much of Tabbie's stuff had been stolen? Her mind went to the man Charles Howarth. Could he be responsible for this? Why should he do it? That wouldn't make sense. It wasn't him. It was some greedy individual who had come to see what Tabbie had left after her death.

Slowly stretching out an arm she put her hand on the door to see how empty her home was. Her heart thundering all the way up to her throat, her head strangely numb but her senses nervously alert, she pushed on the door. It moved only a fraction, something was blocking it. Sarah stifled a cry. Were the thieves inside and pushing on it to prevent entry? She listened, she could hear nothing. She pushed again, as hard as she could. The door gave way a little more. It was stuck on a rush mat. Bending, she reached inside, fearful her hand might be grabbed. Grasping the mat she pulled and shook it until she'd wrenched it free and tossed it aside.

She stepped inside, holding the lantern up high, her eyes shooting to the four corners in fear she would see intruders. There was no one. She took a longer look round and everything inside her collapsed. The essence of her life, like a golden circle around her heart, shattered, breaking into tinier and tinier pieces and seeping out of her in a river of despair. The table had been overturned and hurled into a corner and the screen smashed up and everything else was gone. The thieves had even taken the presents she'd bought for Aunt Molly, Arthur and Tamsyn. The carpets and mats had been ripped up into tangles. The logs beside the hearth had been tossed about and the ashes from the fire had been thrown at the walls. The shutters at the windows were hanging at crazy angles in an attempt to yank them off the hinges. This wasn't just a robbery. Those responsible for this must hate her. They had wrecked all her hopes for a new life. She had nothing to go to her family with now, nothing worth going on for.

The money! They might have missed the money hidden in a cleft in the wall behind the door. Stepping gingerly through the mess and chaos she located the triangular stone that disguised the hidey-hole and pulled it out. She pushed her hand inside the small recess. She gave a cry of relief. She still had the twenty pounds. The coins were there, safely inside a leather pouch. She pulled the pouch out. The money would keep her comfortably for several months until she could get a job. Her family should find that agreeable. She would buy some new clothes tomorrow and present herself to them without delay. In that respect she had stalled long enough.

She heard a noise, a shuffle. It was coming from the corner where the table lay on its side. She shot round. She saw nothing. It must be some small creature that had crept in. Her heart was hammering and she didn't want to stay here. What else could she do? She'd hate to ask anyone to take her in. Jowan Kivell would have to be told there was nothing here for his acquaintance to collect and buy. She could go to Chy-Henver. Jowan and his kinfolk would not deny her shelter for the night. She hesitated, her reserve making her consider if she could actually ask a Kivell, even Jowan, for more help. There was another shuffling sound. She gasped, staring at the upturned table. She couldn't bear to spend the night here. She would go to Jowan straightaway.

A ghastly wail came from behind the table and a small, bent figure rose up clad in a black dress and a black bonnet with its ribbons dangling free. A cry climbed up inside Sarah but got stuck in her throat. She went rigid.

There came a croak of a voice. 'Hello, Sarah.'

'Tabbie . . . ?' No. All reason told her this wasn't her aged friend.

The figure came round the end of the table and flew straight at her. She was mesmerized for a moment, then started to flee from the shack. There was something mad and unholy about the creature. Keeping a tight grip on the money pouch and with the lantern swinging in her hand she got to the doorway, screaming as the creature came after her with high-pitched wails.

A terrible pain across the back of her leg made her buckle at the knee and she was falling. Another heavy blow hit her shoulder as she went down. The lantern glass broke but the flame still burned. Sarah still had the pouch in her hand. She hurled herself round to face her attacker with her hands raised to protect herself. 'Who are you?' she yelled as the creature raised the log that had struck her before.

The next assault was halted. The person pulled off the bonnet. 'Don't you recognize me, Sarah?'

Sarah stared at the leering face above, eerily shadowed in the flickering light. 'Dinah! Why are you doing this? Did you steal my things?' She tried to get up but Dinah Greep kicked her viciously in the legs.

'Not me,' Dinah rasped in her raw voice. 'Abner Jago did it. Ah!' she spied the pouch. 'I'll have that!'

While Sarah struggled to get away the crazed girl reached down and snatched the pouch out of her hand. 'No!'

'Yes, you bitch. You owe me this.' Dinah jangled the coins, laughing, gloating.

'What are you talking about? I owe you nothing! You've no right to be doing this.' From where she was sprawled, Sarah lunged and grabbed Dinah round the legs. She tugged on her and tried to bring the girl down. While trying to kick her legs free and shrieking insanely, Dinah launched her upper body down towards Sarah and grabbed her hair. Screaming, Sarah clung on with one arm while scrabbling to clutch Dinah's skirt to unbalance her. Dinah sank her teeth into Sarah's scalp. Sarah cried in pain, and screaming in anger she forced Dinah to the ground.

Clawing and rolling, kicking and lashing out, they fought for dominance. Sarah realized she was fighting for her life. Dinah had gone off her head and would stop at nothing until she had killed her.

Down on her back, with Dinah putting her hands round her neck, Sarah managed to get hold of one of the scattered logs and struck Dinah on the neck. She expected Dinah to attempt to wrestle the log from her. Dinah threw back her head and butted her full in the face. Completely dazed, Sarah was helpless. Dinah wrenched the log from her hand and Sarah felt blow after blow rain down on her body. Stark lights were before her eyes and her head rang in shrill agony. She fought against the coming darkness but knew it was hopeless. It wasn't Titus in some form back from the grave that was a danger to her. For no real reason a bitter, crazed girl from the village was going to beat her to death.

It took a while before Dinah grasped that Sarah was limp and still. 'There you are, bitch! You got what you deserved.'

In the fight she had dropped the pouch. Swiping up the lantern she dropped low and scrambled about for it. Triumph. She held the light over Sarah's body. Dinah's eyes bulged like a reptile's as she revelled in tracing the paths of blood on Sarah's face, hands, legs and ripped clothes. A lump of tangled hair lay on her chest where it had been torn out of her head. 'See who finds you beautiful now.'

She saw Sarah's pendant flung to the side of her neck. 'Aha, I'll have that.' She went outside. The mist was thick and the lantern gave no more than a faint glow. She couldn't see an inch ahead or in any direction. The flame flickered. It would die soon. It didn't matter. She had nothing to worry about. She had money, a lot of money by the weight of the bag. She'd soon be away from here and no one would ever find her. She would go across the downs. No one would know which way she had gone. No one would ever know she had been in Tabbie's Shack, that it was she who had murdered the ridiculous young widow lying there.

Off she went, round the shack, past the garden patch and was soon stumbling over the rough hostile ground. She sang the first line of a hymn at the top of her voice, 'Guide me O thou great Jehovah.' She cackled through the cloak of cold, wet, ground-level cloud. 'I don't need anyone to guide me. I've got money. I've got this necklace. I can do anything I like. I'm free . . . free!'

Ten

K it ran his fingers along the expertly carved end scroll on a cabinet top. He was in the Chy-Henver workshop, a long stone building, whitewashed on the inside, the walls neatly displayed with a vast miscellany of tools. Workbenches ran on three sides of the walls, a square trestle for fitting jobs was in the middle of the floor, and the whole was lighted by long windows and by the double doors left open. Kit found the wood dust irritated his nose and made his eyes gritty. He wouldn't be able to stand this atmosphere for long; far better the smoky confines of a gambling room. 'This is exceedingly well done, Jowan. If I may say so, you are very young to have reached such excellence.'

'Kivells are started off young on their given craft,' Jowan replied, secretly pleased with the compliments he had received while showing his half-brother the premises. Charles Howarth seemed genuinely interested, asking about everything from wood lacquers to inlay designs, and the various specialist tools.

'Are you allotted your craft or allowed to choose your own, Jowan?' Kit wiped a speck of dust from his eye. He wished Jowan would call him Charles to show he was getting friendly, but the younger man was staying firmly aloof, as if he didn't have a name at all. This hurt, for Kit all too often felt he had no real identity. He wished he had not presented himself to the Kivell family as the real Charles Howarth. He hated to be called Charles, each time it accused him as a liar and made him feel more than ever that he belonged nowhere at all. The real Charles Howarth was an understanding sort of fellow. Somehow getting wind of Kit's probings into his family he had sought Kit out and had been delighted to meet him. He'd wanted to make a friend of Kit, to see him occasionally, but while remaining anxious that the truth of Kit's identity should never be revealed. Kit loathed Charles for that. He shunned all idea of forming a friendship with him.

'We tend to follow the work we show a natural feel for. Most boys and girls follow their parents' skills. All of my Aunt Eula's girls are quilters like her and the boys are metal-workers like Uncle Jack. Shall we go outside? You can take a look at the wood store.' Jowan wasn't oblivious to the other man's discomfort.

'Yes. I'd like to see the raw timber.' Kit nodded goodbye to the cousin of Jowan's, his cousin too, who worked and lived at Chy-Henver. Thad Kivell was quiet and serious for a Kivell, even rather shy. He nodded back with a smile and got on with sanding down a turned chair leg. Kit felt he had at least won Thad over. The other Kivell who worked there was out on a job.

Out in the chilled air, a high natural bank at the back of the workshop gave shelter and cut off the sharp wind. Kit offered Jowan a cigarette from a gold case. Jowan accepted and they lit up. 'Our father was never a carpenter, though, was he?'

Jowan frowned. 'He never did anything useful.'

'You were not close to him?'

'No.' He gazed at Kit. 'Were you hoping to hear good things about him, after this romantic affair he was said to have had with your mother?'

'I didn't know what to expect.' Kit couldn't help sounding grim.

'Your mother was fortunate not to stay in Falmouth. Titus wouldn't have stayed good to her for long. This must be hard for you to hear.'

'Yes, very hard.' Jowan couldn't guess how hard. Kit was here not to gain Jowan's acceptance but to seek the best way to get back at Tempest, yet he wanted Jowan to like him. The more he got to know the Kivells, took part in their lives – last evening he had been entertained to a musical evening at Burnt Oak, with regional instruments and fiddles being played, with raucous dancing and much drinking – he was wanting to be a part of it all. He met Jowan's eyes. 'You

don't trust me. You're right not to. I'm a stranger and you
want to protect your family, especially your grandmother. I
hope that will change when you get to know me better.'

'We'll see.'

Jowan had said it softly and Kit hoped he had made some
headway with him. He saw something peculiar out in the
lane, low on the ground and inching slowly towards the
cottage. 'What on earth . . . ?'

Jowan looked. 'My God, it's a girl. It's Sarah!' He threw
the cigarette down and ran to her, appalled at the state of
her, bloodied and clothes in shreds, meaning she could only
have crawled and clawed her way along.

Kit ran with him. Jowan pushed him aside to ensure he
was the one who picked Sarah up. He was very careful, her
leg had been viciously attacked and her left shoulder was
dislocated. He was sure some of her ribs were broken. She
was limp and slight in his arms, her eyelids flickering, barely
conscious. He surmised she must have come here by impulse,
probably thinking to get to Amy, her friend. He was shocked
and sickened by her injuries, she seemed near to death. 'It's
all right, Sarah, you're safe now. Charles, fetch Rachel from
the house and tell Thad to run at once for the doctor.'

Sarah had no idea where she was. Her eyelids opened a
shade, but desperate not to wake up she allowed her weakness and pain to pull her back into deep, deep sleep. Now
she was wide awake, lying on a soft bed in a large darkened
room, looking up at a white ceiling. From time to time in
her muddled state she thought she'd heard voices, male and
female, and noises, but she had no notion what they were.
She heard something now, a gentle swish. Then something
soft and warm was touching her hand where it lay on the
bedcover. She turned her head, a stiff and painful movement,
and waiting for her vision to clear she saw a figure, a young
woman sitting close beside the bed. 'Amy . . .' Her voice
came in a dry cracked whisper.

'No, Sarah, it's Tara Nankervis. It reached my ears that
you had been hurt and I've been here most days to see you.'
Tara stroked Sarah's bruised and battered brow. Most of
her face was florid with marks and scratches but the rest of

her skin was deathly white. Tara had cried when she'd first seen Sarah. She had been savaged as if by a madman.

'Where . . . am I?'

'You're at Chy-Henver. Only God knows how you managed to get here. You'd crawled all the way on your hands and knees.'

Sarah found the effort of keeping her head turned too much and she gazed up at the ceiling and then closed her eyes to try to remember why she had made such a painful journey. 'Amy's not here, is she?'

'No, she's abroad with her family, in California, America. Jowan Kivell lives here now and some of his family.'

'Jowan? Jowan?' It was exhausting just to think. 'Yes, I had to see him. Tabbie's Shack . . . oh no!' The horror of her home being cleared and wrecked, of the violent beating she'd received made her gulp in torment.

'It's all right, Sarah. You're safe now. Jowan knows what happened. I'm so sorry about your little home and what's happened to you, but you're going to be looked after from now on. Try not to upset yourself.' Tara spoke soothingly while caressing Sarah's hand and face, hoping the contact was comforting.

There was a knock on the door.

'Come in,' Tara called softly.

Jowan came in slowly. 'I heard talking. Is Sarah awake?'

'Yes. She's remembered what happened. She's very tired, we must go gently,' Tara cautioned.

'Of course,' Jowan tiptoed to the bedside. 'Hello, Sarah. It's good to see you awake after all this time.'

Sarah did not understand. 'How long have I been here?'

'For just over two weeks. You've been very poorly.' That was an understatement. The doctor had reset her shoulder, strapped up her ribs and stitched a long gash in her leg, but he had expected Sarah to die within forty-eight hours from brain or internal injuries. He had announced it was a miracle she had survived. Despite all her past sufferings, her depression and hopelessness, and having her new future so maliciously cheated from her, somewhere inside had been a spark of strength to bring her through. Thank God. She had come to him, she had needed him, and he would have hated to lose her. 'Sarah, don't distress yourself, have you any idea who did this to you?'

Sarah put her mind back in Tabbie's Shack. She squeezed on Tara's hand. 'I came home from the mine . . . all Tabbie's things were gone.' She creased her forehead and put her free hand there. 'The money Tabbie left me was still there. Then I heard something. She was there.'

'Who was there, Sarah?' Tara prompted as Sarah fell into a tormented silence.

The vision of the figure in Tabbie's clothes coming at her filled her with revulsion. 'It was . . .' Just who had been waiting for her? Someone who'd hated her and wanted her dead. In her mind she saw Tabbie's bonnet being tossed away by the terrifying figure. 'It was Dinah Greep! She was like a mad woman. She wanted to kill me.'

Tara glanced at Jowan. He said, 'That makes sense, Sarah. Dinah Greep disappeared on the same day, after she'd done a terrible thing at home. She tried to hurt the Greep children but thankfully Miriam got to them just in time. The girl must have gone insane. I'm afraid she must have taken your money. There was none in the shack.'

'She's taken everything from me,' Sarah croaked, tears of despair melting down her face. 'Tabbie left her things to me to give me a new life and it was all for nothing.'

'You will have a new life, Sarah. You mustn't worry about a thing. You're among friends,' Jowan said, reaching down to gently touch her arm.

'We're all rallying round you,' Tara said, drying Sarah's eyes. 'All you need to do is rest and get well again.'

Sarah closed her eyes. All she wanted was to sleep for a very long time. A name popped into her mind and she snapped her eyelids open. 'Jowan, she told me it was Abner Jago who stole my things.'

A dark look passed over Jowan's strong features but he was quick to smile down on Sarah. 'I've already asked about but drew a blank. I'll get on to it, straightaway. With luck I might be able to get something back for you, Sarah.' He wouldn't rest until he did.

'Thank you. I'd be . . . so . . . grateful . . .' Her voice faded away and she sank into a deep sleep.

Tara and Jowan decided to leave her in peace.

'Well, we know the full story now, Mr Kivell,' Tara said at the foot of the stairs. 'Poor dear Sarah. Could we not get in touch with her family? It would help her greatly to recover if she saw them. Do you know where they live?'

'No, but my grandmother does. I'll go to see them.'

'Perhaps you'd allow me to do that while you concentrate on retrieving something of Sarah's property. I'd so like to help her.'

The agreement made, Jowan escorted Tara to her pony in the stables. Kit had just dismounted and tethered his mount. 'Mrs Nankervis, it's a pleasure to see you again.' It was more than a pleasure to view her in her dark-blue riding habit and veiled hat, gliding with the grace of a gazelle. He'd been disappointed not to have been invited to Poltraze after his call there but he had been compensated by seeing her here twice.

'Good afternoon, Mr Howarth.' Tara wasn't sure about this man, but she took a second look at his mix of refinement and ruggedness. How could a man have such magnetic eyes? They were as beautiful as crystals and strangely mysterious. They were somehow forbidding, yet when he looked at her he tempered them until they showed a smooth richness. She knew there was predatory sexual desire in the manner in which he turned on the charm and easy smiles but also that he genuinely admired her. She reminded herself she would be a fool to allow herself to be flattered by him. He shouldn't be trusted. He was on his guard every second. He invited no one to his rented house at Gwennap. She had observed Jowan Kivell's reserve with him and he seemed a sensible young man.

'Hello, Jowan, is there any change in Sarah's condition?' Kit resented Jowan's stony face, which showed he disapproved of him being familiar about what he saw only as family matters. He had been civil to Jowan without being ingratiating, and he had been polite and interested without being nosy. What did he have to do to get his half-brother to drop his surliness?

Jowan told him the news.

'I'm so pleased. I've just come from Burnt Oak. Grandmama

Tempest was wondering whether when this happy day arrived, Sarah would agree to receive her.'

'It will be a long time before she's well enough for any visitors other than Mrs Nankervis.'

'Well, she will be delighted to hear of the progress in Sarah's recovery. I shall return presently to tell her about it.' As soon as he had said the words he regretted them. He needed time to himself, to unravel the torrent of confused emotions after a recent occurrence at Burnt Oak.

His grandmother had as usual been delighted to see him. She had been charming over morning coffee and the midday meal, full of energy while telling him more about the proud aspects of the Kivell history. It was a mild day and she had shown him over her garden. It was a miniature of any garden that would grace a great house. There was a rose arbour, a fish pond, shaped hedges, herbaceous borders, giant ferns, camellias and azaleas. A glasshouse was hidden away behind a box hedge. It was utterly peaceful, and Kit could imagine the wonderful spectacle there would be in subsequent seasons.

'My nephew Laketon designed all this,' Tempest said, venerable in dark green, a lace-trimmed bonnet, a fur-trimmed mantlet and carrying a fur muff. 'He went into carpentry but then developed a love for new species of flowers and plants. He's a thoroughly dislikeable individual, and I never cared to ask where he procured many of the plants. It's my belief there are some grander gardens in the county that are bereft of their rightful enhancement.'

'It's certainly very pleasant here.' Kit was at ease. It was the first place he felt he could linger in for some time. He stepped away to look up at a robin singing lustily to advertise its territory. His heart lurched strangely as Tempest surprised him by easing her arm through his. 'I call the robin Bobby. He's been my little friend for many a year now.'

Part of Kit froze and the rest of him squirmed. She had offered her hand on each of his arrivals and departures, but she had never touched him like this before. Manners dictated he should offer to escort her properly around the garden but he was not able to bring himself to. He did not want to get close to her. She did not deserve any more consideration than was necessary for politeness. He must never get to like her. He must remember he hated her.

After a while she said in a careful tone, 'Charles, would you like to see your father's grave?'

It was the worst time she could have asked him. He tried to fend it off but it was no use. The debilitating dark mood that invaded him so often gripped him in its chilled fingers. The anger, frustration and emptiness would come next and he would need to lash out, to break something or hurt himself to release his unbearable pain. There had been times when he had ripped apart things he'd valued, feeling a little release each time the broken pieces got smaller and smaller and more irreparable. He had banged his head against walls and doors and bedposts until he'd made his head bleed; there were scars hidden beneath his wealth of black hair. Then to get oblivion before he went totally out of his mind he had drowned himself in alcohol or smoked opium. Sometimes he wondered if these Kivell people detected he was muggy-headed or edgy. There were times he was sure whispers had been passed about him.

'Charles.' Tempest patted his hand, and Kit realized it was trembling. 'I'm sorry. I should have allowed you to come to that decision in your own time. It will be hard for you.'

Hard – it would almost be impossible not to desecrate the grave of the diabolical Titus Kivell. It was not the remains of his mother's wonderful lover down there in the ground but her evil rapist, a beast, and the originator of his misery. He couldn't do it and he swung away from Tempest.

'Ohh!'

Next instant he'd cried out, 'Grandmama!' He had moved so roughly Tempest had been toppled towards the ground. Instinctively he'd reached out and caught her and held her steady. 'I'm so sorry. I never meant to hurt you.'

Why did he say that? It was the very thing he had come to do, to punish her for her cold-heartedness. But from what he had seen she had only been cold towards her husband and Titus. No one could be blamed for hating the man who had kidnapped and raped her, forcing her into marriage when just a girl and then isolating her from her own family. It must follow that a child born after a rape would be hated too. His own mother hated him; the whole experience had reduced her to madness. He was right to hate himself, for he had no worth at all, but was he right to hate his mother? She had been unable to love him, she had wanted nothing to do with him, but she had ordered he be brought up as a gentleman, with an excellent education, while she could have had him abandoned to an orphanage or the workhouse. He had needed to blame someone for the lack of love and the subsequent desolation in his life, but was it fair to hate the grandmother who had known nothing about his existence until a few weeks ago and, who, after some initial fright and misgivings, had seemed to take to him from the very first day? She doted on him now, he couldn't deny that. As soon as she had realized his taste in food and drink she'd made sure he had been given it at meals. She had shown him over Morn O' May, and played his favourite tunes on the piano. Every time their eyes met she smiled at him, she listened attentively to whatever he said, and she encouraged all the others at Burnt Oak to accept him as one of their own. If he had been brought up here he would almost certainly have been nurtured in the same close manner as all the Kivells. Ironically, even his father, so fond of siring children, would have been proud to have known of his existence.

His grandmother had stayed in his arms as he'd supported her, then it was she who was embracing him. She had sensed his melancholy, and he had felt her joyful emotion at his cry of acknowledgement that she was his grandmother. Kit had succumbed to the moment, the sudden affection, and had rested his face on her shoulder and for the first time in his life he had experienced the sort of inner reaction that was a positive release. He had nearly been responsible for causing Tempest physical harm but his immediate response had been to save her, to protect her. He would never have believed he'd welcome her arms around him.

He checked himself quickly; he was not one to display his weaknesses.

'You have a lot to tell me, haven't you, Kit?'

He cleared his throat. 'More than you could ever know.'

'Well, I am your grandmother and you can come to me at any time.'

He had revealed a lot about himself and it sat uneasily. 'I am a very private man.'

'I've gathered that.' She smiled. 'Shall we go in and have some spiced tea? Your Aunt Eula has made ginger biscuits, the ones you like so much. It will warm us through.'

He nodded, raw emotion rising and preventing him from speaking. He left soon afterwards, eager to get away on his own to think things through. Then as on his second visit to Poltraze he found himself not wanting to be alone and rode to Chy-Henver. It was a bonus to find Tara Nankervis here.

'If you are about to leave, Mrs Nankervis, may I escort you part of the way?'

'Very well, Mr Howarth,' Tara said. It would be churlish to refuse as they would start off in the same direction. She would at least find his company interesting.

Hugh Kivell ran into Morn O' May. 'Mama Tempest, a gentleman's arrived and he says his name is Mr Charles Howarth, from Bristol.'

Tempest called for Eula and they went outside to meet this new stranger, an impostor. Someone from Bristol must have known about Charles's quest to find his father and had travelled down to exploit the family. Genesis had not allowed him to dismount from his hired mount.

'Whoever you are and whatever you've come for, young man, I can tell you that you're out of luck.' Tempest seethed in anger, ready like a tigress to protect its young. 'My grandson, Mr Charles Howarth, has been in Cornwall for some weeks. Leave this place immediately or the men and the dogs will run you off.' He was so unlike Charles. Compact, neat and slim, hair that was fair with a hint of light brown, as well-bred as royalty, self-confident, and owning a ramrod-straight posture.

'Madam, I can assure you that I am who I say I am, Charles Howarth, of the Howarth Shipping Line. The man masquerading locally under my name, who greatly resembles the Kivell menfolk, is undoubtedly your grandson, and he is also my half-brother. We have the same mother. His real identity is Christopher Woodburne but he goes by the name of Kit. I have only known of him in recent months. I knew of his intention to come here, and as sadly I think him to be a little unstable, I begged him to allow me time to see to some important business matters and then to allow me to accompany him. He agreed. I immediately discovered he had deceived me and now at last I've been able to follow him down. I need to see him. Is he here?'

Fidgeting with her hands, Tempest looked from Genesis to Eula. She did not need a sixth sense to know this man was telling the truth. She had been sure from the start that Charles, or rather Kit Woodburne, was hiding a good deal. His true identity, the most important omission, was just one thing. 'You had better come inside and tell us the full story, Mr Howarth.'

Eleven

'You had no right to come here!' Kit snarled in Tempest's sitting room. God in heaven, he could put his hands round his half-brother's throat and squeeze the life out of him.

'You had no right to pretend you are me,' Charles Howarth replied coldly, 'and to have told lies about my mother. How dare you! In the light of what really happened it's an insult to her.' He was on his feet, hands behind his back in front of the fireplace, in command. Also there were Tempest, Eula, Jack and Genesis.

Kit felt he was the subject of an inquisition. Damn them all. They could think what they liked. They would not get the better of him. 'It's an insult what she did to me. She cut me off as if I'd had no right to be alive!'

'Kit, it grieves me to say this, but your father had no right to perpetrate the offence that saw you conceived.'

Kit flinched. So did Tempest; she hoped Titus was burning in hellfire for raping Prudence Howarth.

'So I've no right to be alive, is that it? God knows I've wished often enough that I'd never been born,' Kit bawled, glaring round the room, settling his blazing eyes on Tempest.

'Kit, I want you to know I'm still happy to accept you as my grandson. Nothing could change that. Did you lie because the truth was too painful? It's easy to tell you have suffered. Mr Howarth has told us about your childhood. That you resent me in particular,' Tempest said, hating to see him like an animal both on the defensive and about to attack.

He saw the understanding in her eyes and for a moment had to look away. He wanted to rail against her but it was impossible with her reaching out to him with genuine concern. 'You were cruel to Titus.' His voice was only mildly accusing and he felt he was shrinking in size. 'He didn't ask to be born. If you had shown him a mother's love he wouldn't have turned out to be so bad. That poor girl at Chy-Henver is still going through hell as a consequence of what he did to her. You and Titus have ruined lives. Don't you feel some responsibility for it all?'

'Yes I do, Kit, every day since Titus's birth. I rejected him at first. I didn't want to see or hold my son.' Tempest tried to keep her head up but she was soon looking down and tears were sprinkling her lashes. 'I was just sixteen years old, and Garth punished me for not loving him by making me give birth tied to the bed by my hands and feet. He was drunk throughout my labour and threatened he'd cut me up with his hunting knife if I didn't produce a healthy son. I nearly died, but two days later he came to me and forced on me a husband's right. I hated him, and although I tried so hard to, I couldn't love his son. But I was never cruel to Titus. I gave him time and indulged him. It was only when he turned out to be cunning and nasty like his father that I started to ignore him. Having to live on my wits to survive I discovered other senses and began to dream of the future and make accurate predictions. That terrible day I killed Garth still haunts me, but I had to do it, he was about to abuse Eula in the worst way imaginable. It was only fear of me that kept Titus from doing a great many more evil things.' She was weeping now, but shook her head to prevent Eula from comforting her. 'Kit, I'm not proud of the things I've done. I don't know what eternity has in store for me. I'm very sorry about what happened to your mother and how it's made you suffer too. I'm also sorry for Mr Howarth and his father. It grieves my heart every day to know I gave birth to a monster.

'Please, Kit, I beg you, whatever you had in mind when you came here, don't go on allowing it to make you a victim. I don't care about your deception, and nor will the rest of the family, even Jowan, when they hear the full story. If you want to, you can be part of us. At least don't do anything until you take time to consider all that I've said.'

Kit said nothing. From all her words it seemed he had no just reason to have sought retribution. His head thundered, his brain was thumping inside his skull as if it was about to split open. The people in the room went in and out of focus and he thought he would be sick. The air was not getting into his lungs and he was sure he was about to faint.

'I have to get out of here. Don't try to stop me.' Forming his hands into a battering ram in case someone stood in front of him he rushed out of the room, then out through a side door into the garden. He took a long breath of cold air, shivering and shuddering but in a fever at the same time. He couldn't bear to take his leave in front of a crowd of staring Kivells and began to thread his way through the garden towards a door in the outer wall. Tempest had shown him where the large ornamental key was kept. He would go out in the fields beyond. After that, he didn't know . . . with any luck he'd get lost and never be found, to die somewhere lonely where this rotten world could never bother him with the business of trying to live in it again.

'Kit! Wait! Wait for me.' Charles was running after him.

'Go away!' he hurled over his shoulder. 'I don't want you or anyone else near me.'

'But I want you.' Charles caught up with him easily for Kit's steps were blundering and shaky. He grabbed Kit's arm and clung on. 'You don't have to do this. You have people in this world who care for you. You have kinfolk. You don't have to be alone, to feel unwanted. You haven't given any of us a chance to get to know you, to perhaps love you. It's what you want more than anything, isn't it?'

'You don't mind the people here knowing we share the same blood but you took pains to let me know you don't want that in Bristol. You care too much what society thinks.' He would not be anyone's sordid secret. He was either this man's brother or he was not.

'Position in the world is a consideration, I don't deny that, but the reason I asked you to keep your identity a secret was for my parents' sake. I didn't want gossip circulating about my mother, to run the risk of evil-minded people sullying her name. It wouldn't have been fair on my father either, do you see? My decision was to protect them. You never gave me the chance to fully explain. Kit, you keep running away to avoid more rejection. I understand that. Please, stop for a minute and just think, like your grandmother implored you to do. Do you think I'd have come down all this way to Meryen if I didn't care about you? Why do you think I've just followed you out here?'

Kit put his hand to his head. He was trembling, incapable of speech.

'I know where you're staying. I paid well to discover your tracks. I'm going to take you there. I shall stay and not leave you until we've had a long talk, and this time, Kit, you will listen to the facts and not shut everything out and torment your soul.'

Twelve

S arah and Kit gazed down at Titus's grave. It was at the back of the burial plot, lying at a right angle to the other graves, at a distance that showed it was set apart. The headstone was smaller than the others, and bore only his name, age and date of death, 1838.

'What do you feel?' Kit asked.

'Nothing at all,' Sarah said, in a shrug of a voice. 'After everything that's happened, all his influence on me has been wiped out. I don't feel love, hate or even resentment towards him. And there's no point in regrets. Titus has no power over me any more, thank God. The danger my friend Tabbie saw heading for me was from Dinah Greep, not Titus. And you, Kit? Have you come to terms with everything?'

'It's getting easier, I think. I was beginning to warm towards Grandmama before my brother Charles turned up, and then he put me right, eventually. It was good of him to stay with me for a few days, until he'd hammered home the facts as to how I should really see them, that I would have gained nothing by hurting my grandmother, and that the aching void I've always had would have been made worse. He pointed out that I could have that void filled by becoming a member of the Kivell family; deep down it was what I'd wanted after coming here a couple of times. Charles surprised me by telling me I should feel proud of myself, that although Titus may have followed his father's ways, I did not. I don't know about feeling proud. I did need Charles to take me to task for being so selfish. That's what getting my sort of revenge is about. Grandmama has been so understanding. I want to make things up to her. She says her vision was so frightening because I really had meant danger to her at the beginning. Well, that's all over and can be left where it deserves to be, in the past.

I'm so pleased that you feel ready to move on with your life too, Sarah.'

She wrapped her arms about herself. 'It's a good feeling.'

'Well, we've no need to linger here or to ever come back. Shall we go in? I'm looking forward to my first family Christmas Day.'

The air was crisp and a simple sun was low in a powder-blue, pink-tinged sky. Sarah thought, we're two little figures under the heavens for a tiny space of time in history. Kivells walked this land before us and new generations will walk here long after we're gone. The observation did not make her feel unimportant but rather more determined to keep her resolve. She had recovered from the attack and now wanted to grasp life, make some happiness for herself, while she was young enough and able to do it.

'Are you going back to Bristol in the new year, Mr Woodburne?'

'Call me Kit, we're friends now. I've instructed my lawyer to sell my house there. I'm planning to have a property built at Gwennap. It's a very good area and it means I will remain close to Burnt Oak. You'll be very welcome to visit and stay at any time. What do you intend to do, Sarah? I was sorry to hear that Mrs Nankervis's appeal to your family did not bring about the desired response. Do you have any plans for the future?'

Sarah did not answer. It still hurt that although Tara's visit to Redruth had been met with politeness there had been an emphatic refusal to see her. 'They said they are happy in their new life and don't wish to be connected again to the Kivell name,' Tara had reported in an apologetic and sad voice. 'They prefer to be left alone, they said, and were sorry about your distress but they didn't think you could be happy living with them. They wish you well for the future.'

Sitting up in bed at Chy-Henver, she'd answered, 'I expect they think I'll bring them trouble. God knows I've brought enough on myself. I understand.' She saw Aunt Molly, Arthur and Tamsyn's point of view but it had crushed her to be shunned, to have that hope taken away.

Her spirit had picked up when Jowan had returned home later the same day with a purse full of money for her. 'It didn't take me long to locate Abner Jago. He took me to the old barn where he keeps his stock. Most of it was either stolen or bought for an unfair price, I'm sure. He was, shall I say, a *little* scared of me and blubbed that he hadn't sold many of your things. I made him pay up double what he'd got and then I took your things on to my friend. There's nearly ninety pounds in there.' He'd nodded at the silk purse, a gift from himself. 'You're a woman of some means now, Sarah. I remembered what you said about Tabbie's drapes meaning a lot to you. I've brought them back with me. Rachel will clean them for you.'

'Wherever I go when I leave here I'll have something of Tabbie's to take with me.' She'd wept with the relief and poignancy of the event. She could support herself for some time to come. 'Thank you, Jowan. I'll never forget all that you've done for me.'

She owed Jowan her lifelong gratitude and Tara too. Having friends to support her during the worst time of her life had helped her see things in the right perspective. Her inwardness was a natural occurrence for protection but by not mixing with others she had denied herself loyal friends, and denied them the help they might need. It was over now and she would put her selfishness aside and make a new beginning. She had that in common with Kit.

'Mrs Nankervis has asked me to become her companion,' she told Kit. 'It's a kind offer.'

'How did you reply?'

'I said I'd think about it. I'm not sure about living up at the big house. She pointed out I'd be free to come and go as I wish, but neither the gentry nor the servants would approve of me.'

'Don't let that bother you. There's little entertaining at Poltraze. Mrs Nankervis is very short of good company. She only has her daughter. She must be very lonely,' Kit said. Tara had shunned his company since she'd heard of his deception. He had called at Poltraze two days ago and had been told the mistress was not at home. While riding away he had spotted Tara at the drawing-room window. Of course, he couldn't expect to be received. The tale of his false identity had caused a good deal of gossip. He couldn't blame Tara for thinking him unsuitable to receive. It was a pity. He had a genuine liking for her. He held her in high esteem. There were not many ladies who would care about the welfare of a lowly mine girl. 'She would appreciate having someone to play cards or sew with, and fill in the lonely hours. It's sad to see such a fine lady weighed down by so much sorrow.'

'I agree. It's kind of you to think of Tara in that way, Kit.' She had formed a respectful friendship with Kit, understanding his subterfuge and earlier bitterness in the light of her own experiences. She had talked Jowan round to her point of view and he now accepted Kit as his brother, although he was still reserved with him. 'I hadn't thought about Tara's situation. It must be awful living in that gloomy old house. Everyone knows she and the squire don't have a proper marriage. Perhaps I will accept her offer. I don't have to stay there forever.'

'It could be a worthwhile opportunity for you. My advice is that you take the position. It's got to be better than finding a little place in a new neighbourhood where everyone will want to know your business. Stay on in Meryen, Sarah. People care about you here. That's worth more than all the treasure in the world. I can hear music. The present-giving and merry-making is about to begin. Let's go in and enjoy ourselves.'

Tara broke the custom and had Rosa Grace brought down from the nursery for Christmas dinner or she would have eaten alone. Joshua had not slept in the house the night before, which was unusual these days, and he had not put in an appearance so far. In previous years Michael had brought Cecily and Jemima to join in the festivities for the whole day, but today, after popping in after breakfast and exchanging presents, he had announced the girls were to go to their maternal grandparents in Truro for a few weeks.

'I take it you won't be accompanying them,' Tara had said, stiff in disappointment.

'Actually, I shall stay with them for Christmas dinner and then go on to an address close by.' He was rocking on his toes and smiling broadly, showing lots of teeth. 'You might as well know, Tara, and I hope you will be pleased for me, I have been paying court to a Miss Adeline Phillipps, of

Lemon Street. I am very taken with her and she has confessed she shares my feelings.'

Tara saw the twinkling light in his eyes and the dark pink highlighting his flat cheeks. He appeared younger and boyishly energized, which she had not witnessed in him before. 'I'm amazed, Michael. If you've fallen in love then of course I am pleased for you.' And she was envious of him. If this happiness was the result of being in love and being loved in return she was unlikely to ever know what it was like. 'But when and where did you meet this lady? You don't keep me informed of your whereabouts any more and I'm totally unaware of you travelling abroad.'

'A month ago I went to a literary evening at Tehidy. The Bassetts were entertaining Sir Henry Welcomming, a talented historian. I thought it would prove interesting. Adeline and her parents were there. They are a somewhat serious and a bookish family and we all struck up a pleasing conversation. At the end of the evening Mr Phillipps invited me to dine at his house. Adeline is not a particular beauty but she is witty and intelligent. It proved to be sheer pleasure to learn we have a lot in common. She is helping her father to form an account of their family history. I would like to invite her to Poltraze to see my works in the library. Joshua is not here for me to ask his permission but he has been in good spirits lately so I am sure he would not object. How would you feel, Tara, in view of our past association, if Adeline was to come here?'

'It is thoughtful of you to ask me, Michael. I would not mind at all. I'm sure Miss Phillipps is delightful.'

'Thank you. I didn't want to take it for granted. I must say, it's a very poor show for Joshua not to be here. I hope he won't be leaving it to you to hand out the servants' presents alone.'

'The despicable Laketon Kivell must be keeping him away. I wish there was a way of getting rid of that man. Anyway, Rosa Grace and I will be staying at Truro ourselves in the New Year. So our girls will have the opportunity to play together.' Hopefully Sarah would be going with them. She prayed Sarah would accept her proposal. She felt she could easily go mad with loneliness. If Miss Adeline Phillipps was as quiet and pursued her history records as passionately as Michael, she was hardly the material to make a diverting friend.

After the goose and plum pudding had been eaten, Tara took Rosa Grace up to the drawing room. Rosa Grace was enraptured with the fir tree which stood in a decorated tub and was as high as the picture rail. Tiny baskets of sweetmeats, gilt gingerbread, pomanders, paper roses, papier-mâché robins and baubles hung from red ribbon on the lavish boughs. Small toys were propped on or hung from the boughs. Fawcett had just lit the taper candles. 'The tree in the hall is the biggest but I like this one best,' Rosa Grace said in an awestruck whisper.

'It's time for you to choose something from the tree, darling.' Tara smiled down on her, sad that there were only the two of them for this.

'Shouldn't we wait for Papa? Why didn't he have dinner with us?' Rosa Grace was a little less bouncy than usual.

'I don't know, but it must be something really important for him to have been detained. I'm sure he'll arrive as soon as he can.' Joshua had mentioned he was looking forward to Christmas. He had chosen the fir trees and the holly and ivy off the estate for the house himself. Of late he had taken a little interest in Rosa Grace. He had ordered a large doll's house for her and had planned to have it brought in after dinner. Laketon Kivell had probably hurt him again. Tara had been expecting Joshua to have the jauntiness wiped out of him at any time, but why did it have to be today? It was the worst time to have her loneliness reinforced and her little girl's dreams shattered.

'I thought he was beginning to like me.' Rosa Grace bowed her head and pulled in her lower lip.

'Oh, darling.' Tara knelt down to her daughter's level. 'Why do you say that? Papa does love you. I know he doesn't spend a lot of time with you, but nor does Uncle Michael with Cecily and Jemima. Some fathers are like that. It doesn't mean they don't love their children. I know that Papa has a special present for you. Hopefully, he will be here soon to give it to you himself.'

Rosa Grace seemed happy with Tara's explanation and she

roamed the tree. 'Ooh, there is a little brown horse on red rockers. Can I have that, Mama, please?'

Tara reached up for the gift, careful to avoid the taper flames. If Kivell really was keeping Joshua away then the man was being particularly malicious to do so on Christmas Day. It meant his hold on Joshua was getting out of hand. The man was a blight on Poltraze, he was dangerous. He must be ousted from the estate. She would tell Joshua if he didn't eject his lover, she would not return from Truro with Rosa Grace. The trouble was that Joshua was powerless against Kivell, and Michael wasn't up to the task. It seemed to Tara there was only one way to get rid of a dangerous Kivell and that was by another fearless Kivell. She had no influence over any of them so it seemed Laketon Kivell was invincible and getting ever more deadly.

Joshua had slept heavily since the early hours. Laketon removed the glass that had contained a strong concoction of valerian and other herbs. Combined with the lashings of champagne he had encouraged down Joshua's throat last night it would keep him out for hours yet.

Dressed in elegance, groomed to perfection, misted in cologne, Laketon perched on the bed and leaned over Joshua and pressed a hard fingertip across his sweaty forehead. He would have a thundering headache when he finally woke up, he would feel violently sick and hardly be able to find his feet. The wild antics of a few hours ago would ensure his muscles would ache for days. 'Thank you for last night, Joshua. It was one of our best times ever.' Laketon's tone turned from sarcastic to icy-cold and razor-sharp, 'Although it took a lot of drink to get you up to par, but then I am not Aaron Hobbs.'

Joshua's face, flawless and glowing with health from all the recent pampering and acquired happiness, was now puffy and blotched. Laketon put his thumbs and fingers on the delicate skin under Joshua's eyes and pinched and pinched along his cheekbones. 'You really love him, don't you? You adore Aaron Hobbs. I know all about the fabulous present you've bought him for today. The gold and diamond tiepin. How could you use the same jeweller where you buy gifts for me? I'm glad you love him so deeply, Joshua, that you think he's all yours. It's what I've been waiting for, because when I take him away from you it's going to hurt you all the more.'

Throwing back his head Laketon brought it forward and butted Joshua's brow. There was an instant red mark; an ugly bruise would appear soon. The headache he'd have would be as bad as if cymbals were crashing next to his ears and a brutal hand was gripping his brain. He got up and with his eyes blazing like red coals he ripped the covers off Joshua. There were bruises all over his body. 'You cheating bastard! You know what happens to those who cross me or get in my way. I caved in your beastly father's head and I burned him and his grasping wife in their bed, and she was alive at the time. I poisoned Michael's wife for threatening to blackmail us, and I drowned your mealy-mouthed elder brother Jeremy all those years ago for taunting me. I allow no one to treat me as if I'm dirt. I take what I want and I do what I want. I loved you once but not any more. But no one will ever take you away from me, Joshua, because I'm using you and I will do so for as long as it pleases me.'

Picking up a jug of water he went to the fireplace and, careful not to cause blackened smoke to spoil his appearance, he poured the water over the embers. He would not be back for hours. Joshua would lie naked and freeze. At the door he looked back at the pathetic figure. 'It's the season for giving. I'm off to give your valet the present you've got him and one of my own. Happy Christmas, Joshua.'

He slipped into the big house, slumbering now for the afternoon. He crept upstairs and into the master suite in the west wing. Much of it was rebuilt by himself in his carpentry days, and furnished in the neoclassical style, with Grecian friezes and sculptures; it was all slightly decadent. He had a good idea where Joshua had hidden the present and he wasn't wrong. He took the brightly wrapped gift, tied with red and gold ribbon and finished with elaborate bows, out of the drawer of a table displaying a glass Elgin vase. Joshua would have spent many blissful hours picturing how he would flourish his gift to Hobbs and how he would make love to him afterwards.

He went through to the dressing room. As he'd expected, Aaron Hobbs was there waiting for his master, and with so many hours having passed since his expected arrival the youth was slouching in a chair, head down despondently.

He jumped up. 'At last! I—' Hobbs's excited beatific smile drained away and a blush flew up from his milk-white neck to the curls nestling on his brow. He had reached out with both arms and dropped them down smartly to his sides. 'Sir, I am sorry. I thought you were Mr Nankervis.'

'Do you know who I am?' Laketon asked in a tone any master of a big house would use, but he had made it kindly.

'I think so, sir. Is it Mr Laketon Kivell?' Aaron felt his knees go weak and a chill shearing his backbone. It had happened, the one thing his master feared, they had been found out by his sadistic lover.

'You are correct, Hobbs. Good afternoon to you.' The youth trembled as Laketon kept him prisoner in a lengthy searching gaze. Laketon could almost hear his brain wondering feverishly what he was doing here. Hobbs would know he was Joshua's lover and how he treated him. His expression on the youth was soft, interested and without a trace of threat. 'I'm sorry you've been kept waiting. I'm afraid Mr Nankervis woke with a chill, and sadly, despite brave attempts to rise from his bed, will remain indisposed for the day, and tomorrow too, I should say. He was anxious that you received a little token gift from him for Christmas in appreciation for all you've done for him. He rates your services very highly. I offered to bring the gift along myself. He so wanted you to have it today. And so do I.'

Aaron gulped, his Adam's apple moved awkwardly up and down his throat. The dark red of his cheeks, the gleaming whites of his eyes showed his fear. 'Th-that's very thoughtful of you, sir. I'm sorry to hear about the master.'

'Thank you. I'll pass on your good wishes, shall I? He'll be so disappointed not to have seen you today. Christmas this year will be quite ruined for him. Well, here you are, Hobbs.' Laketon held out the small square box. 'Open it. Joshua wants to know what you think.'

Aaron stepped up to him, avoiding eye contact. Putting his hand out as if afraid he was about to reach into a snare and have it snapped off he took the gift then backed away as if the ground between them was on fire. 'Please relay my thanks to Mr Nankervis, sir. It's very kind of him.' He had difficulty pulling off the ribbon and paper his hands were shaking so much. He stared at the black leather box as if it was something horrendous. It was an inappropriate and expensive gift to give to a servant. Laketon Kivell was a violently jealous man and this might send him into one of the rages Joshua had told him about.

'Ah, it looks like jewellery,' Laketon said in a chatty voice, coming up close to him. 'Joshua gave me a beautiful time-piece. I wish I had brought it with me to show it to you. He's so generous. He always gives his valets something of excellent value.' Laketon had demanded his gift last night and had been secretly infuriated to receive some paltry silver-ware for his desk.

Aaron had no choice, he lifted up the lid. The tiepin was exquisite. It would have been a dream of an experience to have opened this with Joshua looking on, to bask in his devotion. It was terrifying to be ordered to do so by this man. What would he do to him for bedding his long-time lover? 'It's . . . it's . . .'

'It's what I told Joshua to get you, Aaron. Actually, we chose it together for you.' Laketon beamed warm smiles at him.

'You did?' What was he to make of this?

'I wanted you to have something beautiful. You've made Joshua very happy since you arrived. He's a victim of depression, don't you know. He can mope for days and days and see nothing ahead but dark clouds. I was in despair to know what to do to help him this time and then, the saints be praised, you turned up. I know how close you and Joshua have become.'

Aaron dropped the box and pressed his back against a wardrobe. Joshua had said this man enjoyed baiting and playing out tortuous games followed by acts of cruelty. He screwed up his face and shut his eyes, terrified at what would come next.

'Oh, my dear boy,' Laketon exclaimed as if shocked and apologetic. He kept his distance. 'I don't mind. Joshua and I agreed from the beginning we would take other lovers as long the other approved of the choice. We've found it's helped

to keep our love strong over the years and to never take each
other for granted. I've been perfectly content to keep myself
out of the picture while Joshua has been enjoying the first
fruits of your union. Please don't think I'm jealous or angry
with you. I owe you a great debt of thanks. You've returned
my dear Joshua to his best. He hasn't been so happy for
years. It was being forced to marry and having to behave as
a husband that was bringing him down. I'm so grateful to
you, Aaron. Actually, I've brought you a little Christmas
present myself.'

Aaron opened his eyes. Laketon Kivell had picked up the
box and tiepin and was gazing straight at him, exuding gratitude and something unreadable. Rather than frighten Aaron
it excited him. The big man had one eyebrow curved in a
sensuous manner. He was taller, stronger and more handsome
than Joshua, and rugged and masterful. The overt wicked-
ness about him, something he could never successfully
conceal, was powerfully appealing. Aaron was used to lovers
who, although occasionally wild, were mainly gentle and
considerate, demanding his love and adoration while lavishing
it back upon him. It was a pain to have to keep telling his
masters he loved them. One master had liked a reversal of
positions with him acting as the valet while encouraging Aaron
to give him orders. The man in the room had a beast in him
and although that was scary it was electrifying also. 'You
have, sir?'

'I don't like talking in this room. It's quite claustrophobic
with all these wardrobes and clothes hanging about. We'll go
into the bedroom. Joshua wouldn't mind. You lead the way.'

Aaron obeyed, his stomach churning both with dread and
an exhilarated tension. Laketon Kivell was going to do something to him, he knew it. Every nerve in his body was growing
to a painful high pitch. His whole body was tingling. He
could hardly bear it. Was this man about to take revenge on
him for indulging his lover? Or . . . it would be so wonderful
if . . .

Laketon closed the door and came up behind Aaron until
he was close enough to touch him. 'Stop,' he breathed huskily
in the youth's ear.

Aaron stopped walking and heaved a jittery sigh. Hurt me

in a pleasurable way. Let it be that, he pleaded silently. He'd welcome that. Joshua didn't do anything of the kind. He felt Laketon's arm come round the front of his body. He looked down at the man's large hand. There was a jeweller's box in it.

'This is for you from me. Take a look, Aaron. I hope you like it.'

'Oh, sir, it's so kind of you!' Aaron effervesced with delight. He had thought this was going to be a boring Christmas Day, now it was exactly the opposite. He lifted the box lid. Inside was a pair of diamond-set cufflinks. 'I don't know what to say. Thank you. Thank you so much.'

Laketon put his other arm round the youth and held him by the waist. He was as slim and soft as an adolescent. He stroked his golden curls.

'Oh, sir,' Aaron murmured.

'I think you and I will get on very well, don't you, Aaron?'

'Oh, yes sir.'

'Turn round to me.'

Aaron complied eagerly.

'I think we enjoy the same things.'

'I'm sure we do, sir.'

'You know what to do,' Laketon said in a voice that ordered Aaron to get on with it.

Reaching to pose at a bedpost, Aaron purred, 'I'm entirely at your service, sir.'

Thirteen

S arah arrived at Poltraze in a small Kivell carriage, made in the community's workshops and a rather plush affair. She was wearing a mantlet over a two-piece dress, a bonnet, gloves and shoes, all bought with her own money. A footman appeared in a flash and opened the carriage door and had an umbrella ready to shelter her from the miserable steady rain. The butler was waiting for her in a reverent manner up under the portico. She had never thought to be given a reception like this. There seemed to be hundreds of windows in the house and tiny rivulets of rain were running down what seemed to be a thousand small windowpanes. Morn O' May had seemed huge to her the first time she'd gone there, but this house was vast. Until now, because of rumours, she'd thought the house only a grey bleak creepy place, but used to things so basic and having no sense of what might be considered ill-designed she saw it as grand. She was sure there would be many things inside and outside to amaze her.

Determined not to let herself down in front of the servants – it was well known that some servants behaved more high and mighty than their masters or mistresses – she would take a long interested look at everything as the days passed. She didn't want the servants to think she had never seen anything splendid in her life before. Amy had come here once with her mother to take part in Tara's very first charity committee and they had never returned, finding the genteel ladies condescending and the stateliness of the house daunting. Sarah would not allow anyone or anything to make her feel unworthy. In contrast to the grandeur a definite gloom hung about the place. The January rain had turned the stone of the walls, the lofty pillars and balustrades a murky grey. Much of the ground was recently replanted with small shrubs but there was some colour from berries and winter blooms. She frowned at the whole aspect. It was unfair that one small family should live in a house with so many, many rooms while large working families had to cram themselves into tiny cramped dwellings.

She was careful mounting the curved stone steps, still sore throughout her body from the attack. The footman ensured no more than a few drops of rain landed on her. This treatment would have been unwelcome and alien to her once, but she had allowed the Kivells, Jowan and Tempest, in particular, and Rachel, a laughing, eye-catching girl, as free-spirited as any Kivell male, to dole out every consideration on her during her recovery. Isolation was no longer her goal. She did not really have one. Life had taken so many unexpected turns she saw no point in making plans. She would just let things happen, while staying careful not to bring trouble to herself or her friends. Fate had taken this next uncharacteristic twist, she was coming to live in the big house of Meryen, and not up in the attics as a servant. Tara said she was to think of herself as a long-term guest, and to feel free to go out as often as she wanted and receive her own visitors. Tempest had urged her not to become a stranger at Burnt Oak, and Jowan had done the same concerning Chy-Henver. She had promised not to cut herself off from them. It would be good to see Kit again also. But that might not happen for some time; she was to travel with Tara to Truro in a few days for an undetermined stay. It would be quite an experience to live in the foremost town of the county gentry.

'I'm here to see Mrs Nankervis. She's expecting me. Miss Sarah Hichens.' She wasn't shy to announce her business but she was both annoyed and amused as her strong Cornish accent cleared the deferential expression off butler's narrow face. His eyes seemed to vanish under his heavy brows, so great was his disapproval of her. No doubt he was thinking she should have gone round to the tradesmen's entrance.

'Oh yes . . . Madam is waiting for you in the morning room, miss. If you would care to follow me . . .'

Sarah did not bother to reply. The butler had been told his mistress was expecting a visitor and he obviously assumed she would be a lady of high birth. She wouldn't allow this stiff-backed individual to intimidate her and she was pleased that at first she had passed for a lady. Her dainty shoes tapped through the vestibule and she was at the beginning of the hall which seemed to be as wide as the entire village and to stretch without an end. She slowed to a snail's pace – there was so much to take in she couldn't possibly hurry. Such space there was, with carved cabinets, and tables and stands swathed with cloths and runners and all displaying ornaments and figurines of which she had never seen the like before, some brightly painted, even with gold paint. Why did the gentry want such big vases? Some had great curving handles. Did the squire grow flowers large enough for these vases? It did not occur to her that some of them were purely ornamental.

There were mirrors and chairs and even a sofa. Jowan would be fascinated to see the fine turning and carving on them. The fireplace and mantelpiece alone would swamp an ordinary house and it went right up to the ceiling, and that seemed at least twenty feet above the hearth. There was half a tree trunk burning in the hearth! The whole of Meryen could be warmed by it. The beautiful crystal objects hanging down from the ceiling must be chandeliers; such magnificence. The ceiling itself was a work of art, with mouldings and suchlike. Doors showed that many rooms led off from the hall, plus two corridors; she was easily going to get lost here. There was painting after painting and huge cloth banners and a good deal of weaponry crowding the walls. She glanced up the stairs. They were wide enough for a horde to run up and down side by side, and they went on and up to a gallery.

'Ahem . . .'

She came to as if from a dream. It seemed as if she had been on a long journey. The butler had opened a door and was waiting for her to follow him through it.

'Miss Sarah Hichens, ma'am,' he intoned as if a bee had stung his tongue.

'Sarah! How wonderful that you're actually here.' Tara rose from a Chesterfield sofa and rushed to greet her. 'We'll have tea, Fawcett, and ask cook to send up something tasty.'

She laughed after he'd left with his superior nose held aloft. 'Don't take any notice of Fawcett. He disapproves of everyone. Take off your outdoor things, Sarah, and sit beside the fire. Make yourself comfortable. I'll take you up to your room shortly and show you over as much of the house as you like. I'll take you along to the nursery and introduce you to Rosa Grace. I'm sure you'll both get along very well.'

In awe of what she had just seen and now by the opulence of this room, Sarah took a few seconds to carry out Tara's invitation. This house was like something out of heaven; what must the Queen's palace be like? Some of the furniture was well worn and repairs were needed to the panelling; Sarah had no idea that it was a shameful state not to have all things perfect. She lowered herself into an armchair that was plump and so comfortable she was sure she could sleep in it with ease. She set her eyes on Tara but could hardly contain her curiosity to look over the rest of this wonderland. 'I'm looking forward to meeting your little girl. I've only seen her once or twice when you've taken her to church. What will she think of me? I'm not the usual sort of company you keep, Tara.'

'Rosa Grace is quite excited to think I'm having a friend come to stay.' Tara was studying Sarah's every expression. Was she as happy to be here as she herself was to have had her arrive? She'd been afraid Sarah would change her mind and not come at all. It was a big step for her to give up her independence, to live in an environment that was totally strange and where most quarters would not be at all friendly. Her fears had been unnecessary. She could see Sarah was enjoying all she found in her new home. 'You look very well, I'm glad to say.'

'So do you,' Sarah replied. She had thought often that Tara seemed to have something on her mind, something bringing her down, but she didn't feel close enough to her, or that it was right, in view of their different stations, that she should mention it.

'It's the relief of having you here. I can hardly begin to tell you how lonely I've been, Sarah. If not for Rosa Grace there have been some days when there seemed little point in getting out of bed. Now all that will change. I promise

you that you won't get bored. There are so many things we
can enjoy doing together.'

'Is the squire at home?' This was Sarah's one concern
which she had voiced to Tara before Kit's encouragement
on Christmas Day that she should take the position. Mr
Nankervis couldn't possibly approve of Tara taking on such
lowly company.

'He won't say much about you being here, if that's what
you're worried about, Sarah. He took to his bed with a very
bad chill over Christmas and has still not recovered. He sent
word that I should not disturb him. Actually he's rarely in
the house at all.' Tara would not allow Joshua to dictate to
her who she had as a friend. He had no grounds for complaint
with the terrible company he continued to keep. Joshua had
been carried to his suite after spending two nights at Paradise
Cottage. She had not been allowed at his bedside, but Laketon
Kivell was there every evening and it was an insult to her
that he even had the audacity to stay the night. 'Sarah, we
live separate lives. His interest lies elsewhere.'

'I'm sorry.' Sarah glanced down, not knowing what to say.
So it was true what Tempest had hinted about the squire.
Sarah hadn't wanted to believe it – she'd had no idea such
a thing went on. She had thought Tempest indelicate, but
saw now she had kindly passed on useful information. Joshua
Nankervis was having an affair with the obnoxious Laketon
Kivell. She hoped she and Tara would get away to Truro
before she encountered either of them.

'I thought that while we're alone we would dine together
but if Joshua does happen to want to come to the table I'll
order a tray to be taken up to your room,' Tara said. 'I don't
want you to feel uncomfortable, Sarah. Do tell me at once
if anything, even the slightest thing, troubles you. It will be
a little strange for you at first, but I'm sure we'll get along
very well. We could write to Amy together. She'll be delighted
with our news. It's a new start for both of us.'

A week passed in which the two women packed for the
stay at Truro, or rather the maidservants packed for them.
Sarah found it strange to have everything done for her as if
she was a real lady. Tara's personal maid had astonished her
on the first evening, when, after seeing to her mistress's

change of clothes and hair, she had come to Sarah to do the same. It seemed ridiculous to her to change so many times a day and she thought she would never get used to being waited on. Elvira Dunn spoke only when necessary and moved with an economy of energy. She was perhaps in her thirties; she was tall, slim and wore spectacles. Her mousey hair was combed in a severe centre parting with a topknot stuck through with tortoiseshell pins. Her clothes never varied from untrimmed dark grey. Her touch was light, and Sarah found her a shadowy presence and was always glad when she'd finished her task and was gone.

'Thank you, Miss Dunn,' she had said after the first occasion she had been corseted and eased into a lovely dinner gown, of silvery-coloured satin, a gift from Tara, and coiffured and adorned with her own jewellery: a single string of pearls, a Christmas present from Tempest. She knew a moment of sorrow; she had been robbed of the pendant Tabbie had given her, her precious possession.

'It's just Dunn, miss,' the woman had replied mildly before slipping out of the room, as quiet as a whisper.

'You look beautiful, Sarah!' Tara had exclaimed a moment later when she'd appeared to take her down to the dining room. Tara had noticed the servants sneaking reluctant admiring glances at Sarah. Even Fawcett had raised his usually gloomy brows in surprise that one of Sarah's breeding presented such a refined figure. If Sarah ever went to a ball or soirée she would be surrounded in seconds by eager young men. Her beauty would ensure her voice and humble origins would, in the main, be overlooked. Her early womanhood had been wasted on Titus Kivell, just as Tara's had been wasted on Joshua Nankervis. Life had been unfair to both of them. That would now change. Tara would use the last breath in her body to make it so.

The evening before the leave-taking, Tara went along to Joshua's suite, determined to see him. He had been indisposed a long time. Hobbs had informed her that Laketon Kivell had insisted the doctor need not be sent for. This struck Tara now as odd. If Joshua did not need the services of a doctor then why had he stayed so long abed? Fawcett had reported that all his meals were eaten, so he couldn't be very ill. Was he hiding away? Damn Laketon Kivell. He must have beaten Joshua so badly he was ashamed to show the results. This had to stop.

She usually knocked on Joshua's bedroom door and Hobbs would answer and inform her that the master was either sleeping or desired to be left to rest. She wouldn't be turned away today. She went straight into the room ready to face Hobbs and even Laketon Kivell if he was there. Thankfully they were not. Joshua was lying flat on his back in bed, the covers tucked up under his chin. A single candle on the bedside cabinet provided a feeble light in the room.

'Joshua, are you awake?' she whispered. Her hands gripped together, she felt like an intruder on Laketon Kivell's territory. People who crossed him often came to grief. She could be putting herself in danger. She must be careful what she did here. 'I'm leaving for Truro tomorrow. I've come to say goodbye.'

'Agh, no, no,' Joshua muttered, twisting to one side and pushing the covers away.

Tara crept round the side of the bed. Joshua was sweating and twitching. He was running a high fever and his greying hair was plastered in rat's tails to his forehead. He needed the doctor and had needed him days ago. Peering closer she saw the mottled fading of bruises on his face, neck, arms and chest. She brought a hand to her mouth. The depth of Laketon Kivell's cruelty was becoming ever more chilling. He obviously had Hobbs in his evil grip. From the evidence of the youth's arrogance when she had spoken to him he was in collusion with Kivell. Joshua had been happy with his young valet and had said Hobbs was devoted to his service, but Kivell had seen to it that it had altered. She should have guessed the reason, for Joshua's sudden newfound happiness was the extent of the valet's services. Joshua had fallen in love. It accounted for his good moods, his kindness to Rosa Grace. Laketon Kivell was no fool. He had realized this and had vindictively chosen Christmas Day to punish Joshua. He had been brutal to Joshua then and since.

Joshua groaned and thrashed about. Tara gasped to see how thin he was, his ribs protruding under his flesh. The door from the dressing room opened and her heart leapt in fright. Laketon Kivell, followed by Hobbs in unseemly closeness, lost the gleam in his devil's eyes and fixed a stare on her as hard as granite. 'Mrs Nankervis . . . ?'

The insolent swine! He was the one who had no right to be here, not her. She knew she had to be clever. She had the safety of Rosa Grace, Sarah, herself and Joshua to think of. 'Mr Kivell. Good evening to you. I'd just come in to say goodbye to Joshua. I found him like this. I'm afraid it seems he has taken a turn for the worse, poor fellow. I'm worried he's contracted pneumonia. I think we should send for the doctor, don't you?'

A woman's soft voice entered Joshua's nightmare. He tried to cling to it as to some hope but he failed to halt the terrible moments he was reliving. Immediately after he'd been brought and laid out here, feeble and with aches and pains plaguing every scrap of his body, he'd made out Laketon's mocking tones. 'We're going to look after you, Joshua, Aaron and I.'

'Aaron . . .' He had called for his love, barely able to hold his eyes open.

'I'm here right beside you, Joshua darling.' A kiss had been planted on his cheek. He had smiled. Everything would be all right now. Aaron would treat and soothe his wounds and take care of him.

'Open your eyes wide, Joshua,' Laketon had demanded.

He did so. Aaron's face was close to his and he was smiling at him. Then he was wrenched away. *Oh God!* Laketon knew about their love affair. Now he understood why Laketon had been so vicious to him on Christmas Day. He had punished him and now he was going to punish Aaron. 'No! Please don't hurt him, Laketon, I beg you.'

'Oh, there, there,' Laketon mocked. 'I've got no intention of hurting the one you love, Joshua. Watch and I'll show you what I will do.'

Turning the boy to him, Laketon caressed his face with the backs of his fingers then fluttered them about his body. Joshua stared, not wanting to believe what he was seeing. Laketon bent his great dark head and brought his open mouth down on Aaron's. He was going to rape him! 'No! No!' Joshua cried. He tried to get up from the bed, he had to save Aaron. He would die to protect him.

He fell back in horror. What was going on? Aaron was reaching up and putting his arms round Laketon's neck and bringing his fine body in intimately close. He was kissing Laketon enthusiastically. They were laughing and their coats were coming off. They were kissing again and again and doing more and more. He didn't want to watch but he couldn't help himself. This was the ultimate punishment from Laketon, to seduce away from him the one he loved so deeply. Worse still Aaron was enjoying it and instigating things. Joshua cried and screamed and it would have alerted someone in the house but his voice was too weak. If only he had killed himself that day then he wouldn't be going through this now. The instant he was able to, he would kill himself. Laketon, the utter bastard, would not be able to keep a grip on this place then. He'd been thrown out of Poltraze.

Staring at Tara, Laketon saw that if he didn't act quickly his cushy life here would soon be over. Joshua was very ill. 'You are right, ma'am. The squire is most uncomfortable. The doctor should be sent for straight away.' He turned on Aaron and gave him a wink that Tara didn't see. 'Hobbs, you are a fool! You have been unforgivably lax in your duties. Could you not see your master's condition has deteriorated? We will have to pray he will fully recover. He may well consider whether you deserve to be kept on in his service.'

Tara did not listen to Hobbs's grovelling apologies. She rang for Fawcett to order the doctor be fetched with all haste. When Fawcett had withdrawn, the room was in silence except for Joshua's heavy breathing and mutterings. 'Hobbs, sponge your master down with tepid water and fetch him a clean nightshirt,' she ordered. 'Light the lanterns but do not place them where they will hurt his eyes. I'll bring in some potpourri, the room smells most unwholesome.'

She went down to the winter parlour where Sarah was, stitching needlepoint before dinner was announced.

'Is something wrong? You look worried,' Sarah said.

'I hope not,' she replied, furious with Laketon Kivell for causing this latest anxiety. 'I've sent for a doctor to attend Joshua. His chill has turned into a raging fever. If he's very ill our trip to Truro will have to be postponed.'

*   *   *

'I went too far.' Laketon marched into Aaron's small bedroom, on the other connecting side of Joshua's dressing room. He spat, something he abhorred in others but something he did when furious with himself. The spittle hit the square wood-framed mirror on the wall. If Joshua died – and the doctor was going to ask questions about the distressed state of his body – then he would be promptly ejected off the property by the miserable bookworm Michael. He wouldn't be destitute – he had been leaching money off Joshua for years and stashing it away; he owned a lot of top-class jewellery and other valuables so he'd be able set himself up nicely elsewhere and he'd have no trouble finding another wealthy lover – but he liked it here. He wanted to stay here for years and see the gardens re-established under his guidance. The grounds of Poltraze were *his*. If Joshua died he'd somehow make sure they became his, the estate wouldn't get rid of him easily.

His reflection in the mirror was glacial and he turned that coldest of cold stares on to Aaron. The swaggering little bastard, he wasn't a bit concerned by the recent event. He had no heart, he was nothing but a profiteer and he certainly couldn't be relied upon to be loyal. Any other servant would be in fear of his position over the poor quality of his duties but he was taking it for granted that Laketon would sort it all out. He didn't care about Joshua's heartache and suffering. It didn't occur to him that his master was the one man Laketon had ever loved. The fact that Laketon abused Joshua was immaterial. 'Are you sure you've attended to your master properly this time?'

'Yes, he's as tidy as one of your flowerbeds and smells as fresh as a daisy. Mrs Nankervis was satisfied with the result when she went to sit with him.' Aaron smiled in self-satisfaction, unaware of the simmering rage in the man who loomed over him.

'Good, but this means she and my uncle's damned widow will be staying on instead of leaving tomorrow.' Laketon banged one fist against the other. Blood and hell's damnation! How could he have been so stupid as to allow Joshua to suffer for so long?

'You're all tense, my dear sir.' Aaron put on a child's voice and fluttered his exquisite eyelashes. 'Would you like me to relieve you of that?'

'Not now, you fool!' Laketon ached to slap his simpering face. 'You need to write a letter of apology to the squire, one that's full of remorse. Do it quickly. The doctor will be expecting you to be dismissed. Tara Nankervis would already have done so if she wasn't nervous of me. I'll dictate the words.'

Aaron wasn't happy with what he was forced to write down but accepted he had to take the responsibility for his master's neglect. Laketon read it through, grunted in satisfaction and placed it on the youth's pillow. 'Pull up the window, I need some fresh air,' he growled. He joined Aaron at the window. 'Any sound of the doctor arriving?'

Aaron stuck his head outside, blinking through the drenching rain. 'Not yet.' He made to get back inside to shelter. The wind was fierce and battering against the side of his face.

Laketon put one hand on the youth's collar and one on the seat of his breeches. 'I've had enough of you, you loathsome frog.'

'Sir? Laketon, what are you doing? Not here, please.' Aaron felt the icy fingers of fear. He hated heights and the lantern-lit ground immediately below was swimming in crazy circles. 'This isn't what I like.'

'You think I want to do *that*? God damn you, I wouldn't dream of such a thing with Joshua so ill. What I want, Hobbs, is you out of my life and Joshua's for good.'

Aaron realized Laketon's intention. He opened his mouth to scream in terror. A violent wrench on his neck forbade it. His neck wasn't broken and he didn't lose consciousness, and he was fully aware of every terrifying second as he was sent plummeting to the ground.

His eyes glowing in dark ecstasy, Laketon smiled a sated smile. After a moment he dusted his hands and straightened his cuffs. 'Off to hell with you, Hobbs. You'd better not have crushed my new bay shrubs.'

Fourteen

'Here, girl! Missy! Missy, will you obey me? Come back!' Kit threw a hand up in resignation. He had got over his dislike of dogs and had taken on a Burnt Oak lurcher puppy but he'd not got to grips yet with the training of the young bitch. He was riding to Burnt Oak, taking his time on a long way round that skirted the downs. The weather was dry, crisp and fresh, and after years of locking himself away in unhealthy atmospheres he took advantage of every moment to be outside. He had stopped several times to allow Missy to explore the bleak landscape of old gorse, ragged heather, sprawling brambles and wind-bent spindly trees, but now she was just in sight down in a dip sniffing and worrying at something and ignoring his calls.

Sighing light-heartedly, he dismounted the black stallion, also a recent acquisition, and pushed through the hostile growth which scratched his riding boots and snagged his riding breeches. Here and there his feet were twisted to the side by odd-shaped stones which threatened to sprain an ankle or unbalance him. He slithered in some places and sank an inch or two in soggy patches, making him fear he might have lumbered into a bog. 'Missy! Come here, I say!'

He imagined his grandmother as if she was actually witnessing the scene, smiling softly at his impatience and ineptitude. She had a smile for everything he did or said. She seemed fascinated by all there was to know about him and she questioned him endlessly about his life, while listening to him intently without interrupting. It was a warm, amazing thing to have someone genuinely interested in him at last, who sought to understand and soothe him. He was beginning to believe that the woman he had hated so much, on whom he had planned revenge, had actually come to love him. He couldn't say he loved her, not yet, but he liked her, approved of her and respected her and fully appreciated the comfort she lavished on him. Sometimes he thought he felt a glimmer of what it would be like to be a small child given a treat, a child who was cherished, and to feel the delight taken in its delight. He had never thought about getting married and raising a family, assuming his former unhealthy existence would burn him out and kill him while young. He had been sure he'd be unable to relate to a life of commitment. But perhaps if he did meet the right woman one day, someone who would be devoted to him, and they had a family, he'd make sure his children would know what real parental love and attention was all about.

'Missy, what have you got there?' The dog was fussing with and growling at what looked like a bundle of black rags. 'Here, girl. Here!'

Missy was too absorbed in her find to heed him. Kit marched up the last few feet and pulled her away by the collar. Missy whined, eager to get back to sniffing and pawing the object. Kit crouched down for a closer look. What was so interesting about some old rags? He reached out and pulled on the black cloth. 'Dear God!' His guts gave a tremendous jolt. The cloth was a dress on the bones and remnants of flesh of a woman. She had been dead for some time. Some poor unfortunate, who had wandered in the wrong direction, got lost in the dark and had perished in the cold. There wasn't much left of her; as well as the putrefaction, animals and crows had taken advantage of the carrion.

Missy rounded him and began investigating the body again. Kit tried to ease her away. 'No, Missy, leave it!' The dog had one of the corpse's arms in its mouth and was tugging on it. Kit saw something down on the dark flattened ground where the arm had been. It was a leather pouch and with it was something that glinted in the sharp winter sunlight. He picked them up. The pouch chinked, it obviously had coins in it. He rubbed the dirt off the other item. It was an exquisite piece of jewellery, a topaz and silver pendant. It seemed the dead creature had been a thief, fleeing with her pickings.

He knew whose body it was. Dinah Greep, the girl who had attacked Sarah and stolen her money and her most precious belonging. He got up and slipped the pendant into his coat pocket.

'Leave, Missy!' This time he got the right authority into his voice and Missy dropped the skeletal arm, which fell down with a flop, the bones loosening from shoulder to the smallest finger joint. Missy sat at his side, fidgeting sheepishly. So after running off into the night Dinah Greep had come to grief. From Sarah's statement, the girl had been seized by madness. She had died lost and alone. Kit shook his head. Apparently, there had been no need for the girl to cheat and steal. She'd had a roof over her head, had never starved, and had lived under the protection of a kind and God-fearing brother. Yet she had become bitter and envious, the two most self-harming of emotions, which all too easily led to hatred and instability. He had come so close to a wretched end himself.

He owed Dinah Greep nothing. If he had seen her when alive he would have demanded she was hanged for attempting to murder Sarah. She had tried to maim her brother's babies. She had been rotten right through. But he couldn't just leave her like this. Something had made the girl, just sixteen years of age, bitter and vengeful. She had probably had a distressing story to tell. The weather was turning damp, the wind was getting keen and ruffling his hair and chilling his face. He cared not for his discomfort but for the girl's dignity. Taking off his coat he laid it over her body.

He rode for the village to seek the Greep home. Afterwards he would leave Missy at Burnt Oak and go on to Poltraze. Sadly, Tara Nankervis did not welcome him there but he now had a reason to go to Sarah, to return her treasured property. Perhaps her friend would see him in a kinder light.

'I have urgent business with Miss Sarah Hichens,' he breathed down on the butler's scrawny frame at the entrance of the grim place. 'I'm sure that in the circumstances Mrs Nankervis will allow me entrance.'

'I'll enquire for you, sir,' Fawcett intoned, as grave as a judge and as haughty as a duke.

'Be quick about it,' Kit snapped. Damnable little prig, if

he narrowed his eyes any tighter he wouldn't be able to see at all. If Kit was master of this house the pompous flunkey would be turned out with a strategically placed boot. 'I'll wait in the hall.'

Sarah was on her way down the stairs, carrying a basket overflowing with materials and lace. 'Kit! This is a pleasant surprise.' She hastened her steps.

'Hello, Sarah, my dear.' He came to the foot of the stairs and gazed up at her. How well she looked. More than that, she was as lovely as a spring day. Her raven-black hair was pinned up with ringlets about her ears. She seemed content but he hoped she wouldn't dry up in this gloomy environment. She had gained her freedom and dignity and she should always stay that way. He leaned his head to the side and brought his fingers up to his chin. He could picture Sarah running barefoot through a meadow, a daisy chain circling her long flowing tresses, and dancing beside a stream. It made him smile deeply; he had never been given to romanticism before.

Tara came out of the winter parlour to meet Sarah. They were there busy making scented gifts for her next fund-raising event. Her hand holding up yards of trailing ribbon fell to her side. Kit Woodburne was there and he and Sarah were smiling at each other, obviously firm friends and perhaps more. There was no denying they would make a handsome couple. No! She couldn't lose Sarah's companionship so soon, not now she was forced to stay here and oversee Joshua's nursing. He was still debilitated from the pneumonia. It would have been easy to desert him, but how could she after he had begged her not to leave him, grasping her sleeve so tightly it had left a weal in her arm. He was like a helpless child, heartbroken over the suicide of his valet, who had rightly been full of shame over his master's decline. He was terrified of Laketon Kivell. 'Don't let him near me again, Tara. I can hardly bear another day.'

She had engaged a nurse, a formidable-looking woman of masculine build and a manner fit for a navvy. She excelled at her job and was loyal to her charge and to Tara. 'Don't leave Mr Nankervis for a minute,' she had ordered. 'I'll relieve you twice a day.' Thankfully, at the moment Kivell was keeping low. He sent Joshua caring messages and kept his visits brief. She had lain awake night after night pondering on how Poltraze could be rid of the loathsome man, even to arranging for an assassin to dispose of him, but every option seemed either futile or too dangerous. Kivell was deadly in his intelligence. He was keeping a close watch on the house and seemed to anticipate all that went on. Now she was suffering another Kivell in all but name under her roof.

'Mr Woodburne,' Tara said coolly, after dismissing the hovering Fawcett. Kit Woodburne's closeness to Sarah was going to cause gossip in the servants' hall. 'I take it you are here on some business or other with Sarah?'

'Good morning to you, Mrs Nankervis. Yes, I have some news for her.'

'What possible news could you have that would interest Sarah?'

Kit was disappointed with the frosty reception but not for his own sake. It was a pity the lady's stifled life was making her cold and unfriendly. She was as fair as a snowdrop, as delicate as thistledown, but a continuing unfair fate would inevitably lead to her making a frosted shadow of herself. Serious now, he turned to Sarah, who had descended the stairs and was facing him. 'If we could go somewhere to talk . . .'

'Is it something dreadful?' Frown lines creased Sarah's brow.

'Yes, it is really, but you have nothing to worry about. It concerns the money and property stolen from you.'

'You had better come into the winter parlour,' Tara said, before Sarah could reply.

Sarah dropped the basket on the table where she and Tara had been sewing. The room was filled with the scent of rose pot-pourri. She looked expectantly at Kit.

First, Kit glanced at Tara. She was close beside Sarah, her hands folded in front of her slender waist, her expression grim. She made her dislike of him obvious. Sarah was the only one to light up her day and she begrudged giving away even a few moments of her time to others. 'A short while ago while riding by the downs I happened to come across the body of a girl. There's no doubt it was Dinah Greep, and

I discovered your money and pendant under her body.' He produced the items from his coat pockets.

'My pendant!' Ignoring the pouch of money, which held little importance to her, she took the pendant from him. 'Thank you, Kit. This is the best thing ever.'

'It was good of you to bring it to Sarah straight away, Mr Woodburne,' Tara said, delighted for her. 'Don't put it on now, Sarah. It needs to be cleaned properly. It's a really beautiful piece.'

Laughing, Sarah went to a window for clearer light, studying the pendant in the palm of her hand. Having it back was like having part of Tabbie with her again.

Tara started to follow her. Kit saw this for what it was meant to be, a dismissal of him. He wasn't having that. She should at least be polite to him. He stepped into her path, ignoring her irritation. 'I was sorry to hear about Mr Nankervis succumbing to illness. I do hope he is progressing well.'

Tara held herself stiff and formal. Insolent man, how dare he act as if an equal, his subterfuge gave him no right to authority. Apparently, he had been called on at Trengrove House by some curious socialites, but only because he was attractive and rich and would have a fine new house by the end of the year. He had made a good impression on some silly females who'd reported he was a gentleman of charm – contrived charm they would have seen if they didn't have feathers for brains. Again, because he was rich, men of business and speculators had been sniffing round him. He would, no doubt, be putting money into the mining ventures. 'He is. Thank you for your enquiry.'

'Would there be an opportunity to see him for a few minutes? I would so like to meet him.'

'My husband is still confined to his room.'

'I am sorry to hear that.'

'How did she die?' Sarah rejoined them, shivering at the memory of the terrifying night of the attack. 'Have you any idea, Kit?'

'I beg your pardon?' Kit's mind fought to unscramble her words for he was so absorbed in Tara. 'Oh, the girl . . . I should say she got lost and perished during that very same night. Her brother and one of the parish constables will have collected her body by now.'

'You went to the Greeps' cottage?' Sarah asked.

'Well, yes, it seemed the decent thing to do.'

'That was very thoughtful of you,' Sarah replied with admiration, glancing at Tara to include her in the comment, aware that her friend hated Kit being here.

Tara nodded. It was a thoughtful act. Kit Woodburne had some kindness in him. In the circumstances, rather than going to a lowly cottage to inform the kin, many a gentleman would have informed the first person he met of his find and forgotten about the matter. It was what Michael would have done. Joshua would have gone to the Greeps', albeit a little reluctantly. Joshua had been a good man in the old days. He had comforted Amy when her younger brother had been found dead in Poltraze woods. It was only since the beast Laketon Kivell had tightened his hold over him that he had become weak and hard-hearted. She hated seeing him so scared and defeated.

'You must know the family, Sarah. How do you feel about the girl's death?' Kit said.

'Jeb Greep is one of the kindest, most genuine people I've ever known.' As for Dinah Greep, she couldn't be wholly unforgiving now her life was so much better. Poltraze had dejection overhanging it but she had found a lot in its merit. It was good to have formed a close friendship with Tara and she got on well with Rosa Grace. 'I suppose I feel sorry more than anything for Dinah. Jeb will be relieved to be able to lay her to rest.'

There was silence. Sarah would like to invite Kit to sit down but felt it wasn't her place to.

He said, 'You have not been to Burnt Oak since you moved in here, Sarah. Grandmama Tempest misses you. And so does Jowan. He asked me to pass on his regards if I saw you before he did.'

'I haven't forgotten them. Actually I'll be seeing Jowan later in the week. He's going to do some work in the house.'

Silence fell again, longer this time. Tara knew her inhospitality was out of order. Kit Woodburne was here for a legitimate reason, on an act of kindness. She shouldn't continue to be churlish, and she had promised Sarah she would always make her feel comfortable here. 'Would you care for some tea, Mr Woodburne?'

Kit raised a careless eyebrow – Tara Nankervis deserved to be teased. If he flirted with her no doubt she would grow as cold as iron. It was tempting, but poor Sarah was feeling awkward enough. 'That would be delightful, Mrs Nankervis.'

'How are you finding it here, Sarah?' he asked when they were all seated about the dark wood fireplace. 'I hope the servants are being respectful towards you.'

'It's like living in a different world.' She was gazing at the pendant; none of the wonders here matched it for its sheer simple beauty. 'I'm getting quite used to all the changes. As I've told Mrs Nankervis, there are some creepy places. The Long Corridor is definitely haunted. I'm convinced I saw a shadowy figure flitting along there on my second day here. It gave me goosepimples all over. Most of the servants don't know what to make of me but I don't mind them. There's only one fly in the ointment here, a very big nasty one.'

'The disdainful butler, I dare say.'

'Not him, I think he's rather funny.'

'Who is it, then?' Tara asked, determined to know even her friend's smallest thoughts. 'Mr Michael Nankervis? His fiancée, Miss Phillipps? Have they been rude to you?'

'No, I've only seen them from a distance. I was talking about Laketon Kivell, that devil who is terrifying the house.'

'Sarah! You should not say such things in front of outsiders.' Tara was vexed and blushed, embarrassed.

'Kit is not an outsider, he's my friend.' Sarah shrugged. 'It doesn't alter the fact that Laketon Kivell is all but running things here and there's no one who can stop him.'

'I know all about the dark side of this kinsman of mine,' Kit interjected. 'It's time I introduced myself to him. Are you sure you ladies are safe here?'

'It's none of your business, Mr Woodburne.' Tara went redder, with anger. Between them Sarah and this man had caused her to lose her dignity and now she was even more worried about the predicament of Joshua, and his lover's actions. 'As it is, we'll be leaving here as soon as my husband is well again.'

Kit was unconcerned by the rebuke, many a thought ticked away inside his head as he witnessed the anxiety in the eyes of both women. 'It will be interesting to get to know the fellow.'

'Be careful of him, Kit,' Sarah warned.

'There is no need for you to worry. I shall see if I can do something about Laketon Kivell.'

'Why should you want to concern yourself with Poltraze's problem?' Tara asked bluntly. She knew the answer, he saw Sarah as more than a friend. He was out to impress her. Perhaps he intended to put a bride into his new house. Sarah was from a humble background but she would grace any house.

'I like to see justice done, but most of all I want to see Sarah safe and content. You too, ma'am, if you'll allow me to befriend you,' Kit said seriously. He was looking forward to the challenge. He had rid himself of his taunting bullying nursemaid, and to rid these two delightful women of a deadly threat would fill him with satisfaction. Grandmama Tempest and the other Kivells would approve. Laketon was an embarrassment to the Kivell name. 'I know I have used deception in the recent past but you can trust me.'

'What do you think, Tara?'

'Well, it would be a tremendous relief to see Kivell put out of here for good' – she stared at Kit with hope and dread – 'but the thought of you trying to do so frightens me. He's very vindictive. I believe the man's quite mad.'

'Don't worry, Mrs Nankervis, I have years of successful bluff at the card table to call on. I shall patiently learn the right ploy to attempt to unseat him.'

After he had gone, with the intention of roaming the grounds to seek out his quarry, Tara was in no mood to stitch scented sachets. Pacing up and down, pausing to gaze anxiously out of the windows, she cried, 'I should never have agreed to let that man do what he is about. If he fails, and that is very likely as Kivell is far too shrewd, it could bring the whole house down. He may punish Joshua again. Anyone in the house could be in danger. Perhaps I should send Rosa

Grace away. I don't want to risk any harm coming to her. She was greatly distressed by Hobbs jumping out of the window. I tried to suppress the facts but servants' gossip spreads as quickly as a disease. I don't want any more harm to come to you, Sarah. I'll arrange for you to accompany Rosa Grace to Truro immediately.'

'I won't go, Tara,' Sarah said firmly. 'Send Rosa Grace away with her nanny if you must, but I shall stay here with you. Jowan is due here this week, and if Mama Tempest is called on to help Kit, then Laketon will have the might of the Kivells against him.'

'You're very fond of Kit Woodburne, and he you,' Tara glowered. 'Is there anything between you?'

'In what way?' Sarah frowned at the question and Tara's manner. 'I know you are worried and that you don't approve of Kit coming here but there's no need to get mazed.'

'Mazed? What does that mean?' Tara saw her folly and herself as unreasonable. 'Forgive me, Sarah. I'm fearful there are romantic feelings between you and Mr Woodburne, and that I might soon be denied of your company. I'd hate to lose you now. But your personal life is none of my business.' Sarah was smiling at her and suddenly she was smiling too.

'Tara, Kit is the son of my late husband, I couldn't possibly think of him in that way. I'm pleased to have him as a friend. Like you, I took an instant dislike to Kit but now I know him I would trust him with my life. Mama Tempest explained things to me. Because of his loveless childhood Kit needed to blame someone for his miseries. As soon as he was shown some concern he responded to it rather like a child. He was vulnerable, still is really. Kit has a lot of honour, Tara, and he's strong and clever. This is your best chance to rid Poltraze of its devil, don't let anything ruin that.'

'You could be right. If I send Rosa Grace away Kivell might get suspicious, he knows we're inseparable. Anyway, Mr Woodburne may decide to do nothing and I don't want to send Rosa Grace without a good reason. We must go on as usual but keep very much on our guard.'

*   *   *

Kit walked along the path beside the croquet lawn, taking little notice of the renewed shrubberies; the plants were protected against the winter winds and frosts with circles of sacking. He hoped if he wandered about the grounds long enough he'd come across Laketon Kivell. The hothouses were the best bet. There was a pair of curious-looking trees and he stopped and stared at them. The trees were not tall, and their trunks were rather narrow and had a crisscross arrangement building up to coarse tufts under huge spreading leaves like those of the palm. 'How very strange . . .'

'Can I help you?' Someone with a strident voice was coming up fast beside him.

Kit gazed nonchalantly towards the voice's owner. The two men of similar dark rugged features sized each other up. With wary eyes wandering about Kit's person, Laketon said, 'You, sir, can be none other than Kit Woodburne. I suppose you will know who I am? Should I be pleased to make your acquaintance?'

'I hope you will find it so,' Kit replied lightly. The gardener exuded an insidious reptilian quality. He half-expected him to flick out a long, forked tongue. 'I was actually wandering about in the hope of meeting you at last. Would you mind telling me the name of these fascinating trees?'

'Not at all, they're *Berberis*, this species is monkey puzzle, from Chile,' Laketon informed him proudly. 'So called because it's said monkeys are puzzled about how to climb them. Have you never seen the like before?'

'Nothing like these, Mr Kivell.' Kit smiled warmly into the other man's eyes. To get rid of this garden pest he first had to get him to trust him. 'You may be aware I'm having my own property built. I would be delighted if the gardens ended up as well as Poltraze's once were. I regret that I did not see them in their heyday, but I can see the old glory reflected here and there and that you are getting everything under control again.'

'I'm doing my best. Would you care for me to show you around?'

Kit knew this was a ploy to study him as much as an opportunity to show off. 'That's good of you.' He strolled off with his hands behind his back. 'I'm afraid I know little about plants and flowers. I just like to admire their pleasing effect. My grandmother told me you are responsible for the establishment of her garden. I congratulate you on its beauty. I find it peaceful there. Tell me, Laketon, how you came by such a love of the earth.'

Kit could tell Laketon was as puzzled about him as a monkey was about the trees they were leaving. Laketon would know him as a liar, and that his earlier plan for Burnt Oak meant he could be a hard man underneath the agreeable manner he was portraying. Laketon would soon experience that side of him.

Fifteen

'What the blazes! I've had enough of this day in and day out.' Michael ripped the spectacles off his long learned nose and leapt up from the red leather club chair. 'I'll have it stopped.' Until the noise of the carpentry had started up again he had been almost as still as the rows of antiquated books in the darkened musty library. Seated at the long table, copying up his notes on the Nankervis history during Tudor times, was his bride-to-be, Adeline Phillipps.

'But can you order it to be stopped, dear? The work has to go ahead, I suppose,' the bespectacled and wafer-thin Adeline said, in her strange floating speech. Behind her, the fireplace was carefully lit and attended so as not to harm the precious books and maps, and the butterfly and moth collections. The plaster mantelpiece was an ugly affair featuring faces of Nankervis children who had died young. In dark basic clothes, Adeline was waxen pale and ghost-like and looked as if she only had to step back to be incorporated into the grim tableau. She never seemed to mind anything, and had the enviable ability to shut herself off from the world.

Michael found her uninspiring and he did not lust to take her to bed, but after enduring the incessant nagging of his first wife, Adeline was perfect for him. It was good to have a woman who, apart from sharing the same interests, rarely sought to offer an opinion. God willing, she would bear him a healthy son. He had come to think his life would be complete if he was squire of Poltraze. Strangely, that prospect, which he had never wanted the responsibility of before, seemed a not unlikely occurrence. Joshua was slowly killing himself – or rather Laketon Kivell was doing it for him. The only work to be done anywhere on the estate then would be at his behest. 'I suppose you are right, my dear, but how is one to concentrate with all this hammering and scratching going on? I shall have a word with Tara. She omitted to tell me the repairs were going ahead in the morning room. It was not her place to order it to be done.'

'That was disrespectful of her, dear. Mrs Nankervis takes too much upon herself.' Adeline only glanced up briefly from her labour.

'She does indeed, my dear. I shall see that it comes to a stop. I have other issues with her also.'

Satisfied and encouraged by her loyalty, he left on determined strides but closed the door in whisper quietness. Adeline didn't seem to be aware he had gone.

'Tara, I want a word with you this minute.' Michael barged into the winter parlour, wrinkling his nose in disgust at the heady fusion of rose and lavender scents.

'It seems you do,' Tara snapped from the sewing table. 'But I will not listen while you are in such an aggressive mood.' She continued to fill a china pomander with pot-pourri, hiding her surprise that her normally placid brother-in-law was being so rude. She couldn't imagine what he had come to gripe about.

'Damn it, Tara, you will heed me, and alone if you please. Perhaps your companion could withdraw for ten minutes.' He grimaced at Sarah, although not without fleetingly admiring her dark beauty. He certainly wouldn't mind spending a covert afternoon with her.

Sarah headed for the door. 'I'll come back in a while,' she said, worried that Tara was in for an upset.

Up on her feet, Tara glared at Michael. 'How dare you come in here and throw your weight about like a ruffian and order Miss Hichens away!'

'The girl is a Kivell and she is part of the two complaints I have against you. Damn it, Tara, you are filling the house with Kivells. It's bad enough that we have to endure a Kivell as Joshua's lover, who does exactly as he pleases, now you not only have the widow of the most infamous of that ragbag clan living here, you are freely inviting one of their bastard breed here too, a man who masquerades as a gentleman, a rogue who admits to being an impostor, and who probably should be incarcerated in an asylum. Damn it, Tara, he was speaking to our daughter for some time the other day. Don't you care?'

'Mr Woodburne was talking to Rosa Grace? Where was this?' Tara was not troubled, rather she found herself pleased by the information.

'Her nursemaid was taking her outside for a walk. Woodburne engaged both in conversation and even allowed Rosa Grace to show him her doll. He had no right to go anywhere near her.'

'Well, he takes more notice of Rosa Grace than you do. No doubt you shot away to avoid being delayed from your precious books. I have no fears about Mr Woodburne's integrity.'

'Then you are a fool, Tara. And you have had the audacity to engage a carpenter in the house, a Kivell at that. Joshua left that sort of thing to me years ago!' The more he went on the more Tara expected to see steam blowing out of his ears. 'None of it is appropriate. I demand that you behave as the wife of the squire should. You're making Poltraze a laughing stock. My dear fiancée finds it all very strange.'

'I'm not in the least interested in what Miss Phillipps thinks. She will quickly discover being a Nankervis wife offers no advantages. You are the one who does not see to his duties. I've asked you many times to arrange to have the panelling in the morning room repaired. Joshua kindly asked me recently if all was well with the house and I mentioned the repair to him. He sent word for the steward to take the appropriate course. It was Atkins who engaged Jowan Kivell, as the best craftsman for the task, and not I. Before you intrude on me again in such a vulgar manner do get your facts right. You would have known about the woodwork if you'd had the courtesy to call on Joshua since he came out of his delirium. You care about no one except yourself, Michael. If you have finished, go!'

'Don't think to try to degrade me, Tara. I won't put up with it.' He wagged a finger at her. 'Poltraze was once a quiet place and it will be again.' He turned on his heel and strode out, going straight up to Joshua.

Cheek of the man! Tara balled her fists. He hated Laketon

Kivell's dominance here but he did not have the courage or
foresight to do anything about dislodging him. Michael had
no use in the world. What was the point in delving into the
Nankervis history? It didn't have a particularly glorious past
and its future was doubtful. The moment Joshua was well
she would take Rosa Grace and Sarah to Truro and nothing
would induce her to return.

She went to the window. Kivell was out there somewhere,
giving orders to the gardeners as if he was the squire. Kit
Woodburne had befriended the wretch to glean a way of
dealing with him. He would do anything for Sarah. Tara bit
her lip, she hoped he would take things very carefully and
not put himself or others into danger.

She shuddered. Pray God, Kivell did not take an intimate
interest in him. Kit was amazingly handsome. Kivell probably was attracted to him. She was attracted to him, if she
would only admit it. No, I'm not, she stressed to her reflection in the windowpane. My interest in him lies solely in the
fact that he is the only hope of ridding Poltraze of its beast.
She turned back in the room to recall him chatting with Sarah
and smiling at her on her subsequent visits. He had a nice
smile, well a stunning smile actually. He did not try to include
Tara in their conversation, merely being polite to her. She
hated to know it but it rankled. There was no need for her
to stay offhand with him, particularly now she knew he had
a heart to be fond of children. It would be good to be his
friend too.

Joshua gingerly pushed back the bedcovers. He felt as weak
as water and his muscles ached without mercy. He was able
to sit up on the couch for part of each day but now he was
in bed and supposed to be taking a nap. This time he had
ordered the nurse out of the room, saying he could not easily
fall asleep with her clinging presence. Screwing up his face
in the effort to sit up, he inched his heavy legs to flop down
over the edge of the bed. Everything was an effort. His chest
still hurt from the infection, his sandpaper-dry mouth retained
a bitter taste and he sweated all day and night.

He took a minute to allow his head to clear, then bending
to the doors of the bedside cabinet he opened them, and with

his head spinning, searched about until he found the pair of nail scissors he had furtively procured from the nurse that morning. He got back into bed, pulled up the covers, making sure the scissors were hidden, and lay panting to recover. The scissors were small with curved tips but they were good enough to open up the veins in his wrists and enable him to bleed to death. The nurse would ensure he wouldn't be disturbed, so this suicide attempt should be a successful one.

He had been planning it for days. It was the only way he could find the peace he longed for and get revenge on Laketon Kivell, the man he hated more than all the powers of hell for seducing the boy he had loved. Tara would have her wish and thanks to the conditions of her dowry she and her child would be well provided for. Death was the only way out of his misery. Even if Laketon was to meet his end first, he couldn't go on knowing what he had become, a snivelling, useless wreck of a man, conned by a velvet-smooth valet.

He felt about one wrist to determine the best place to make the first cut. He opened the scissors and put the point into place. He wouldn't be able to make a quick job of it but he was determined to go ahead, not caring about the pain. He paused and whispered, 'God forgive me. Please take me into Your arms.'

The bedroom door opened and he whipped the scissors beneath his body. He could have screamed. Must he be thwarted at everything? His rapid movements were a give-away that he was not asleep.

'Joshua, may I come in?' Michael called softly. 'I've slipped past the nurse. I need to talk to you.'

'For a moment, if you must.' Joshua could not keep the irritation out of his voice. Damn his brother to hell! Of all the times to finally come to him, and then only for his own ends . . . Michael and everyone else didn't really care about him. How he hated this life and craved to be out of it.

Michael tiptoed to the bedside. 'Sorry to disturb you. Just a quick word, are you allowing Tara to give orders concerning the estate?'

'Tara's been good to me. She's the only one I can trust. She may do exactly what she pleases. There, that's your answer. Now leave me in peace.' Joshua shifted, pushing his body into the mattress. 'Ouch!' God in heaven, how could he have forgotten the scissors?

'What is it?' Joshua's feeble face was twisted in so much pain that Michael flung back the bedcovers. 'Is it your back? I'll fetch the nurse.'

'It's nothing! I don't want her making a fuss.' The scissor points were sticking into him but Joshua would bear it until Michael left the room.

'Maybe you don't want a fuss but something hurt you very badly. Has that monster been beating you again?' Joshua struggled against him but Michael was determined to learn the facts. Gathering Joshua up to face him he looked down at his back. The blood in Michael's veins ran cold. 'My God, you've been impaled by a pair of scissors. Is Kivell making you lie on sharp things to torture you?'

'No,' Joshua wailed. 'It's an accident. The nurse must have left the scissors behind. Don't say anything, I beg you, Michael. Laketon will go into a rage. He'll have the nurse thrown out and have me guarded more tightly. I'll be even more of a prisoner. Don't say anything to anyone, please!'

'But this is outrageous negligence,' Michael seethed, gently tugging out the scissors and watching in horror as a fat trickle of blood further wetted Joshua's nightshirt. 'Of course the nurse must go. This can't be kept a secret, your nightshirt is slashed and there's blood on it and the sheet. I'll fetch Tara. She should deal with this.'

'No! It wasn't the nurse's fault.' Joshua gripped Michael by the shoulders and burst into a drench of tears. 'I stole the scissors from the nurse to kill myself. I was about to cut my wrists when you came in.'

Michael was so shocked he thrust Joshua away from him to flop down on the bed. 'Suicide? You were about to bring shame on the Nankervis name? Damn you, damn you, Joshua.' Standing back from the bed he was appalled by his brother's blubbering but he couldn't stay entirely angry. 'Are things so very bad?'

It was an effort for Joshua to bring himself under control. He gulped on enormous sobs and Michael proffered his handkerchief. 'I'm living in hell, Michael. L-Laketon has taken everything from me. Death is my only way out.' An unquiet desperation gave him the strength to sit up and plead with his hands. 'Don't hate me, Michael. Leave me alone so I can do what I want and find my peace. Think about it, Michael. My death will benefit you. You'll be the squire. You're the only one who's ever really loved this house. You deserve to have it. You'll be able to move your daughters in and bring your bride here as mistress. Tara hates Poltraze. She'll be relieved to get away. She can find a husband who will be a real husband to her. And Laketon will have no sway here any longer. It's the best thing for all of us, Michael, you must see that. Help me, please! If you've got one scrap of decency in your body, don't let me go on like this.'

One moment Michael was shrinking back in horror at the suggestion, the next he was edging forward as he found himself agreeing with it. Back and forth he went, but he ended up almost at the door. He had no brotherly bond with Joshua but he did not want him dead, and he couldn't possibly help him to commit suicide. 'There's got to be some other way. I mean, you could simply sign Poltraze over to me.'

'Then Laketon would kill me, as slowly and as painfully as he knows how. I don't want to leave this earth by his evil hands.'

Michael's head spun with a rush of thoughts and tension took him in an unnerving grip. After years of methodically easing himself through a selfish life he had never before had to consider anything so vital and dreadful. Putting up his hands for silence he went back to the bedside and sat down, feeling as if all his breath had been knocked out of him.

Weakness overtook Joshua and he fell back on the pillows. 'I haven't really thought about how you've suffered,' said Michael. 'I can understand how you feel you have nothing to live for with Kivell controlling your every second. It isn't you who should die, Joshua, it's him. We must think of a way to push him out, or better still be rid of him forever.'

'Kill him or have him killed? It's impossible. I've gone over everything I can think of to do just that. He seems to be aware of everything that goes on here. Anything we try could bring us into danger. He might hurt your children. It's hopeless for me, Michael. I can't stand another day here, the memories are too terrible. Listen, please, I agree my suicide would bring disgrace to Poltraze and make it difficult for you. I could have an accident of some kind that would be classed as a tragedy. Help me to arrange something, a fall from a window; that would be easy. No chance of survival to mess things up.'

Michael shook his head. 'I don't know how you can discuss your death so coolly. Don't you dare jump from a window; your dying the same way as Hobbs would lead to speculation. It would cause a scandal. I need time to think this all through, to come up with a way to get us out of this bloody awful situation. Grin and bear it until then, promise me, Joshua?'

With fresh painful tears, Joshua closed his eyes and nodded. 'What about the scissors?'

'The nurse can take the blame for that. Kivell need never know, or Tara. We'll tell the woman we'll hush it up this time because her services are valued.'

After giving the nurse a furious dressing-down, Michael went straight down to the library. 'Adeline, my dear, leave that. I suddenly feel stuffy in the house. Let's get away from the noise and take a little fresh air. It's a dry day. We'll take Cecily and Jemima for a ride in the carriage. Rosa Grace can join us.' The suggestion that Laketon Kivell might seek revenge on his children if Joshua signed Poltraze over to him had made Michael for the very first instance want to spend some time with all three of his daughters.

Jowan was fully occupied in fitting a new wall panel in the morning room but his mind was on Sarah. Most days he saw her but he wanted to pass more than a few friendly words with her. She didn't look right in these grand surroundings. She didn't belong here with these people. Sarah should be mistress of her own household. She would be perfect for Chy-Henver. He was a little younger than her but he could give her everything she'd ever want, he would give her all the love and respect she deserved. She could never have children; it would be a hard sacrifice but one he'd willingly make for her. She haunted him, not just because she was so lovely but for her pride, dignity and strengths that had seen her through so many ordeals. Her touching vulnerability appealed to him as no other woman's could. She wasn't greedy nor did she flaunt her new position. Sarah was simply who she was and would never change. He wouldn't leave here today until he'd got the chance to invite her formally to a meal at Chy-Henver.

Leaving Tara with her angry brother-in-law, Sarah went to the morning room. She knew from before the work had started that Michael Nankervis demanded hush while in the library; if he objected to the inevitable sounds of Jowan at work that was ridiculous. The morning room was at the other end of the house anyway, and how could someone work without making a sound? It was a strange world that was occupied by the gentry and their servants. The former made unreasonable demands and complaints and the latter genuinely grovelled to do their bidding as if their masters were gods.

She found Jowan standing on a dust sheet sizing up his handiwork. 'How are you getting on?'

'Sarah!' His dark eyes sparkled like gems at seeing her. 'That's the last panel, there's only the oak to treat to produce the same colour and the decorative moulding to put back in place. Dismal sort of place here, like everyone says it is, don't you think? I wouldn't like to live here. You seem content, but are you really?'

'In a way it's easier here for me than those born to the life. I don't have the same expectations and the only role I need to play is Tara's companion. How are things in the village? I confess I've lost touch with what's going on there.'

'Things are really grim. Mrs Nankervis's generosity at Christmas was a help but there's a lot of hungry bellies, among the mining folk in particular. People are dying from the usual round of fevers and diseases. Grandmama tried to help but some people were too proud and turned her down. Some will be able to call on poor relief but there will be no help for others.'

'I should do something more for them than just sitting comfortably and sewing. I could make some simple gestures without it seeming too much like charity. I could leave things on doorsteps and hope it will be seen as a gift from God. It's what people like Jeb Greep would believe.'

'When you are in the village you must come to Chy-Henver, have a meal with us. Rachel misses the women's chats she had with you. We all miss you.'

'I'll do that. I like being there, thinking about the old days when Amy was there. She's been gone for two years now. She and Sol must be coming back soon. A letter is on the way to tell her I'm living here now. I hope she's not moved on from the New Territories and doesn't get it.'

Jowan became serious. 'Sarah . . .'

'What is it?'

'Grandmama Tempest has had a letter from Sol, she's deeply upset. You and Mrs Nankervis should be hearing from Amy yourselves soon. The thing is . . .' He edged closer to Sarah, how was she going to take the news?

She was beginning to worry. 'What, Jowan? What are you trying to say?'

'Sol and Amy are having another baby, and the thing is they've decided to live in America for good, in California. They like the vast beautiful land there. A man can own thousands of acres. Sol's going to build his own ranch and take up farming. They're not coming back, Sarah. Thad and I are going to buy the carpentry business from them.'

'You mean I'll never see Amy again?' Sarah walked away in a daze. 'But I've dreamt about her returning home. It was the one thing that kept me going when I lived with Tabbie.'

Jowan went up behind her. Now was the time to tell her of his feelings. The nerves in his stomach started up a wild dance and sweat pricked his neck. 'Y-you have the rest of us, Sarah. You have me. You need never be lonely or fear homelessness again. If you ever want to leave this life at Poltraze you can go to Burnt Oak or to Kit's house, or – or to me, Sarah.'

Sarah stayed put. This was awful. She had heard Jowan's admiration and desire for her in his nervous husky tone. She'd had no idea that sort of thing was going through his mind, and it could never be. This man had been her stepson and now he was her friend. She could offer him nothing else. She turned round slowly. 'I'm sorry, Jowan. I'm sure you'll understand why.'

Jowan knew at once he had made a tremendous mistake

and it could have been much worse. Sarah could have been horrified and offended by his declaration. How could he ever have contemplated she would consider tying herself to a son of a man who had virtually torn her heart out? His cheeks burned with shame. 'No, I'm sorry. I've been a fool. Please forgive me.'

She owed him so much and thought only of his feelings. 'Can we forget this ever happened? Go on as before?'

'Yes. Thank you. I'll just get on with my work.' He was grateful to Sarah for being kind. Thank God he would be finished here today. The moment he was alone in the room he pressed a hand to his eyes to prevent tears. It would never do for a Kivell male to cry but how he wanted to. He was in love with Sarah more than he'd realized. No woman could ever match her. He knew now the kind of raw loneliness she had experienced.

Sarah dragged her feet back to the winter parlour. Poor Jowan, she hoped he'd soon get over her. Amy was starting yet another new adventure in her life, leaving her and Tara behind as increasingly sad characters in comparison. A truly satisfying life seemed set on passing them by. The only thing life ever threw at them was more complications.

Sixteen

Kit was getting a lesson in botany. Inside one of the hothouses Laketon was pointing out his new collection of orchids. 'These have been brought over from the southeast of Asia. There's a great many species but I'm sure you don't want to be bored with their Latin names. They will flower at various times from spring to autumn.'

'I have much to look forward to,' Kit said, making mental notes. He wanted such treasures in his own gardens. He particularly liked the red-brick walled garden. Its contents unspoiled by Laketon's dark deed, it was of considerable size; its sheltered effect created a microclimate and it had over one hundred species, including fruit trees, herb bushes and climbers. *Liatris* grew over a row of arches. What a blaze of colour there would be when everything was in bloom. There were quiet nooks and secluded benches, weathered statues and a magnificent sundial. It was a perfect place to meet for an assignation. He would settle for a stroll inside with Tara Nankervis; she was quite friendly these days. She seemed delighted that he had spoken to her daughter. He took a good look around the hothouse. 'So you would recommend tinted glass in the structure, Laketon?'

'Every time, it tempers the scorching effect of the sun, Kit. I hope you will allow me to assist you when you are ready to start the landscaping of your gardens.'

Laketon turned his full attention on his distant cousin. What a magnificent beast he was. Such a pity he preferred women. Could he be coaxed to try something different? No, he knew exactly what he was and at this moment he wanted Tara Nankervis. But as Kit seemed not to care that he had opposing tastes, he might agree to some diverting company in the establishments where both genders' appetites were

catered for. Joshua would be of no use to him in that depart-
ment again, he'd respond only with fear. Let his wife namby-
pamby him, it was all he deserved, to be treated as a needy
child. Tara Nankervis was to stay on in Truro after the numb-
skull Michael Nankervis's wedding. She could take Joshua
with her, keep him there indefinitely, and then he'd have free
rein here with no one to prevent his will being obeyed.
Michael Nankervis was getting smug; he would, no doubt,
give him notice. Laketon would ignore it. Michael would
never stand up to him; he didn't have the guts.

'I shall be delighted to call on your expertise. I hope the
squire won't become anxious that I'll poach you away.' Kit,
as always, watched the other man for telltale signs of rancour
or suspicion. 'It's good he is well enough to come downstairs now. It's a pity he feels he won't be able to attend his
brother's wedding.' Unfortunately, the squire spent a lot of
time with Tara, denying Kit the chance to get to know her
better, and her him. Joshua Nankervis was a singularly tiresome, pathetic individual. Like an infant he sought comfort
from his wife, and Sarah too, and both women were quick
to attend to his demands. Michael Nankervis had taken to
sitting in with them too; he made a point of scowling at Kit.
The brothers had closed ranks against Laketon. What could
they do against him, hunched up like rabbits caught in a
trap? It was pitiable.

'Mr Nankervis is a very generous man, Kit. I'm sure he'd
be willing to loan my expertise to you,' Laketon answered
as if his position amounted to no more than head gardener.
Then he gazed at Kit. 'Sadly, the squire will never be the
man he once was, can't see him ever being up to socializing again. I understand you're quite a card shark, Kit. I
know a place where a game could be played, with the right
sort of entertainment thrown in afterward, if you get my
meaning?'

'I do indeed, Laketon. I shall be happy to visit it. Yes, the
squire is too frail for junketing, it can't have been much fun
for you lately, but then he hasn't got Kivell blood in his
veins. Kivells have one thing in common, to know how to
live life to the full.' Kit laughed uproariously and Laketon
followed suit. Had he fooled Laketon that he had an ally?

He was seeking out Laketon's weaknesses and that was more easily attained when a man was well gone in drink.

'I'll arrange something,' Laketon said. Then he eyed the delicate growth of his orchids, eager to get back to them.

'If you'll excuse me, I'll slip inside in the hope that the delightful Mrs Nankervis will offer me some refreshment.' Kit had tolerated enough the other's dull and sinister company.

'Of course, good day to you, Kit.'

Kit hoped to win a smile from Tara. Rosa Grace formed an easy topic of conversation but progress with Tara was hard. Sarah engaged him a lot, and then there were the two maudlin Nankervis brothers, tied to their chairs and bringing down the ambience. He would, however, forgo the pleasure of seeing Tara for a while. He concealed himself behind the nearest hedge to keep watch on the hothouse. He wasn't disappointed. The footman, Hankins, was approaching. Kit had noticed the young man in the vicinity of Laketon Kivell once before. He watched as Hankins went into the hothouse, clearly nervous, so Kit assumed, of the service he was about to provide for his superior. Laketon didn't seem pleased to see him but inclined his ear. Kit couldn't make out what was being said but he understood the situation: Hankins was supplying information, no wonder Laketon knew about everything that went on in the house. Moments later Laketon tossed Hankins a penny and waved a hand to dismiss him.

Kit moved off some distance then waylaid the footman in a quiet leafy spot at the back of the house. 'Hankins, I wish to speak to you.' Each of his words was like a thud and at each one Hankins blinked in alarm.

'I-I'm sorry, sir. I can't stop. I have to get back to my duties. Mr Fawcett will be after my blood if I'm late to help serve afternoon tea.'

'And I'll have your blood if you don't do exactly what I say from now on. Don't look so worried. I'm not nearly as ruthless as the man you've just offloaded information to. What I intend to do will benefit the whole of Poltraze and if you play your part well it will set you up here nicely for the future.' Kit produced a florin and the servant's fear abated with a greedy lick of the lips. 'This won't take long if you cooperate.'

Michael was in the library with a book open in his hand, standing beside the library ladder he had just descended, without a clue why he had chosen this particular volume or what it was he had wanted to look up. He couldn't keep his mind on anything except Joshua's wish to die. 'I've got a very good idea,' Joshua had said quite calmly, and even looking rather bright, during his next time up to his room. 'It's foolproof.'

'What do you mean? You can't still be considering ending your life?' The more Michael thought about actually helping Joshua do what he wanted, the more he felt sick. And scared, scared of Laketon Kivell yes, but also he felt that a legion of disapproving angels was watching over him to see if he'd take part. Any manner of things could go wrong with such a dire scheme, and then there would be Kivell out for revenge and the authorities to answer to. He would not be elevated to grieving squire if he was dead or locked up in jail.

'I've been thinking about nothing else. It's the only thing that's keeping me from despair or madness.'

Michael had brought his hands up to his ears. 'I won't listen to you. I shall leave the room. I'll give you my support in anything but that.'

'Hear me out!' Joshua hissed, clutching his brother's coat. 'I haven't got long. As soon as Laketon considers I'm well enough to go to his cottage, goodness knows what will happen to me. You've got no choice, Michael. You must help me. It would be too cruel of you to let me suffer for years and years ahead.'

Michael pushed Joshua's hand down. 'I'll listen to you but I'm not promising anything. It's a dreadful thing to ask someone to do, don't you realize that? Have you thought about how I am supposed to live with my conscience?'

'I'm sorry,' Joshua replied flatly. 'This is what I've worked out. I'm strong enough to go downstairs. I'll play up on being really frail and stay close by the fireplace. Then, on a mild day, I'll suggest you take me for a short walk. We'll go to the pool—'

'The pool? Don't be stupid. It's too far away for an invalid to walk.'

'Well, you can push me in the bath chair, then. Anyway, at some point you will look away and I'll drown in the pool. It wouldn't be your fault. You can tell everyone that you did all you could to save me but couldn't reach me in time. It will be a tragic accident. Quite apt, really, our elder brother Jeffrey, who should have been squire, drowned in the pool. Sorry that you'll have to get wet, Michael.'

'Get wet? I can't do it. I'll be consumed with mortification watching you kill yourself. How am I supposed to lie convincingly? God, Joshua, think again for pity's sake.'

'I won't change my mind,' Joshua whispered, his throat choked with tears. 'I'm sorry, Michael, I really am, but if you refuse to help me to go ahead with this more honourable way out, I swear I will kill myself. I can't, I won't go on living a life of hell. You'd best think what you're going to do about Laketon after I'm gone.'

Now here he was with Joshua's morbid proposition going through his mind, relentlessly pushing him ever further into a corner. Perhaps the best thing was for Joshua to die, he was going to cause a lot of trouble otherwise, and he didn't want him to go on suffering. What to do about Laketon Kivell? That was the thorny question. The only way to be safe from him was if he was dead. Kivell's death could be contrived. A bullet through the brain would do. It could be said he shot himself cleaning a gun. But who could he get to be the assassin?

Shortly after leaving the footman, Kit made his way to the library. With luck he'd find Michael Nankervis there, he couldn't resist some time there every day.

'What the hell do you want?' Michael growled at him, slamming shut the book in his hand then regretting it, fearful he had damaged the musty delicate pages. 'How dare you come in here, Woodburne. I didn't even hear you knock.'

'Actually I did, but no matter. I'm sorry to disturb you, Nankervis, but we should talk. Allow me to speak. I think you will be very interested in what I have to say.'

Seventeen

It was unusually quiet in the village. Sarah peered up and down the High Street and the little lanes and byways. There were no small children running about or anyone out to the shops. Her steps echoed where there were cobbles and stamped on the frost-hardened ground. The more she went along the more conspicuous she felt in her tailor-made clothes and feminine boots. She was more a stranger here now and had the self-conscious expectation that at any moment someone would come out of their mean little cottage and order her to clear off.

She had come to distribute the things she'd helped Tara put together to sustain the most vulnerable in Meryen through the harsh winter months. She'd been driven in a carriage, but had ordered the Poltraze groom to stop on the village outskirts, her intention being to go to the Greeps first to ask for their advice and a favour. The carriage was loaded with food, candles and lamp oil. There were also seed potatoes, enough for a row or two for every poor family, and other seedlings, the surplus left over from Poltraze's abundance. All the preparations would have been enjoyable if not for the squire joining her and Tara for part of each day. He treated her presence in his home with faint politeness but he had brought the atmosphere down. In the end he had unexpectedly taken a brief interest in the charity doings and ordered two sheep to be slaughtered to provide mutton. Sarah wanted to glean from the Greeps which families were the most deserving and how best to get the gift to certain families to make sure no drunken fathers or neglectful mothers misused it.

Her knock on the Greeps' back door was answered by an old woman. 'Sarah Hichens, indeed, you've heard, then?'

she muttered grimly. Sarah thought she was unwelcome until she added, beckoning her inside, 'It's good of you to come.'

'Heard what, Mrs Endean?' Although pleased to feel she was still considered part of Meryen, Sarah, alarmed, asked the obvious question. 'Has something bad happened?' Frettie Endean, of stout build and frank manner, acted as the local midwife and was also the layer-out of dead bodies. The Greep infants were on the kitchen mat, the boy playing with a few clothes pegs, the baby on her back, gurgling while kicking out her legs. Sarah hoped Frettie Endean wasn't here for her second occupation; perhaps Miriam had suffered a miscarriage, which wouldn't be as bad as her death, but what accounted for the desertion of the village? Then she knew, she should have guessed. 'There's been an accident at the mine, hasn't there?'

' 'Fraid so.'

'Oh, my God! Are many dead or injured? Is Jeb among them? Is that why Miriam isn't here?' It wasn't dramatic to take the worst for granted. Her own mother's life had been destroyed in an accident on the mine surface. Death and maiming were all too common above and below grass. The last day she'd worked at the Carn Croft a miner had lost his arm in a dynamite explosion. Only the quick ascent to the surface with the help of another miner and the prompt attention of the mine surgeon had saved him from bleeding to death. 'When did it happen?'

'About a couple of hours ago. All I know is that some men and boys are trapped underground from a rock fall. A scat was heard and then 'tis believed up to forty ton went crashing down. 'Tis thought the men below, Jeb included, I've prayed to God, are safe in an air pocket, but they can't get up till the way's cleared for 'em.' Frettie shook her wise head, wiping away a tear with her starched white apron; the rest of her clothes were black, she had lost two husbands and a son to the mine. 'We're in for another long vigil, Sarah.'

'What can I do to help?' Sarah was bobbing on tenter-hooks, wanting to dash off to the mine.

'Can't see you can do anything but pray, maid. The village is practically empty, though there's some in the chapels down on their knees.' Frettie pulled out a chair from the table. 'Sit down. Reckon I can squeeze out a drop of tea from the pot. So, Sarah, what are you on upon coming here, then? What's it like living up at the squire's? I heard he's back on his legs again. And the man who's really called Mr Woodburne's been spending time there. That was a turn up, eh, he being partly a Kivell? It must have been a very strange time for 'ee.'

Sarah answered all the questions. 'I'm wondering now what to do about the things I've brought. They'll be needed more than ever. There's likely to be a lot of grieving in Meryen. I'm sure Mrs Nankervis will do all she can to help.'

'I can tell you what you need to know, if that's a help. You can drop the things on back doorsteps.'

'Thank you, Mrs Endean.' Sarah sipped the bitter stewed tea. 'What about yourself? Do you need anything?'

'The lodgers I take in provide me with enough keep to get by. They're all miners. Sadly, if any of 'em have perished others will come along to take their place soon as word gets round. Give the stuff out to the young families and the frail, my handsome.' After she'd rattled off the names of the most deserving needy, little Job Greep tugged shyly on Frettie's apron. 'Aw, the dear of him wants something to eat. Let's see what your mummy's got in the larder, shall we?' she cooed to the boy.

'I'll set about giving out the things from the carriage. Goodbye, Mrs Endean.' Before she left Sarah took a lingering look at the children, sad for a second, as she was from time to time, that she would never be a mother.

She got the groom to bring the carriage into the village, and trudged up and down the weedy or ash paths to rough back doors, each home telling a different story of near poverty, of much needing to be fixed. The groom helped her to carry the goods, which she tailored to each family or individual. Hardly anyone locked their doors until bedtime, so if no one was at home they left the goods in the kitchens so they wouldn't go astray. They wend their way through Meryen, travelling on foot along the very narrow byways, squeezing past the damp overgrowth of the hedges, getting their boots muddy and becoming none too tidy.

'This seems to be the last, Miss Sarah,' the groom said,

as he pulled out the final bundle from the carriage. They were at a tiny lonely wayside place, a long distance past Chy-Henver; the mine buildings were in clear sight, and the only noise reaching across the short stretch of scrubland was the thump and boom from the engine house. 'Was there enough to go around?'

Sarah's eyes went to the lofty Carn Marth rearing up away in the distance; today it seemed to provide a sorrowful fatherly watch. 'Well, all the neediest have got something. It's surprising how the littlest thing can be a great help when you've got virtually nothing. Thank you for helping me, Moyle.'

'It's my duty and my pleasure, miss. Here, let me carry that parcel for you too. The mistress won't be happy with me if I bring you back wearied out.' As he placed her parcel on top of the bundle, John Moyle glanced at her rather than keep a distant gaze somewhere above her head. Servants were to do the latter out of respect, but things were different with Miss Sarah. People elevated to a higher position often took on high and mighty ways but she had kept her ordinary manner and never put anyone to trouble. It was good to dwell on her lovely face at close quarters.

Sarah led the way through an opening in a tumbledown stone wall to what amounted to a narrow muddy track. 'A family called Kent lives here,' she announced sadly. She had told John Moyle a little about each householder; he was not from Meryen and was curious about each inhabitant. 'The old grandmother died last autumn. Her son Elias works under grass, and his young son David is a lappior, buddling on the surface. Elias's wife died from typhus. If Elias perishes, poor David will have nobody and could end up in the workhouse.'

'Hopefully someone will take him in.' John shook his head grimly. 'That's where I come from. It's a harsh life. If a child's not careful he can grow as hard and cold as the winter ground. A farmer took me to work with the beasts and beat me nearly every day. Working with the horses came as natural as breathing to me. The head groom at Poltraze noticed and poached me to work for the squire. Sorry, miss, you don't want to hear about my life.'

Sarah looked into his apologetic eyes. 'That's all right.

And now you're the head groom.' Most of the servants at Poltraze seemed as if they had been dropped exactly as they were out of the sky, moving, curtseying or bowing creatures living and breathing only to perform their utmost for their master or mistress, and then to complain in the servants' hall about their lot. John Moyle was one of the human ones, more his own man. His eyes were a mellow fawn colour, which reflected resignation to his place yet retained a strong element of self-respect. He was quick to tip his hat but he did not grovel. More than a six-footer, he was mildly spoken, his voice holding an interesting range of tones. He had an inner smile. Sarah had seen him a few times and had noticed he sometimes smiled for no specific reason, and his thoughts seemed to drift off as if he was seeing something only he could see, a different future for himself perhaps. Life could take you anywhere, she mused, who'd have thought she would be handing out succour in this way to the needy of the village, with a groom in the distinct pale-blue and buff livery from the big house? Tabbie would be proud of her. 'Let's just pray all will work out well for Elias and David.'

Leaving the cheerless Kent home, she said, 'I'd like to go to the mine now. See what I can do to help.'

'Begging your pardon, Miss Sarah, do you think that's wise?'

'What do you mean?'

'Well, meaning no disrespect, but although your intentions are of the highest order the folk there might not entirely welcome you. I've heard they like to keep to their own in times like this.'

Recalling the occasions she had huddled at the mine face after an accident, although her aloofness had set her a little apart back then, she too would have resented anyone turning up in a grand carriage and finery, a stark contrast to the mining folk's own shabbiness. The only outsider welcome there was the mine surgeon. Gentlefolk were considered to want only to stare and get in the way, and were a nuisance because they'd still insist to be waited upon. She wasn't a lady and she wouldn't expect any such thing, but she didn't belong at the mine either. 'I don't want to just go as if all I care about is to hand out charity and leave the people to it.'

'Well, there were some lonely housebound people, I'd noticed, who might be glad of some company.'

Sarah gave him a grateful smile. 'You're right. They were so frightened. I'll spend some time with each one. Thank you for the suggestion.'

'Thank you, miss.' He had thanked her because normally if a servant made a personal remark he was severely chastised. His attention was taken to the downs. 'There's a rider coming, a gentleman. It's Mr Woodburne.'

'He must have heard about the disaster and gone to the mine.' Sarah waited beside John. Her insides were in knots. What would be the news from Carn Croft? She hoped Jeb Greep wasn't among any killed. If he and the others were safe in an air pocket she prayed they would be reached before the oxygen ran out.

'Sarah, what are you doing out here?' Kit said, reining in but not dismounting. He had something vitally important to get on with.

She explained.

'That's very worthy of you.' Kit was thinking fast, he could use this situation for something he had planned today; this would provide a better way. 'Moyle can take you to where you want to go next. He must return to Poltraze now. He'll have duties to attend to. What time would you like him to return? Make it before dark or you'll have Mrs Nankervis worrying about you.'

'Yes, of course.' Kit was right, although she couldn't grasp his emphasis on John Moyle's duties. 'What news from the mine? Has anyone been brought up? Are there any more casualties? You know Jeb Greep, is there any news of him?'

'There's nothing yet about Greep or the men on the same level. Two men who were crushed to death have been brought up, their names Wearn and Kent.'

'Oh no!' Sarah pressed her fists together. 'Poor David. Do you know what he's doing now?'

'He's with Miriam Greep, he's to stay with her. Sarah, I'm going to ride on to Poltraze to inform Mrs Nankervis. I'm sure she'll want to know about this. I'll tell her you'll be fetched back later.'

Numb and cold, Sarah watched for a moment as Kit rode

off at a canter. More than ever she experienced the difference of being on the other side of the tragedy.

'Where would you like to go, Miss Sarah?' John asked
softly.

'Oh, I'll go back to the Greeps' place and tell Mrs Endean
what's happened. We'll take the things we've left here.
Miriam Greep will take care of David for the time being.'

'I'm sorry for the village and sorry for you, miss.'

'Thank you, John.'

Kit was drinking tea with Tara and the Nankervis brothers
in the winter parlour.

'Sarah will know the best way for the estate to help all
those poor people.' Tara sighed over the tragedy at the mine.
'Last week a miner died of lung congestion; a family man
of only five and thirty years. The sexton will have a busy
time digging more graves.'

Joshua turned to Michael. Talk of something worthy might
help settle his nerves – if the next few hours went wrong,
God help him and the others here too. 'Yes, we should do
something for these poor unfortunates, don't you agree,
brother?'

'Yes, indeed.' Michael pounced on the suggestion, glad
for a moment for the distraction. 'I'll set something up.'

'A disaster fund is what is needed, for now and future
occasions,' Tara said quickly, taking advantage of Joshua's
generosity. He had changed considerably since his pneumonia, as if his near death had given him a different perspective on life. He valued people more than plants now. He was
still frail, reed-thin and pale like dust on alabaster. Hopefully
when he was stronger he'd take charge of his land and properties and not leave everything to Michael. He was in a very
peculiar mood today, fidgeting impatiently one moment, still
and contemplative the next, all the while glancing at the
clock as if wishing the time away. Michael was acting
strangely too. He had grown pompous of late but today he
was vague and edgy, pulling at his hair, his collar and cuffs.
'It will help people to rebuild their lives. Thank you, Joshua,
and you too, Michael.'

Kit was tense and he was studying the brothers, but it did

not stop him running his eyes over Tara. At every brief eye contact with her he had been rewarded with a smile. She was more than warming to him, he was sure. He knew a woman's body language, the meaning behind her looks. He wished this day was over and he was alone with her, not in mere lustful anticipation – that would be totally out of the question after what was about to happen. He just wanted to be with Tara, to gaze at her without end, it would be a gift most wonderful.

He addressed Joshua. 'You're looking quite well today, if I may say so, Mr Nankervis.'

'Forgive me, Mr Woodburne, but I don't see how you can say that,' Tara said.

'I am feeling a little better every day, Mr Woodburne.' Joshua frowned at Tara and turned wide smiles on Kit. He had taken to Kit from the first, and he was the one who had come up with the best plan to put an end his misery.

'But you do seem rather on edge, brother,' Michael put in. 'Are you sure nothing is troubling you?'

Tara glanced at her husband. Of course he had troubles, namely how to keep out of the malicious clutches of Laketon Kivell. Thank heavens the brute was almost totally absorbed with the gardens nowadays, but Joshua clung to her presence and invaded her days. It was even worse now Michael had taken a belatedly guilty interest in him, almost becoming his shadow. Michael had slipped away to Truro one day and quietly married Miss Phillipps. It obviously wasn't a love match but he should be spending his time with his bride. She envied Sarah's freedom to come and go with less restriction. She wished she was with her, Sarah was all alone and anxious for her friends.

'Nothing is wrong, I assure you,' Joshua said, glad that all eyes were on him sympathetically. 'However, I am feeling terribly cooped up. It's been ages since I've taken a breath of fresh air. I'd like to take a short wander about the grounds.'

'Are you sure that's wise? You might take a chill,' Michael cautioned; playing a part.

'I think it will fare me better than staying fireside-bound. I shall end up getting stiff and lazy.' Joshua rose and stretched up his arms. Even this exertion made his limbs tremble.

'You're clearly not well enough for a walk, Joshua,' Tara said. There was another reason the notion wasn't wise: he might encounter Kivell. 'Why not sit in the conservatory? It's the next best thing.' *And take Michael with you.* She would appreciate being left alone with Kit. Another thing that wasn't wise but she didn't care. There was an attraction between them; once given the chance to explore it they would inevitably become lovers, an affair might not last and it might break her heart because her feelings for him were very strong, but she didn't have the will to deny herself.

'I really want to go outside,' Joshua stressed. He would not be put off, time had run out for him here and he welcomed it. 'It's not raining. If I'm well attired it will do me the power of good. I'll ring for Fawcett to have the bath chair prepared. That should satisfy you, Tara.'

'If you are determined then I shall accompany you,' Tara said, it was her duty, and Kit would probably suggest joining them.

'No, no, my dear, I've encroached on your time and space enough. Besides, you should stay here in case Miss Hichens arrives back shortly. She may be somewhat distressed and will have need of you.'

'Then allow me to join you,' Kit offered.

'Wouldn't dream of it, Woodburne. Miss Hichens is close to you also, she may have need of you too. A footman will be quite capable to push me and I really would prefer to be alone.' Joshua was impatient now. 'There really is no need for anyone to fuss.'

'Nevertheless,' Michael said, heading for the door, 'I won't have you venturing out alone on your first occasion. Someone should be with you to ensure that you are not exerted. I shall take you and have no argument about it. We'll go to the summer house and you can rest there a while before I bring you back.'

'Oh, if you insist,' Joshua grumbled crossly. 'Don't you dare treat me like a child. I will have my pride in front of the staff.' He halted a moment at the door. 'Goodbye, Tara.'

'Be sure you wrap up well, Joshua. Ask Fawcett to arrange some hot chocolate for when you get back.'

When both brothers were out of the room, Tara felt as if a

great weight had been lifted off her, that there was more air to breathe. 'Would you like some more tea, Mr Woodburne?' She stifled a giggle, it would have been an awful thing to do in light of the tragic event at the Carn Croft Mine, but it seemed such a silly polite question to ask the wholly desirable man she wanted an affair with.

Kit caught her light mood. 'I'd rather have something stronger but it would mean you ringing for that pompous butler, so tea will do.'

Tara poured from the silver teapot. 'Remind me please of the time Moyle is to return for Sarah.'

'It will be in about half an hour. She asked him to meet her on the outskirts of the village so as not to disturb the peace, although I suspect the peace will be broken there by much weeping and wailing.' Kit put the silly little teacup down and smiled into her eyes. 'Tara, I would like to make a contribution towards the fund you are to set up.'

'Thank you, Mr Woodburne. It will be very much appreciated.' She made it obvious she invited his interest with a long gaze. 'What made you go to the mine?'

'I confess that at first I was merely curious. Having spent the first part of my life shut in a dark old house, then away at school, and then leading a rather nocturnal life, I have seen little of the real world. Of course, I've seen the poor conditions of the working man, woman and child before in various circumstances, but just taken it all for granted. It was a blow to my system to witness the dignity of those people as they waited and hoped and prayed for their men and boys to emerge alive and unhurt. It was humbling to see their suffering and their pain.' It was good sharing his thoughts with her. 'I'm ashamed to admit that I've never considered that the poor love their families in the same way as others. I envied my peers at school for the care from their parents, but I've never thought about a parent loving their child very deeply until I saw how much your little girl means to you. Rosa Grace is a delightful little soul and a credit to you, Mrs . . .' He leaned forward. 'May I call you Tara?'

'There is no reason why you should not, Kit. Do you know, this is going to prove such a dreadful day that I'd like to go up to see Rosa Grace, to reassure myself she is happy and well. Would you like to come with me?'

'I would, Tara, very much.'

'Are you sure you want to go through with this?' Michael gulped at the enormity of the question. He was shaking with fear at what he was about to help Joshua do, glancing all around, terrified he would be seen.

'I have no doubts at all. It's the only way out. I've told you so every day since we first discussed it.' Joshua was calm as he got out of the bath chair at the summer house. 'Don't worry. We put up a convincing show just now.'

'But it's so drastic, so final, Joshua. There will be no going back.'

'I thank God for that, and I'm sure He will understand.' For the first time ever Joshua took his brother in a tight hug. 'Thank you for this. I'm sorry to leave you with an even harder task, of getting rid of Laketon, but I'm sure Woodburne will do what's necessary. Listen to him, Michael. He seems just the sort of fearless chap able to carry it through. Take care of Tara. I wish you many, many happy years as the new squire.'

For the first time also Michael felt an emotional link with his brother. He was in tears. 'But, Joshua!' How could he find the strength to do this thing? It was a terrible crime in the eyes of the law and God.

'You can't let me down now. I'm sure I will be fine wherever I end up.'

The men completed a tearful goodbye.

A short time later Michael was wet up to the chest and shivering behind the boathouse as he changed into an identical suit of clothes. The plan had gone well so far, he was sure they hadn't been seen, but he was still in the throes of horror at having to weigh the body, which must not be discovered for some time, down in the pool. When an hour had passed since he and Joshua had left the house he was back inside, red in the face but managing to keep his tremors under control. 'Fawcett, is Mrs Nankervis still in the winter parlour?'

'Actually she's just come down from the nursery, sir.'

Fawcett engaged in a meaningful pause. 'Mr Woodburne had accompanied her. Miss Hichens has just returned.'

Michael glared at him. Now he was the squire this obnoxious individual would soon be put out to grass. He went along to the winter parlour. 'Don't be alarmed, Tara. I need you to come and search the gardens with me. Joshua has given me the slip. He sent me outside the summer house saying he needed to be alone. When I went back in, the bath chair was empty. I'm sure he's just sitting somewhere quietly. I searched but didn't spot him. I don't want to embarrass him by starting up a hue and cry but it really is time he came inside.'

'I agree,' Tara said, glancing at Sarah, who was huddled grimly by the fireside, after reporting there was no more news from the mine. 'It's tiresome of Joshua to do something like this now, but I really don't want to leave Sarah.'

'I'll go,' Kit offered. It was the last part of the plan he had suggested to the brothers, to delay a thorough search, to keep Laketon in ignorance for as long as possible. 'I'm sure the squire can't be far away.'

Tara joined Sarah, keeping an understanding silence. As she held Sarah's hand, watching the twisting red and orange flames in the hearth, her thoughts kept drifting to Kit. He was so kind and helpful. What would they do without him? What would she do without him? It was a thought too dreadful to dwell on.

Eighteen

'Tell me again exactly what you saw,' Laketon ordered Hankins, while treading an agitated path up and down his office.

The footman noisily cleared his throat, fearing the other man might lash out at him. Laketon Kivell had been in a beastly mood ever since he'd realized the squire was missing. 'Like I said before, sir, Mr Fawcett told me to fetch the bath chair and the master's and Mr Michael's hats and coats.'

'Yes, yes, what happened after that, you fool! When they were out in the grounds? You managed to slip upstairs and you saw them from a window, and . . . ?'

'Well, I saw the two gentlemen heading in the direction of the summer house. About an hour later I managed to get back to the window and I saw Mr Michael on his own. He was looking all around and was calling out through his hands – must have been to the squire.

'After Mr Michael and Mr Woodburne failed to find the squire the groundsmen were called out to search through the woods, and the servants were ordered to search the house from top to bottom. You know the rest, Mr Kivell. Since going out for an airing the squire seems to have simply disappeared. It's days now, don't look like the squire's ever coming back. Or . . . ?'

'Or what, God damn you?' Laketon was boiling in ever-increasing fury.

'Well, the mistress is afraid he's been abducted.' Hankins was as taut as a spring, ready to flee for his life if need be.

'Abducted? Highly unlikely. He hasn't been seen out for weeks, there was no way for such plans to be made.' Thundering to his desk, Laketon smashed a fist down on it. He winced in pain and the pain turned his rage into near madness. 'Damn his eyes! How dare he do this to me?'

Hankins blinked and backed away. 'M-may I go now, sir?'

'Yes, get out! If you hear even the slightest thing, report back to me at once.'

Without waiting to see if he would be rewarded with a coin, Hankins flew out of the door as if his heels were burning.

Laketon went behind the desk and sat down, leaning his elbows on the hard wood and putting his mouth against his interlocked fingers. 'You're playing a game with me, Joshua.' His voice was at its deadliest. 'You were pretending to be weaker than you were. Don't think for a minute that you can run away from me. I'll find you and when I do you'll curse the day you were born.'

'What do you think happened to the squire, Kit?' Tempest asked, as they strolled in her garden.

'I've no idea, Grandmama. It's possible he knew of some hidey-hole in the gardens and stayed there for a while until he could get away,' Kit shrugged. 'But I don't know how he would fare. He took no money, food or spare clothes with him. His town house in Truro and all his other properties, including any empty and derelict, have all been thoroughly investigated but there's no sign of him. He could have been abducted, of course. The authorities and Mrs Nankervis are expecting a ransom note at any moment.'

'That's awful. Kit, I've noticed you speak highly of the lady. Would it suit you if the squire doesn't come back? If one day it's apparent he's dead?'

'You know me well, Grandmama. I won't deny that I'm in love with Tara Nankervis and that I'd like to make her mine. I didn't think it would happen to me, it just did. I suppose it's the only way it happens.' It was strange and wonderful, like walking on air, floating on water. Everything had more definition. He saw purpose of nature, flowers and trees and the sky and stars, and things of beauty, sculptures, paintings and fountains, as if he had never seen them before. 'I don't wish ill fortune on the squire but I can't help hoping that one day, somehow . . .'

Tempest thought this through. 'I have the feeling that you will win the lady, Kit.'

'Thank you for the encouragement.' Not that he needed it. It was only the grimness of the present situation that was keeping him and Tara out of each other's arms.

'How's Laketon taking it? I'm presuming there will be an effort to dismiss him?'

'There will be, I am told, in due time.'

'Now is the best time, surely, before the whereabouts of the squire are discovered.'

'It will happen all in good time.' Kit changed the conversation. 'Sarah sends her apologies for not visiting you lately. She's mastering the art of riding so she can get about more easily. She's been much occupied handing out the estate emergency fund and she calls regularly on some of the villagers.'

'The mass funeral must have been a very sad occasion. Seven dead; death stalks among us all the time.'

Kit thought about the time not long ago when he had wished himself dead and his grandmother, so dear to him now, punished and dead. He stooped to kiss her cheek. 'I'm glad I came here to Burnt Oak, and that I've got to know you.'

'If you're telling me that you love me, Kit –' she reached up and stroked his face – 'let me say that I love you too.'

'No one has said that to me before.' He was filled with wonder. *Please let Tara say the same words to me soon.*

Titus Kivell. The name inscribed into the cold stone. Such a desolate memorial, for not even lichens or mosses had encroached on its simple arched shape. 'My son,' Tempest whispered. Kit had not long left for Poltraze and from that moment she had got the intense feeling she must come here. She loved Kit so much, had something called her here to find some love for his father? She tried to evoke feelings for Titus, recalling him as a helpless baby, a boy running about; she looked for special moments, a sweet smile, a funny saying. Perhaps there had been one or two but she couldn't recall them, but this might be her fault and not Titus's. 'I'm sorry, son. I should have been a better mother to you. You might have turned out exactly the same, but it doesn't excuse my neglect of you.'

She laid a posy of snowdrops on the long grass covering the mound then stood back. 'Thank you for giving me lots of lovely grandchildren, including Kit, who will be a comfort to me now I'll never see Sol again. Sol says I could visit him in California but I'm not up to all the travel. I hope you can rest in some sort of peace, Titus.'

Tempest shivered. A cruel east wind was dashing heavy grey clouds across the sky. It was time to go in to her log fire. Turning for the house she was brought to a rigid halt.

Tabbie Sawle was there in her peculiar black garb. Her beady eyes stabbed into Tempest's and she pointed away towards a double grave. It was where Laketon's parents were buried. Tempest knew at once the meaning of the warning. Those that she and Tabbie loved were in danger from the abominable Laketon.

'I understand,' Tempest said clearly.

With a nod Tabbie disappeared.

For Tabbie to appear from the grave meant the danger was imminent and deadly. Tempest couldn't allow the fiend to hurt Kit or Sarah. She knew what she had to do, something she should have done a long time ago.

'You sit a pony very well, Miss Sarah,' John said, his voice ringing with admiration.

'I don't know about that but each time I'm getting more confident,' she replied. She was on Tara's pony, riding side-saddle, as they trotted in Poltraze parkland. 'I'm sorry if training me is taking you away from your duties, John.'

'Teaching people to ride and exercising the horses are part of my duties. Think you're ready to canter?'

'Yes, I've been waiting to go faster.'

'Just press in with your foot and use the reins, the pony will know what to do.'

The sense of freedom as the trees and the countryside seemed to rush by was exhilarating. They left the parkland behind and passed through fields and meadows. Sarah relished the sensations of the wind and the blood pinking her cheeks. She found herself laughing and urging the pony to go faster and faster.

'Miss Sarah, slow down! It's dangerous! Sarah! Sarah!'

She was aware of John shouting to her but his urgent message did not register in her mind. She had tasted a feeling of independence and now she was steeped in her own sovereignty. Nothing could stop her. She was free and invincible. Never had her mind been so clear and complete. She wanted to ride forever and never stop, any minute now the pony would sprout wings and they would be flying. She was a different being now, no longer reliant on the usual rules of nature. It must be like this when you went up to heaven.

The pony was suddenly jerking its head and being slowed down. John had grasped the reins and after several hundred yards he brought both ponies to a halt. Sarah was now staring into his shocked face. Then there was the realization that in her foolhardiness she had nearly killed herself.

'I'm sorry!' Tears welled up in her eyes. Releasing the reins she was gripping so tightly her hands were in pain, she slid down to the ground. She started to run. As fast as she could she was running and running, away from her embarrassment and stupidity, away from life. Her hat which had been half hanging off fell to the ground and the pins in her hair started to fall out and tresses of hair flew out behind her.

'Sarah, come back! You'll fall! You'll hurt yourself! Sarah, wait!'

John was the last person she wanted to face now. He was honest and trustworthy and she was utterly ashamed of herself. She heard hoof beats. He was coming after her. 'No! No! Go away!'

He reached her quickly, dismounting before his pony stopped, and he was running beside her. 'Sarah, stop. Whatever's the matter, it's all right. I'll make it all right.'

She wouldn't stop. He took her round the waist and hauled her off her feet. 'Let me go, John!' She pushed against him. She was weeping, unable to look him in the face.

She couldn't match John's might. She was gathered in against his body, and then she needed his strength and allowed him to cradle her. He was soothing her and stroking her hair. 'It's all right, Sarah. Tell me what's wrong.'

She couldn't stop crying and she couldn't speak. She pulled her arms out from against John's chest and hung on to him for comfort.

'I won't let anything hurt you, Sarah,' he said softly.

It reminded her of Jowan's promise. He had said the very same thing. Why were people so good to her? She didn't deserve it. She stopped snivelling and pulled away, putting her back to John. She was standing in the middle of a wintry field, hating herself. 'It's not that,' she said in a watery voice, brushing away the wetness on her face. 'I'm such a terrible person.'

He came round to face her. 'Sarah, how do you make that out? Think of all you've just done for the village. And you've been a great support to Mrs Nankervis since the squire went missing. She cheered up a lot, you know, when you came to live in the house. All the servants said so.'

'But I'm so selfish! Families in Meryen have lost their loved ones, others have badly hurt men to nurse and will lose their income for ages or for good, and there was me riding a fine pony and going wild and laughing my head off.' She brought her hands up to her fiery face and squeezed hard.

John pulled her hands away and kept them in his own. 'Don't do that, Sarah. Don't hurt yourself. Please don't be such a hard taskmaster on yourself. It's not a wicked thing to find a little enjoyment for a while. You're a good and wonderful woman. Many people admire you. I certainly do and I consider myself a good judge of character. You've forgotten the emergency fund is helping those who're suffering and you played a big part in that.'

All she could do was gaze at him. He meant what he'd said. There was nothing superficial or cunning about John Moyle, he was an admirable man.

He released her hands and touched the tangle of her hair. Then he smiled, such a caring smile, a handsome smile. 'Do you want to go back?'

'No, we were going to the Greeps to see how Jeb's broken leg is healing. I don't want to let him down. I . . .'

'Yes?'

Again she couldn't speak. Instead she stepped up to him. He encircled her in his arms and she leaned into him. After all these years of spurning the idea of a man's physical comfort she was happy to receive it from John.

* * *

Some time later she met up with him as he waited for her at the back of the Greep home. 'Jeb's still in a lot of pain but he's stoical about it, as I'd expected. He's so grateful to be alive. He says he had this strong feeling something was about to happen and he shouted a warning to others to get back or more would've died. Miriam's worried about young David Kent. He's still too shocked to go back to work. He hasn't said a word since seeing his father's body. He went out some time ago and she hasn't seen hide nor hair of him since. I'll walk through the village and see if I can find him. I want to call at Chy-Henver anyway.' All the time she spoke she met John's eyes, noting the more than friendly interest he had for her, and she was pleased to see it. For so long she had thought it would be a stupid, dreadful thing to be attracted to a man again, yet it wasn't so with John.

Tiny stabs of caution crawled about in her stomach. It would be the height of foolishness to get involved with him, and that stage was no more than a breath away. There was only the thinnest of lines to cross before either of them would reach out for the other and they would join in an eager passionate kiss. The raw desire and need of it hung in the air between them.

It was John who looked away, as if remembering his place. 'Shall I look about here in case the boy hasn't gone far?'

'Yes, John, I won't be gone long.' Just a quick hello to Jowan, Rachel and Thad then she would hurry back to John and enjoy the ride back to the big house with him alone.

John cast his eye over the back garden and smallholding for the missing boy. David Kent was receiving a small weekly sum from the emergency fund for the loss of his father. He had something to tide him over until he recovered, a hard thing to do when all alone in the world. Everything seemed in order and the animals and hens were going about their usual routine. Others in the village had rallied round the families of the mine casualties in practical ways. Life was hard for the poor of Meryen but at least there was the comfort of belonging to a close-knit community.

There was a movement near the shed. Just in sight around its far corner was a small boy – David Kent. John walked quietly his way. David saw him and jerked his tousled dusty-brown head away. John waited, and as David didn't run off he guessed he didn't really want to be left alone.

Fiddling casually with his tobacco pouch, leaning his back against the cold stone, he crossed his feet. 'I'm sorry about your father, David.'

The boy made no response. Ghastly pale and undersized, he kept his head down.

'I never knew mine, or my mother for that matter. I know exactly how you're feeling. I know what it's like to have no one and for your home to be no longer your home.' A miner and his family from Twelveheads had moved into the Kent cottage.

David shuffled his feet, an irritable sign, yet John could tell he wanted to hear more.

'Mrs Greep is doing a good job looking after you, I can see that. You're all scrubbed up. The Greeps are good people, aren't they?'

David nodded mournfully.

'Don't worry. I'm sure they or someone else will give you a permanent home.'

David shrugged then held out his small trembling paws in a pleading manner.

'People are good round here,' John persisted. 'No one will let you go homeless. You won't end up in the workhouse.'

There was a jolt in the boy's spare frame and his sharp features filled up with panic. 'B-but—'

'But what, David?' John put a firm hand on his scrawny shoulder. Terror had forced out the boy's voice but it was a good thing to get him talking.

Between terrific sobs, David squealed, 'I heard someone say that Mrs Greep's got enough to do with Mr Greep being laid up and the two young 'uns to care for. That it's too much for her to have me to worry about as well.'

John sighed in anger. There were always those who even in tragic situations used poisonous tongues; in this case they were probably jealous of the boy receiving money from the estate. 'Listen to me, David. My name's John Moyle and I am the head groom up at the big house. I swear to you that you'll not end up in the workhouse or without a proper roof over your head, even if I have to see to it myself. I always stand by my word. Now stop your crying, you're a man now, you don't want Mrs Greep to see your face all red and puffy. Here, do you want to shake on my promise?'

With rapid swipes at his eyes and runny nose, David pulled himself up straight and gave his hand. 'Have you got a family?'

'No, there's only me. I've got a room in the stable block.'

After a moment, David said, 'Things can get better, can't they? Miss Sarah used to work at the mine, now she's living fine and she's like a lady.'

'Not like a lady, David, she *is* a lady,' John corrected him. 'Don't matter where your birth was, it's the heart inside you that makes you good and noble.' He glanced out into the road. How much longer would it be before Sarah came back?

Nineteen

'I still can't believe how different David was after you'd talked to him, John,' Sarah chattered as they journeyed back at a comfortable trot. 'Whatever you said totally reassured him. He says he doesn't want to go back to the mine, not after his father was killed there. Where else could he go, do you think? I'd ask Jowan Kivell to take him on as an apprentice but the Kivells only like to give work to their own kin. I know, I'll ask Kit Woodburne. He'll need a full staff soon for his new house. David could be taken on as a stable boy or gardener's boy. That would be the perfect solution.'

John simply gazed across at her and smiled.

She smiled back. 'What's so amusing?'

'Nothing, I like seeing you in fighting spirit. Your eyes gleam like sunlight on a stream.'

'They do? I didn't take you as one for romantic talk, John Moyle!' She lifted her eyelashes. She was flirting with him, she had never done this kind of thing before and it made her feel her youth and realize what she had stupidly missed out on.

'Oh, I know a phrase or two.' He leaned his head to the side, his eyes glinting and rooted to hers.

On a thought Sarah pulled up her mount. 'Will you be going with us when Mrs Nankervis and I go to stay in Truro? She says she'll wait another week and if the squire doesn't turn up by then we'll leave Poltraze for an indefinite period.'

John eased his pony round so he was facing her and close. 'If I'm not ordered to go to Truro I could easily wangle it. Is that what you want, Sarah? Would you miss me if I wasn't there?'

What was she doing? She had as good as declared to John she didn't want to be without him. A cold panic like a waterfall turned on inside her. How could she be so stupid? She wasn't tied nowadays, she was her own person, and yet here she was encouraging a man to form something deep with her. She trusted John but she knew little about him. 'Can I ask you something?'

'Anything you like. I'm not married and I have no woman in my life at the moment, if that's what you're wondering.'

That at least was a relief. 'Do you want a wife and family one day?'

'If it happens, fine, if not it's also fine,' he shrugged, not wanting to sound too eager. He certainly wouldn't mind having a wife. In fact he wanted Sarah very much, and knowing how independent she was he would take her on her terms. Her question meant she was interested in him. He had to be wise about how fast he could progress with her.

His easygoing manner left her disappointed. She had asked Tara's maid Elvira Dunn a little about the servants simply to edge round to John, and she had learned he was something of a loner and a free agent. She had made a foolish mistake to have voiced her thoughts about him in regard to the move to Truro. He was backing off. She urged her pony forward. 'I must get back. I've been out for far too long.'

John went with her. 'What do you want to do with your life, Sarah? Stay as you are? Do you hope to marry again and have a family?'

'I can't have children! It's why my husband beat me and turned me out, and later intended to kill me,' she blurted out fiercely. The pain of never being able to conceive and give life to a baby of her own hit her ferociously. She had thought she'd never really mind about it but now she felt the burning loss of being barren, and the humiliation. 'So, no, I'm not hoping to marry again. Who would have me? I'm not worthy.'

'I'm sorry I've upset you,' John said, having to increase his pony's speed to keep up with her. 'Wait, Sarah, let's talk about this. Listen to me, just because you can't carry children in your body doesn't mean you can't bring up a family. There's many an orphan in this harsh world desperate for love and a good home. Please, Sarah, stop your pony or I'll do it for you.' In the end he pulled the reins out of her hands and again that day brought both mounts to a halt.

Sarah stared down at the ground, her head twisted away, too hurt and ashamed to face him.

'I said just now that it's fine if I never have a family, but I would like to have a woman in my life. You asked who would want you, Sarah. I do. I want you, Sarah, exactly how you are, here in Meryen or elsewhere. You're in better circumstances than me. The real question is do you want me?'

She looked him full in the face and saw he was absolutely sincere. Then she looked into her own heart and saw that his words meant everything to her. She didn't know how all this would work out but she wasn't afraid to give it a try. She threw out her arms to him and he leaned over and pulled her onto his pony. Their lips searched for the other's and joined in a kiss of ardent concentrated passion. In the past she had offered herself as sacrifice, receiving back only abuse. Now she knew what it was like to be held and cherished by a man who would give her what she wanted and deserved. John had pledged himself in a loving commitment.

'I'd have thought Sarah would have been back by now.' Tara went anxiously to the drawing-room window. There was no sign of her friend and the groom trotting up the carriageway. 'We've both had correspondence from a mutual friend today, all the way from America. Sarah's letter was addressed to care of Tabbie Sawle but the post boy had the forethought to deliver it here.'

'She's really taken to riding,' Kit said, joining her. If all went well in the next hour or so he would soon be in a position to advance their relationship. Michael Nankervis would have business with Laketon Kivell in the next couple of days and it would take a lot of nerve for him to go through with it. Dismissing Kivell, Kit was sure, would prove unsuccessful. His vindictive distant cousin would not rest until he'd achieved revenge for the rejection and that mustn't be allowed to happen. One of his half-brother's ships was about to be moored at Falmouth. Kivell would be put on that ship, Kit would see to it himself. Then the brute who had terrorized Poltraze for so many years would end up in a watery grave. He deserved it, he was a dangerous sadist, and Kit had no compunction about ridding the world of his evil presence.

At irregular moments Kivell had asked to be received to enquire if there was news of the squire. It was thought best to allow him a short interview each time. His mood was always unreadable. But the polite coldness about the man was chilling. Always he was told that there were no clues to the mystery.

Kivell would shake his head. 'It's all so very strange. I don't understand it,' was his stock answer, then, 'I shall keep watch for him.'

And you are being watched, Kivell, Kit thought to himself. It was awful that Tara should suffer the outrage of the loathsome wretch's presence, and that Kivell couldn't simply be thrown out on the spot.

Michael added himself to their company. Kit sighed out his impatience. He was never able to get Tara alone for long. 'Is there something going on out there?' Michael barked. The tension of the last few days was unnerving him. Today it was even worse. He exchanged a secret glance with Kit. Today was *the day.*

'I'm waiting for Sarah to arrive home. She's been out rather a long time,' Tara explained.

'She enjoys going about her saintly acts,' Michael said drily. 'And you too, Tara. I hope you've not promised too much to those villagers, they'll get greedy. I'm glad to say I can trust my wife not to be a spendthrift.'

Tara snapped a maddened look at him. 'I keep to a fair budget. I'm pleased you find Adeline eminently suitable for you.'

Kit gazed down at Tara. She did not belong here. She should not have to put up with buffoons and villains. She should know laughter and excitement and adventure and the attentions of an adoring lover. It struck him that he had never known these things and he longed to share them with Tara.

She noticed his empathy and wanted to reach for his hand. She couldn't have got through these last days if not for Kit. God forgive her, part of her hoped Joshua would not come back, that he was even dead. She wanted to be free, to taste what else life could offer. She would never see her old friend Amy again. One day Sarah might want to leave her and start something new; she seemed to be edging towards being

independent again. Tara was frightened. She needed something permanent and utterly worthwhile. She needed someone
who was dedicated to her. But how could that happen? How
could she be rid of all her troubles? It had been bad enough
not being a proper wife, but if Joshua never turned up she
would be forced to live the rest of her life in limbo, under
the shadow of this damned place.

'What are we doing here, Edmund?' the young kitchen maid
demanded from Hankins, the footman. 'Why have you
brought me to the boathouse? You'll get us into trouble if
we're caught making free in the grounds like this. Mr Kivell
will kill us. Hey, you're not going to try something on me,
are you? I'm not that sort of girl.'

'I wouldn't dream of it, Sally,' Hankins replied, dabbing
at the nervous sweat on his brow. 'I just wanted us to be
somewhere quiet, that's all.'

'Really?' Sally's shiny round face glowed in anticipation.
She had been making eyes at Edmund Hankins for some
time and just lately, he, an austere, reserved individual, who
wasn't too bad-looking, had taken time to pass a few words
with her. It was her afternoon off and she had been delighted
when he'd asked her to take a walk with him. If he wasn't
up to no good, was he about to ask her to be his girl, or
even his wife? Edmund was well thought of by Mr Fawcett,
he had prospects. It hadn't dawned on Sally that he was
taking no interest in her but was looking all about.

Suddenly he grabbed her hand and led her to the side of
the pool. He was shaking like the last leaf on a winter tree.
Sally's heart threw a hopeful leap. This was going to be so
romantic. A kitchen maid was the lowliest of servants and
much put upon by the rest of the staff. How she would enjoy
telling the others about Edmund's romantic proposal, they
would have to show her a little respect then. She dreamed
of Edmund being a butler one day and she the cook in a
more pleasing big house than this one.

It didn't take Hankins long to see what he'd been told to
expect. Even so, the gruesome spectacle of the corpse that
had been kept somewhere secretly in pond water turned his
guts. It was bloated and putrid and tangled in weeds. It took

a mighty act of will to prevent spilling up the contents of his stomach.

Misreading his discomfort Sally took a deep breath and piped up. 'Edmund, does this mean what I think it means?' He was squeezing her hand so tightly, too tightly. 'Ow, you're hurting me.'

'Can you see it? Th-there in the water?' A horrified gasp escaped from the heart of him. He pointed to the water's edge where it was floating, much covered by rushes. 'It's a body. It's the squire. He's in the pool. He's been dead all this time.'

Sally followed his hands then screamed shrilly. 'Oh my God in heaven, it's horrible!'

Hankins was being paid well to play his part in this and promised a swift promotion. He didn't understand why the squire's body couldn't have been retrieved on the day he'd disappeared, when Mr Nankervis had discovered it down there, but he would never question it, thinking it might be for some legal reason. His masters were like demigods to him and had his total loyalty. He would be well set up for the rest of his life and better still his tormentor would soon be kicked off the estate. Nothing, however, could have prepared him for this horrendous sight. Quivering in shock, fighting down the nausea, he somehow managed to get himself and Sally several feet away. 'I'm sorry you had to see that. We must hurry inside and raise the alarm.'

Weak on her feet, Sally was using him for support. 'You'll have to help me in.'

'Come on, then.' He was impatient to get away.

Sally's horror was joined by another concern. 'We can't go in together! I'll lose my reputation.'

'No, you won't, maid. Pick up your feet or we'll never get there.' Hankins dragged her along.

'You mean you'll tell Mr Fawcett and Mrs Nankervis you had no bad intentions towards me, that we're proper sweethearts?'

'Yes, yes, anything. I just want all this to be over.'

Freed from anxiety, Sally was quite satisfied. At least for her the day wasn't going to prove to be a totally bad one.

*   *   *

Fawcett entered the drawing room on inappropriately quick steps and was unusually flushed. Michael jumped up from his chair, aiming a rapid glance at Kit, who was hovering close to Tara.

'What is it?' Tara snapped. Could this lackey get any more disrespectful?

Ignoring her, Fawcett addressed the man who was now his new master. 'Forgive me, sir. Two of the staff, a footman, Hankins, and a kitchen maid, have just run in from the pool and said they stumbled across a body there. They believe it is the squire and he has drowned.'

'What?' Tara brought her hands up to her mouth wide open in horror. 'But it can't be. The pool was searched thoroughly. Michael, you supervised the area.' She appealed to Michael and Kit. 'How could Joshua have turned up there?'

'The pool is very deep in some parts, Tara. Have you any more details, Fawcett?' Michael queried, his voice genuinely shocked, it was a terrible moment. 'Has my brother's body, if indeed it is his, been left unattended?'

'I've taken the liberty of dispatching two men to guard the area, sir,' Fawcett answered in his normal superior tone although he was visibly shaken by the news. 'I'm afraid Hankins recognized the squire's clothes, the ones he was wearing the day he disappeared. He believes the squire has been in the water for some time.'

'I'm so sorry, Tara,' Kit said, wishing he could offer her comfort in a more intimate manner. 'Allow me to be the first to offer my condolences. If I may say,' and Michael's eager eyes were on him, 'it seems the squire may have slipped into the pool and got trapped at the bottom somehow, and remained unseen until now after becoming disentangled.'

'It would seem so. Further examination will tell all the facts.' Michael rose up and down on his toes, getting himself in control. Both he and Joshua had got what they'd wanted. A few formalities, a scoundrel to dispose of, and all would be well. This is my house, he thought, at last, at last. 'Well, we must send for the coroner and the vicar, there are arrangements to be made.'

'But it's so unfair,' Tara gasped. 'Joshua was just getting well again.'

'Quite so,' Michael said. 'Try to stay calm, Tara. It's been a terrible shock for you. Now where is your companion when you need her? I had better go and speak to the two servants.'

'I'll stay with Mrs Nankervis,' Kit said softly. 'Fawcett, bring some tea and the brandy in case it's needed. Order Mrs Nankervis's bed to be turned down, inform her maid she may be required to wait on her mistress.'

'You are very kind, but there's no need, really. I'd rather stay here and wait for Sarah.' Tara was grateful to be left alone with Kit. The various connotations of Joshua's death skimmed through her mind. She wasn't grief-stricken to become a widow but she was dreadfully sorry for Joshua to have met such a terrible end. Pale and stiff, she murmured, 'I can hardly take it in. I will have to go up and tell Rosa Grace that her father is dead.'

'I should wait until you have confirmation and the formalities have been completed,' Kit advised soothingly.

'Yes, of course. It must be Joshua, it couldn't be anyone else. He will have to be buried quickly, tomorrow, and with no lying in state in an open coffin.' She looked up towards the ceiling. 'Things will be different from now on. Michael and his wife and children will move in. I shouldn't say this but I won't be sorry to leave this house for good.'

'I fully understand, Tara.'

'Yes, I suppose you do. You know the truth about Joshua, don't you? He . . . he wasn't Rosa Grace's real father but she is a true Nankervis.' It was important that Kit was aware of the truth.

'I guessed as much. You were never really married in the eyes of God. You had no marriage at all.'

'And you've never thought badly of me?'

'How could I? You have my total admiration, Tara. I could say a lot more but now is not the right time. In a few days—'

'Laketon Kivell!' Tara interrupted. 'What are to do about him?'

'I should imagine Michael will think of something. Please don't worry about a thing, Tara. I am here and I shall stay for as long as you need me. If Michael can't handle the situation then I shall.'

She gazed at him from encouraged eyes. 'I thank God that you came to Meryen, Kit.'

Michael bowled back into the room. Once again he looked at Kit for reassurance. 'I have summoned Laketon Kivell, Tara. It will not be an uplifting occasion but one I think that should be endured.'

Laketon was not pleased to be met by Fawcett and a footman at the house and then ushered into the drawing room without being announced. 'What's happened?' He looked at the stern faces of the men and the disquieted face of the grim woman. 'Why was I dragged away from the hothouses?' He was sure he knew the answer.

'Kivell,' Michael began, swallowing and unable to keep a wobble out of his voice as the other man's snakelike eyes bore into him, 'I am sorry to have to inform you that a short time ago the squire's body was discovered in the grounds.'

'Joshua is dead?' The only emotion Laketon showed was the tightening of one fist. 'Where was he found?'

'He was in the pool. It seems he slipped in and he was caught by weeds at the bottom and was drowned.'

'And suddenly his body became disentangled and floated to the surface,' Laketon said.

It was hard to tell if he was being sarcastic or suspicious as his cold eyes darted between the two men before settling on Michael. 'Who found him?'

'A footman, who had the audacity to take a kitchen maid there for a dalliance,' Michael replied, putting on an aggrieved tone. 'But at least we now know what happened to my poor brother.'

'Do we? And may I ask the name of this footman?' Laketon ground out the question, watching . . .

'That is hardly relevant.' Michael considered he was about to play his trump card, by the suggestion of Kit, but first he presented an expression of mild distaste. 'But as you had a . . . special friendship with the late squire I am prepared to fill you in on the facts. The footman is called Hankins. The appropriate authorities are being informed.'

'And . . . ?' Laketon uttered without civility.

'And what, Kivell?' Michael replied impatiently. He was

scared of the gardener but he had to appear as a disdainful gentleman, indeed as the new squire. 'You should be grateful for this special dispensation to be brought here like this, and that I have deigned to lower myself to acknowledge your illegal association with my brother.'

'Is there not anything else you wish to say to me?'

'Y-yes.' Michael damned himself for faltering. 'I shall probably be considering changes in due course. I shall inform you of how it might affect your position in a few days.'

Laketon narrowed his eyes to slits but he could see those in the room clearly enough. He curled his lips in contempt. These self-righteous so-called superiors were no better than him. Two had an illegitimate child together and the other had condemned himself as a disturbed liar with his own mouth. They were probably expecting him to turn nasty but he would keep them guessing as to what he would do next. They were all on guard against him, and all except the doubly wary Kit Woodburne were nervous of him. He bowed his head. 'I thank you for your kind consideration, sir. I am deeply saddened over Joshua's death and if I may now be allowed to take my leave I'd like to grieve in private. May I see him?'

'I'm afraid that in the circumstances it is out of the question due to— Please,' Michael glanced at Tara, 'I do not want to cause further distress to Mrs Nankervis.'

'I understand.' Bowing again, Laketon took two steps backwards, turned slowly with his head down and left the room.

'Follow me,' Fawcett intoned at his coldest.

Laketon hurled imaginary knives at the butler's stiff back as he was placed centrally in a line with the footman taking up the rear. He was seen out of a small corridor portal.

Rather than return to the hothouses he went round to the front of the house and concealed himself among the shrubbery. So, the time had come for him to leave. The new squire was gloating that he would soon be throwing him out, although he was scared to do so alone, the witless bookworm had got Kit Woodburne to help him; that was obvious. What were they thinking now? Laketon chuckled to himself. In the long lonely days since Joshua's disappearance he had gone through burning rages, near hysteria and a good deal of brandy and wine. Then he had allowed his calculating mind to become as clear as crystal and had put it to work. Why did he care what had happened to Joshua? He didn't love him any more. Joshua had become weak and nervous and a fool. He had not had the capacity or the courage to dupe anyone, to hide away, to go off and start a new life.

The more he had thought about it the more he had become convinced that Joshua was dead. So the news just imparted to him was no surprise. His death was obviously contrived. Joshua had been wilfully murdered and by none other than his brother. Michael Nankervis didn't fool him. His belated brotherly concern for Joshua was a sham. It was not a coincidence that Joshua had disappeared on his first occasion out of the house with Michael, who rarely ventured into the grounds. Michael loved the strange old house and wasn't brought down by its grim atmosphere. He had acquired a pliable wife and no doubt wanted a son and heir, and with Joshua, and Laketon's own grip, removed, then what better than a son who would be heir to Poltraze? Somehow Michael had worked up the guts to drown Joshua in the pool, probably after clubbing him about the head first. Then he had weighted the body down so he would not be discovered until the incriminating wounds on the waterlogged corpse were indistinguishable. No doubt he had kept the search party away from the murder scene. Some time afterward he had made sure the corpse had risen to the surface, just waiting to be discovered. Michael had triumphed. Joshua was an embarrassment to the gentry and no one would pick over his death for long. Michael had everything he'd ever wanted. It was on the cards that Joshua's sickly sweet widow would soon be married to Woodburne and he would have no more responsibility towards her.

Laketon smiled a smile that if seen by another would freeze the blood in their body. Yes, Michael had everything, but not for long. No, it wasn't time for him to leave Poltraze. He was going to kill Michael Nankervis and then he would be the one reigning supreme. With all the others out of the way, Adeline Nankervis would be easy to approach and control. She would have the safety of two stepchildren and perhaps an expected brat of her own to worry about. She would be made to break with the Woodburnes and even her parents in Truro. Poltraze would be all his.

Now he had the pleasure of deciding how to kill Michael Nankervis. Drowning? No, he had taken the life of the elder Nankervis brother, Jeffrey, as a youth, for mocking him that way, and Joshua had met a similar watery end. Poison? No, he'd murdered Michael's vile first wife with poison, for threatening to blackmail him and Joshua for being lovers. In the flames of a fire? No, he had burned the obnoxious old squire and his scheming second wife, Tara's aunt, for getting in his way. Since Joshua's disappearance he had carried a small pistol inside his coat in case there was an attempt to oust him physically from the estate, and he always kept a sharp gardener's knife about him. Shoot him, stab him or slash his throat? Any of those options would do. He would make it look as if the new squire had been robbed and killed by a footpad.

He heard hoof beats. He watched as Sarah Kivell-cum-Hichens was helped to dismount by the groom. As the groom led the ponies away and she dashed up the front steps they turned and looked at each other. Ah, his uncle's little bitch had found romance again. He came out of his hiding place.

Hearing the bushes rustle, Sarah headed back down the steps and peered about. She got the creepy feeling she was being watched. 'Who's there?'

Moments later she was in the drawing room, having refused to take off her outdoor clothes.

Tara rushed to her. 'Sarah, have you heard the terrible news?'

'I've heard nothing . . .' Sarah gasped.

'Then what is it? You're as white as a sheet and you look as if you've just seen a ghost.'

'It was worse than that.' Sarah shuddered. 'I've just seen Laketon Kivell and he was staring at me as if he wanted to kill me, then he smiled. I've never seen such a smile. It was a thousand times worse than the way he looks at you. He seemed insane.'

Twenty

The funeral was over quickly, a necessary decision in view of the foulness of the squire's body, which the double-lined coffin did not entirely keep in. Sarah stood beside Kit at the graveside and with them was Tempest. It was the first time a Kivell had turned out for a Nankervis. To everyone's relief there was no sign of Laketon; he had not been back to the house to enquire about the funeral arrangements. It still did not prevent a feeling of unease that he might suddenly appear and unleash a dreadful surprise.

Such a lot had happened in the last twenty-four hours, Sarah reflected as the mourners filed out of the churchyard. She had found romance and passion with John. She could so easily have made love with him. It was inevitable it would happen the next time they were alone. She was certain John would be caring and masterful and that she would know what tenderness and the sublimity of lovemaking should be like. With the squire dead she and Tara were truly free of Poltraze. After a week of mourning, Tara planned to up sticks and take long-term residence at the Nankervis town house in Truro. Michael had agreed it was better she move away from the estate rather than switch residences with him to Wellspring House, as would be expected. He'd said that when he and Adeline wanted to stay in Truro they would avail themselves of Adeline's family home.

How would this affect her new relationship with John? What did she want for the future? It was too soon to speak of love. The lower position of a groom's wife was not an issue, but only if she fell deeply in love would she ever consider marriage again. If John got a permanent position at Truro she could carry out an affair with him, but the fact that she was in an association with a servant would embarrass Tara. As wonderful as their first kisses had been it was probably better that John stayed at Poltraze and she forgot him.

She had a greater quandary – Amy's letter. *Dear Sarah . . . hope that by the time you receive this you are fully recovered from the dreadful attack . . . pleased Tara has been supporting you. Sol and I and the children, and my mother and sister Hope, really enjoy the wildness and beauty and the challenges of the new life we are starting here. Sarah, we would so like to have you join us. It could be the very thing you need, a fresh start in a new country. We have enclosed the fare for your passage . . . send word and Sol will come to meet you off the ship.*

The invitation had been a welcome distraction after the grim discovery of the squire's body and the fright she'd had from Laketon Kivell. Now she had two different futures to make her up her mind about, Truro with Tara or California with Amy, possibly three futures if she included John after all. Each one held a different appeal. Whatever she did she wouldn't make a quick decision.

The moment she was outside the lychgate and descending the granite steps to the road, Sarah noticed Miriam Greep beckoning to her, clearly anxious. 'What is it? Is Jeb ill or one of the children?'

'We're all fine. It's David, he's taken his few things and run off. I've just tried to talk to John, the groom, but the coachman wouldn't let me get near the carriages.

David listened to him yesterday. I'm hoping he might have an idea where he could have gone.'

'Leave it with me. I'll talk to John,' Sarah promised. 'If we can get away we'll go looking for David.'

John was quieting the horses of Tara and Michael's coach. A striking sight in his livery, he was drawing admiring looks from the village girls. Sarah pressed her way through the retreating gentry to reach his side. She caught his eye and mouthed, 'David's run away.'

'No he hasn't,' he mouthed back, then kept his eyes forward.

Back at the house Sarah was determined to fade into the background, suggesting she take Rosa Grace up to the nursery and keep her company for a while. When the nanny announced it was time the little girl took a nap after her dreadful day, Sarah crept outside to the stable yard. John's response to her statement outside the church could only mean that he knew where David Kent was. David had grown to trust him. It fitted that if he planned to run away he would go to John.

She found John alone in the coach house, where he was cleaning down the small carriage she had travelled in. 'Hello. Where's David?'

'That was straight to the point,' he smiled, dropping the chamois leather. 'David sneaked in here early this morning while I was getting this ready to be pulled out. I had very little time to talk to him and when I bade him to go back to the Greeps he swore he'd run off for good if I didn't let him stay.'

'Where he is now?' She liked the searching way John was gazing at her; she couldn't deny it was good to be in his company, but the matter of David was a serious one.

'Up in the hay loft where I first put him. I've managed to take him something to eat and drink. Don't worry, Sarah, he's fine for now.'

'I'm sure he is. David came to you because he considers you a friend, but what now? He can't sleep in your quarters with the other grooms and stable boys.'

'I promised him in the Greeps' back garden I wouldn't let him be homeless or go to the workhouse. I'm sure I can talk him into returning to the Greeps for a few days until I can find him a job here. I'll take him under my wing. Make sure he gets off to a good start.'

'That's very noble of you, John. Why are you willing to take David on? The new squire will expect you to be responsible for him.'

'He reminds me of myself. I want the boy to have a chance,' John emphasized. 'I like him.'

'You're a good man,' she smiled, meeting his lingering looks. He was leaning ever more towards her and she was gradually moving in on him. 'Have you seen anything of Laketon Kivell?'

'That devil. No, reckon he's keeping his head low. He

knows he'll soon be out on his ear – well, if anyone can get him to go, that is. He's not a man to be crossed.'

'Whatever you do, don't go near him, John.'

'Has he threatened you?' John's strong face darkened with concern.

'No. I just don't want anything to ruin . . . to ruin things for us.' There, the words were out of her mouth, they had just run off her tongue. John meant a lot to her and as if her inner self wanted to confirm it her hand reached up to his face.

'Sarah, darling – ' he kissed her hand – 'in a while I'll send David safely on his way. Will you come back here tonight? Please? I'll be waiting for you.'

'I will, as soon as the house is settled. I won't let you down, John.'

Tempest chose to sit in a quiet corner in Poltraze's drawing room during the wake. She had not been concerned about how the influential men and ladies would treat her, but she found herself the focus of a lot of attention. People approached regularly and engaged her in polite and probing conversation.

'They find you fascinating, Grandmama,' Kit said proudly. 'I gather that much has been said but little has been seen of you over the years.'

'Mainly, I'm sure, because they haven't met someone who has got away with murder.' Tempest sipped her sherry. Female eyes were on Kit voraciously. His origins were not of the highest order but his wealth and looks made him an excellent prospect as a husband or lover. But Kit did not see past Tara and she was more than drawn to him. Tempest saw their future clearly. After a respectable time to allow for mourning, Kit would take Tara as his bride to his new house. Nothing could be better, and all would be well, she would make it so. She had been to Paradise Cottage to carry out her deadly intention but men were there keeping watch on Laketon. He was not there now: at this very moment, unknown to everyone but her, he was skulking somewhere inside Poltraze itself. She sensed it with every strand of her being. If she told Kit he'd search the house and it would put him in terrible danger.

She wouldn't take that risk, but another risk she would take and only by herself, later today.

At her trap, Tempest looked up at the upper regions of the old house. The west wing seemed to have a heavy dark shadow over it. Laketon was up there, in the new master suite he had shared with the dead squire. She must make her move before he made his.

Laketon sniggered as his distant cousin drove his great-aunt home in her trap. Thought they were in with the gentry, did they? They'd never be really accepted. He'd had enough of spying out the guests' movements. He lay down on the bed with his boots on, feeling for the weapons on him, a pistol, two knives and a length of cord, his precaution against sudden attack, weapons to kill. Michael Nankervis wanted him out but he would be the next one to die. He pulled the pistol from his waistband – hard steel with an ebony butt. It had been Joshua's, one of a pair, and his brother had its twin. No doubt Michael now had his gun with him; very useful to Laketon. He'd shoot Michael and switch the guns, make it look as if he had accidentally killed himself. The servants knew their master was jumpy and was keeping close to Kit Woodburne for protection. Once alone he would be even more nervous; understand-able for him to whip out his gun during some sort of fright, trip over and tragically shoot himself up through the chin. Life would progress, and when he felt the time was ripe he would pursue his hold over this property again via the pale-faced Adeline. He would take Poltraze back, by all that was savage and unholy he would, or he would burn it down to the ground.

The idiots in the house thought he was holed up in Paradise Cottage but he had slipped past the other idiots stationed there to keep watch on him. He had taken his personal things and left a letter of resignation. It would seem he had gone for good. He grinned at the opulent drapes above his head, his eyes showing the madness that had taken him over. He would use this bed again, but rather than keep to one lover he would entertain a string of them. He would have every-thing. If only Joshua could see it all.

*　　*　　*

After dark, Kit, Michael and four brawny sailors from a vessel owned by the Howarth Shipping Line surrounded Paradise Cottage, bent cautiously and ready to spring into action.

'There's no lantern lit,' Michael whispered fearfully, near the front door. 'Do you think he's in there?'

'Where else would he be? For his own reason he's keeping out of the way,' Kit replied. 'It's likely he's expecting a visit like this, we must be careful, keep ourselves low. He may have set a trap at the doors. I've ordered the men to break through the back door then to stand back in case they're fired on. We'll do the same here.' His mind travelled to Tara. It would be so good when he got back off the ship and would be able to tell her she need no longer live in fear of his villainous kinsman. Pray God, no one but Laketon got hurt in the process. On his signal, the call of an owl, the assault on the cottage began.

Sarah stole from the house, climbing out of a window of a little-used back room. She reached the stable block quickly, her slippers making no sound on the cobbles. She took no lantern – the moon provided the right sort of light for the meeting she was involved in.

The coach house was nearby. Once she was inside the door, John pulled her into his arms. He took her breath away in a hungry kiss. She kissed him back then pulled her lips away. She could make out his strong outline in the scrap of moonlight filtering in through a high window. 'What if I had been someone else?'

'I could never mistake anyone for you, darling Sarah,' he murmured, threading kisses down her neck. 'I saw David off to the village before darkness fell. We've no one to think of except ourselves. We won't be disturbed. No one ever comes here at night. It's believed to be haunted.'

Sarah looked over her shoulder. The atmosphere in the house was particularly heavy and disturbing tonight, as if something even more sinister than its ghosts was there. Had that horrible sense of presence followed her here? No. There was only John and herself and perhaps a harmless mouse or two.

John pulled her face back to him. Their lips met again in

a powerful kiss that went on and on. He held her face, he stroked her arms. They got to know each other. He squeezed her waist and pulled her in to him tighter and tighter. She gripped his hair, ran her hands along his broad shoulders and down his back. His lips travelled down from her throat, down and down, and she encouraged him to carry on the tantalizing journey. Their breath was coming fast, their hearts were beating the same urgent tune and their lower regions ignited into fire, growing hotter and hotter.

'I want you, Sarah,' he breathed huskily against her ear, nuzzling her there. 'To lie with you will mean everything to me. I've made a comfortable place, if it's what you want. '

'It is what I want, John.' Sarah slid her lips across his chin. 'Take me there.'

He led her past the coach and smaller carriages to the back wall, where he had laid down straw and blankets. The moonlight reached the very spot, turning it into a place of enchantment. Sarah was totally aware of John, as if she had known him for ever. She knew his wonderful smell, the movements of his limbs, the turn of his head, the glitter in his eyes, his smile and the soft and the frantic demand of his lips. It was the most fantastic thing to feel his lips on her, to have a man bestow love on her as a devoted mate, tender and loving and full of giving. She wanted John and she wanted to give all of herself to him.

His heavy breathing of desire filled her with a burning need for him, but he was waiting for her and this meant so much to her, to have a man put her feelings first. She let her shawl fall off her shoulders then took a firm hold of his hands.

'This means more to me than a secret meeting, Sarah. I care for you very much. More than that, I've never said this to a woman before, I love you, Sarah. Whatever happens I want you to know that.'

Could she tell him the same? She had thought she was in love before but that had been something born out of her desperate need to be needed, to have someone take care of her. She could take care of herself now. Did she need someone with her throughout all of her life? She had a future beckoning her in the town or abroad at any time she pleased.

After the recent tragic event all she knew was she had a boundless longing for John.

'You don't have to say anything.' He caressed her face. 'This is enough for now, to have you here with me.' He took her in a lover's hold and showered her with light kisses and touches, quickly building them into something stronger and demanding and exquisitely intimate.

She was lost in the depths of beauty of how it should truly be when lovemaking progressed. John was sensitive and knowledgeable, bringing her to experience the essential dimension of her being. With him she encountered the full mystery of being a woman. This was more than a union of eager bodies. It was a meeting of supreme physical contact and in the end for Sarah, of souls. She lay fully loved and sated in John's arms, only wanting to stay here with him.

Tara couldn't sleep and wondered why she had bothered to get into bed. Her mind was a tumult of emotions, sorrow for Joshua, gladness for her freedom, the love in her heart for Kit. She had felt lonely and empty when he'd driven his grandmother home and anxious for him to return. Kit figured greatly in her future and she was full of fear that Laketon Kivell could so easily devastate everything. Kit and Michael were sure he was keeping low in the cottage and she was worried what they might do. Michael did not have the courage to be in the forefront of a confrontation to demand Kivell get off the property but Kit did. If anything was to happen to him . . .

If only she had thought of something herself to get rid of Kivell but she did not have the physical strength to carry it out, or the authority now. She pummelled the pillows and tossed them down the end of her lonely bed.

She got out of bed. How was she to get through this night? Sarah was probably having a poor time too; she would go to her. Tara's lantern threw ominous shadows on the floor, the wall panels and in window crevices and up on the long ceiling. Sarah wasn't in her room, her bed had been turned down and her nightgown placed ready, but was left untouched. The wardrobe door was open; she had changed her clothes. Fear shot through her Tara. Was Sarah trying to do something about Kivell on her own, or worse still had he snatched her for some reason? What if he wasn't in Paradise Cottage but was actually here in the house? He knew well its many rooms and passages, there were many places where he could be hiding, or concealing a hostage. She must rouse Kit and Michael.

She saw a folded sheet of paper on the dressing table. This could be a clue to Sarah's whereabouts. It was part of the letter from Amy. Tara and Sarah had exchanged the news of their letters, but Tara picked out something Sarah had kept to herself, of Amy encouraging her to join her in California. Was Sarah considering it?

She heard a noise and silenced a gasp. It wasn't close and was rather like the rustle of leaves. Something was very wrong. Rosa Grace! Before she did anything else she had to make sure her daughter was safe and she flew out of the room to the nursery.

Laketon had brought with him a bottle of brandy and because even now he liked to keep up his standards he was drinking out of a glass. It was so funny, hilarious, that these people, probably spending a restless night, could be racking their brains wondering where he was and all the time he was here, lying in comfort on the squire's bed. Kit Woodburne had returned. He must be wishing he was in Tara's bed, perhaps he was. Laketon couldn't imagine Michael had gone down to Wellspring House. He would be in the library, gloating that he'd murdered Joshua and had got away with it, not knowing his biggest problem was still in the house. That's me! Laketon pointed to his chest, gurgling in quiet laughter. In a minute he would go down to the library and kill the new squire, then nip out of the house avoiding the hue and cry and disappear for a few weeks. He had paid the madam of a brothel that serviced his tastes handsomely to provide him with an alibi. He poured another brandy in celebration.

'Uh?' He sat bolt upright and spilt the drink over himself. Someone was there at the foot of the bed. He could just make out a figure in the darkness, the figure of a woman. A ghost . . . ? Chills rode his spine and for the first time in his life he knew real fear, then he scorned himself. Supernatural or not, nothing would get the better of him. His hand shot downwards for his gun.

'Don't move, Laketon.'

He froze, aware now there was a gun trained on his chest.

'Great-aunt? It's you? How . . . ?'

'I knew you were here. At Burnt Oak they thought I went up for an early night but I came here. You're not the only one who has been hiding in this house and waiting for the right moment, Laketon.' Tempest's voice was as hard as frost.

'Why are you here?'

'You know why, to stop you hurting anyone else, Laketon. I won't take the risk that you'll hurt Kit or Sarah, and the world will be better off without you.' Tempest had a firm grip on the gun. 'You can't talk me out of it. I don't care if I hang for this crime or if I'm damned to hell.'

'You'll go to hell and I'll be right there with you,' Laketon hissed, licking his bottom lip. 'Have you thought of that? I won't let you rest in the afterlife.'

'I'll take my chances with God's mercy. But I probably won't hang, I'm sure the Nankervises will be glad to cover for me. All I want is you dead, Laketon. Goodbye.' She fired.

At the same moment Laketon lunged forward and threw the bottle of brandy at her. The bullet hit him with a force that shocked him as it ripped straight through his heart. After the thud in his chest and his yell of terror he plunged down dead, hanging over the footboard of the bed.

The bottle struck Tempest on the shoulder, smashing and showering her with glass and alcohol, making the gun fly from her hand. The force sent her staggering back to lose her footing. She fell to the floor hard. As she went down her neck hit the heavy scrolled foot of a chair.

Tara stopped short of her daughter's bedroom. What was that? A shot! It sounded as if it had come from the west wing.

Kit and Michael were back in the house having discovered Paradise Cottage was empty. Hearing the shot they raced up the stairs, Kit in the lead. They caught up with Tara hurrying down the corridor.

'The shot came from the west wing, Kit. I thought I'd heard someone creeping about. It must have been Kivell.'

Reaching her, he eased her towards Michael. 'Keep her out of the way. Fetch the men.'

'Sarah!' Tara cried. 'She's not in her room. That monster might have hurt her.'

Kit ran on to the suite, his firearm held out before him. If Kivell had hurt Sarah he'd rip him apart with his bare hands, show the barbarous swine no mercy. The door to the suite was open. He listened hard. There were no sounds coming from within. He got the crushing brooding sense that something of untold menace was waiting inside. The first room, the sitting room, was steeped in shadows. Kivell could be anywhere, behind the door, crouching behind a chair.

Kit went in, hardly daring to breathe. He could smell brandy. With the gun held out in front of him he spun round here and there, flinching every now and then, expecting to be hit by a bullet. At one point his throat constricted as if a cord had been wrapped around his neck and would choke out his life force. It was just his imagination. He was allowing himself to face an adversary with all the cunning and intent of a predator and with the madness of a depraved heart and mind. His hand trembled and he brought up his other hand to steady the gun, whipping his body to left and right, behind and ahead, expecting Kivell to suddenly leap out at him with a horrendous scream.

The door to the bedroom was ajar. Putting his side to the wall, he quickly looked inside. Nothing was moving and nothing was making a sound. At first all seemed dark and formless then he made out a strange shape slumped over the foot of the bed. It was a man. Kivell had killed someone. It had to be a servant – Hankins? Had Kivell got the truth out of him?

Letting his eyes stray he saw a second figure down on the floor. It was a woman. Sarah! He let out an anguished moan.

Tara heard him and breaking free from Michael she went in. 'What is it? Sarah!' She saw the body on the floor by the light of her lantern. 'It's not her!'

'Who then? Grandmama!' Kit cried in horror. He glanced at the body over the bed, recognized it was Laketon and he was dead. He fell to his knees beside Tempest, his flesh pierced by splinters of glass. 'What has he done to you?'

Michael was there. 'She shot him, there's a gun beside her. What a brave thing to do, confronting that scum. Is she . . .?'

'No, she's still breathing. He hurled a bottle at her. There's blood where her neck hit the chair,' Kit said, carefully taking Tempest up into his arms.

'Bring her to my room,' Tara said. So it had been the old lady she had heard moving about in the corridors. 'We'll send for the doctor.'

Leaving the coach house, Sarah and John had to be careful not to be seen and to keep away from the dogs. Something serious was happening. Men were running about, some of them curiously in sailors' garb. Now there were urgent voices and the servants had been roused. She got back inside the house and closed the window. She met Michael by the stairs where he was issuing orders. He was in a jubilant mood. 'So there you are! You've caused a lot of worry, girl. I'm happy to say Laketon Kivell is dead and there's now nothing to worry about. Poltraze is about to start a new beginning.'

'Kivell is dead? I'm glad to hear it. Was anyone hurt?'

'Woodburne's grandmother was here. It is she we have to thank for killing the brute. She took a fall and is lying down in Tara's room.'

'Mama Tempest is hurt?' Sarah pushed past him to pound up the stairs.

'Oh, she'll recover,' Michael threw over his shoulder. Nothing could dampen his joy. 'And she'll be a welcome guest here at any time.'

Sarah approached Tara's bed. 'How is she?'

'She won't wake up,' Kit said, his voice heavy with anxiety. 'Her hands are so cold. I don't understand why she was here.'

'I do,' Tara said, dabbing gently to clean away the blood on the side of Tempest's neck. 'She came here to protect those she loves. She knew how deadly Laketon Kivell was, that he was verging on the insane, and she must have been afraid about how he was to be ejected from here. She must have known that he was hiding in the house. We'll never know what he was up to but your grandmother surely saved someone's life tonight, perhaps several.'

'I should have killed him myself ages ago,' Kit reproached himself angrily.

Tempest's chest heaved and she gave a long rasping sigh.

'Grandmama?' His hopes rose and he cried tears of emotion. 'She's waking up. Grandmama?'

He called to her several times then looked at the two women. What was Sarah doing? She had sunk to her knees and was clutching the bedcovers and crying. Shaking his head he ignored her. Sarah was overcome, that was all.

Tara had a creased expression that was full of sympathy. There was no need for that. She should be ordering the maids to bring things, hot water and a nightgown for his grandmother. 'She'll wake up soon.'

'She won't, Kit. You know she won't. Her injury was fatal. Your grandmother has passed away. I'm so very sorry.' Tara's heart was with him. He was in a mist of miscomprehension. She went round the bed to him. She ached to comfort him with her arms but he was standing rigid. His tears fell silently.

He left the bedside. It can't be true, she can't be dead. But when he looked back at the figure in the bed, seeming so small and frail now, he had to admit the terrible truth. The woman he had once wanted to hurt but who he had come to love so much was dead. She had done what she felt she must to protect him and had paid the ultimate price. He went slowly back to her side.

'Tara, please take Sarah with you.' His voice emerged as if from across a barren landscape. 'I wish to be alone with my grandmother.'

Tara ushered Sarah to the door. Kit was partly in denial. He had retreated inside himself, blaming himself for his beloved grandmother's death. Only Tempest's love had brought him out of his former self-destructive brooding. Tara loved him more than ever and now she was afraid he would not allow her love to help him come to terms with his tragic loss.

Twenty-One

'So, we finally leave here tomorrow, I'm glad to say. Everything is packed.' Tara was at her boudoir fireside, with Sarah. The coal had burned down. The grate was nearly as lifeless as their joint mood. In the week since Michael had moved his family into Poltraze they had felt more and more out of place and couldn't wait to leave.

'I'll be up before dawn,' Sarah murmured, as grimly as she felt.

'And I will too. At least it was a pleasant surprise to learn Adeline has a good heart. She seems more than capable of taking over the charities and the emergency fund. But what are we to do from now on, Sarah? I don't want us ending up like a couple of old maids.'

'We can't be accused of that,' Sarah said, sighing, leaning forward with her chin in her hands. 'We're two widows who have never known love.' That wasn't true, but . . .

'Did you form no lasting fondness for John Moyle and he for you?' Tara asked carefully. Sarah had admitted she had been with the groom on the night of the two deaths but she had not mentioned him since.

'He's a good man.' Sarah picked at her skirt. The grief of Tempest Kivell's tragic end had distracted her for days. David Kent had been taken on as a stable boy but the youngster's services were not required in Truro. John had been instructed to teach him how to handle horses and attend to the carriages and he had to stay at Poltraze. He had a commitment to the boy. She didn't want to think about how hard it would be but it was best she go away and leave John in the past. Anyway, she couldn't leave Tara in loneliness. The last place she wanted to go was Truro, to be in a strange town, living a life she was not born into and would never become fully accepted into, far from Burnt Oak, Chy-Henver and Kit. Kit was turning into a stranger. After taking Tempest's body home to Burnt Oak, he had remained there. He had barely spoken at the funeral. Life had taken yet another depressing dip.

Tara judged Sarah's long silence as one that was holding many regrets. 'John Moyle is an attractive man. It's easy to see why you wanted to be with him. Don't be ashamed of your liaison with him, Sarah. Everyone hopes to find love.' She had hoped she'd found it herself but it seemed to have been for nothing. Kit had not been in touch for days and she did not like to intrude on his mourning.

'I'm not ashamed. John and I . . . we weren't meant to be, that's all.' Sarah kept her head down and her tears only just at bay.

'But you do wish you and John had been meant to be?' Tara persisted. 'Please speak frankly, Sarah. I'd hate to think you're putting aside your dreams because of me.'

'I do have feelings for John.' She toyed with her hand-kerchief.

'Just feelings?'

'No, more, I love him. I love him very much. I haven't told him, he's got a commitment to David now.'

'And don't you think he feels the same way about you?'

Sarah recalled John's disappointment as she'd told him it was best they go their separate ways. She had looked back at him all the way out of the stable yard and he had watched her every second, waving to her before she had finally gone. He had not tried to change her mind but she knew that was out of kindness for her feelings, not because he didn't want her. 'Yes he does, but everything's so difficult. What about you and Kit?'

'I've loved Kit for a while now. It's the first time I've been in love. I wish we had become lovers. Kit needs someone, but we didn't get close enough for that someone to be me.'

'But Kit loves you too, I'm sure he does. You're moving away but you should go to him. You should at least reach out and try to grab some happiness.'

'I could say the same thing to you. Some things are only difficult if we allow them to be.'

They stared at each other, drinking in the truth. Sarah sprang to her feet. 'We're both in love and we're moping here and letting it slip away from us.'

'Yes, when we should fight for what we want.' Tara joined her, sharing her new energy.

'We've got nothing to lose if we make our feelings plain to John and Kit. If John agrees to marry me it would mean me staying on here. It will be the right thing. We'll be on the same level. Would you mind terribly, Tara?'

'Sarah, I'd never stand in the way of your happiness. It might not be easy for you living here as a servant's wife.'

'But there is another way, somewhere we could go to make a new start.' Sarah's eyes lit up like stars.

'To Amy, is that what you mean? I haven't mentioned it before but I admit I saw that part of her letter when I came looking for you the other night. It could be the very thing. Why don't you go down to the stable yard and ask for my pony to be saddled, I shall go straight to Burnt Oak. You take John aside and make sure he listens to you. I'll do the same with Kit.'

Sweeping her shawl over her shoulders, Sarah ran all the way to the stables. Glum, John was showing David how to saddle a pony. Spying her huge smile he forsook his duties and went straight to her, smiling back. When they got closer they started running, arms outstretched. There were other grooms and boys about but she didn't care as she flew into his arms. 'Does this mean you're not leaving me, Sarah? I've been so miserable.'

'I'm sorry. With all my heart I love you, John. I want us to be together forever, with David too.'

'I didn't want to take you away from a better life unless it was what you were sure you wanted,.' John squeezed her tight and then David was included in their embrace. 'We'll marry straightaway and we'll adopt David. We'll settle down, the three of us, a proper little family.'

'John, does it matter where we live?'

'Anywhere in the world will do, Sarah darling, as long as we're all together.'

'In that case, how about California?'

* * *

Tara was shown into Morn O' May by Eula and then taken along to Tempest's sitting room. 'I'm so glad you've come, Mrs Nankervis. Kit has been so depressed. He blames himself for my mother's death but there's no need for him to, she knew what she was doing when she went to Poltraze. I'm confident he'll come to terms with it in time but he needs help to see it from a different perspective. We're all very grateful to the new squire for not linking her death with my dreadful cousin's. My mother can rest in peace with no disgrace on her name. Please do your best to cheer Kit. I'll leave you alone with him.'

It was what she was hoping for, to have Kit to herself.

'Hello, Kit.' He was standing at the window, his arm leaning above his head on the pane, gazing out at the garden. She went straight to him. It caught at her heart to see him drawn and lethargic, in a grim world of his own.

'Oh, Tara,' he said, coming out of a daze. 'It's good of you to call.' He rubbed at his eyes in a bid to become more awake. Weariness dragged at his eyes, he had not been sleeping well. 'Forgive me, I've kept meaning to drop you a line. I haven't deliberately been keeping way from you, never you, Tara. I just . . .' No one was a more welcome sight than Tara. She was fresh and fair with her snow-white loveliness. Just looking at her he felt warmth and vigour seeping into him. She was springtime promise and summer beauty. He was a fool to have returned to his old bad habit and lock himself away from the one person he needed most in the world.

Overjoyed that he was pleased to see her, she exuded all her love to him. 'I understand, Kit. Your grandmother's garden is beautiful. Part of her will always be out there and in here, her special room.'

'I know, I do believe that, yet I can't believe I'll never walk out there with her again. If I hadn't come here she wouldn't have come to care for me and gone after that devil.'

'She will walk with you, Kit, wherever you go.' Tara slipped a hand round his. 'She did what she did to ensure your life would continue. She wouldn't want you to feel guilty about it.'

'I know that too. She tells me in my dreams. It's just so hard . . .'

'Of course it is. Would it help if you took a walk round her garden now? Would you like me to go with you?'

He nodded, his eyes fixed to hers. 'I don't know how I could have stayed away from you for so long, Tara. I have to say this, you mean everything to me. I've wanted to tell you that for a long time.'

'And I feel the same way, Kit. It's why I'm here.'

'Tara, after we come in from the garden will you carry on walking with me for the rest of my life?'

'Yes, Kit, I'd like nothing more.'

A fortnight later a vessel of the Howarth Shipping Line set sail from Falmouth for Plymouth, where it would later sail on to America. John, Sarah and young David Moyle stayed in a cosy huddle up on deck until they left the Cornish coastline behind.

Observing them for a short time from shore had been a gentleman, a passenger who had left a local hotel to board a ship bound for the West Indies. He was Irish, apparently, and wore a large hat and muffler and had a full beard. Leaning on a cane, he was only recently fit for the many weeks' journey, having undergone a lengthy convalescence. He wore subdued clothes. The last really fine apparel he had worn had been put on the corpse of a miner who had succumbed to lung congestion, his lowly grave swapped for the finest tomb in the churchyard. Like the Moyles the gentleman was travelling overseas to start a new life. And just like the Moyles he had said goodbye forever to the one place they had in common – Poltraze.